Also by Earl W. Emerson

HELP WANTED: ORPHANS PREFERRED

EARL W. EMERSON

WILLIAM MORROW AND COMPANY, INC.
NEW YORK

Recognizing the importance of preserving what has been written, it is the policy of
William Morrow and Company, Inc., and its imprints and affiliates to have the books
it publishes printed on acid-free paper, and we exert our best efforts to that end.

Library of Congress Cataloging-in-Publication Data

Emerson, Earl W.
　　Help wanted : orphans preferred / Earl W. Emerson.
　　　　p.　cm.
　　ISBN 0-688-09333-7
　　I. Title.
PS3555.M39H45　1990
813'.54—dc20　　　　　　　　　　　　　89-39864
　　　　　　　　　　　　　　　　　　　　CIP

Printed in the United States of America

First Edition

1　2　3　4　5　6　7　8　9　10

BOOK DESIGN BY BARBARA M. BACHMAN

For Brian and Jeffrey

Hell has three gates: lust, anger, and greed.
—*Bhagavadgita*, 16, tr.
P. Lal

1

HOW TO TELL THE DIFFERENCE BETWEEN A DEBUTANTE AND YOUR BASIC DIRTBALL

"I 'm such a slut," Wanda Sheridan announced flatly. Everyone in the room knew she was two-timing Claude. "I wish you guys'd teach me everything. I love this fire stuff."

Lieutenant Allan cleared his throat. "Oh, man. There's a jillion things I could teach you."

"Private lessons?"

"Oh, God," said Lieutenant Allan, who became a buffoon around Wanda.

In the Staircase fire station Wanda murmured "Oooo" like a mantra, using what the expression did to her lips to jack up male blood pressure. She was a throwback to the days when it was thought sexy for a woman to sit on a guy's lap. A tiny person with a tight-waisted Dogpatch physique, she employed a thousand mannerisms to inflame men's fantasies. Her favorite was a stretch-and-yawn where she locked her hands behind her head, flexed from the waist and jutted her goods out for all to inspect.

"Oooo! Firemen have such cute mustaches. Love those uniforms! Always loved uniforms. Can I wear your helmet? It's so heavy!"

Fontana was one of the few Wanda Sheridan hadn't whipsawed into a trance. Wanda treated him with a deference normally reserved for clumsy dentists. "Something about that guy bothers me," she often said to her boyfriend, Claude. It might have been Fontana's dog, which rarely left his side. Everyone in town knew last winter the dog had killed a man in the line of duty.

So far nobody in town could fathom how Wanda, who lived in Seattle but spent most of her time in Staircase, had hooked up with Claude Pettigrew. The consensus seemed to be he'd found her in the classifieds in an underground newspaper: "Fat man with money, drinking problem, seeks relationship with greedy, big-breasted babe."

"My girl," bragged Claude. He was unbelievably tolerant of Wanda's flirtations. Invariably smug over his conquest. "She's *my* girl."

Decked out in his apron and chef's hat, Claude Pettigrew waddled about the beanery like a befuddled character from *In the Night Kitchen*. Unkempt, balding, fifteen years older than Wanda, who was thirty-three going on fourteen, Claude dragged around so much excess blubber his legs could barely cope. Years ago he'd signed on with the volunteers, but his overloaded joints hadn't withstood the Thursday night drills. Watching him wolf down a platter of french fries drowned in pan drippings, Kingsley Pierpont commented, "You oughta tattoo a handprint on your sternum."

"Wha'for?" Claude asked.

"For after your coronary. Underneath we'll write 'Push Here.'"

"Ha-ha. Think you're funny?"

"Yeah, I do."

———

Wanda weighed under a hundred, and the disparity between the petite sexpot and Claude's three-hundred pounds spurred Warren Bounty to observe, "When Claude hugs her, she looks like an M&M in a catcher's mitt."

Judging Claude by his duck-footed walk, facial tics and ill-fitting 1950's J. C. Penney catalog duds, outsiders thought Claude was retarded. But the feebleminded did not gather wealth the way he did. Kingsley said, "When Claude walks into the savings and loan, the vice-president rolls out a red carpet. The tellers stand at attention and blow trumpets."

Claude Pettigrew lived with his mother, chauffeured her immaculate 1956 Buick, which he waxed twice a month, took many of his meals at the station, labored in a local wood mill, and, until Wanda entered his life, still had his first nickel.

An ardent fire buff since the age of eight, Claude had squandered more hours in the fire station than anybody in town. While he puttered about the beanery preparing the noontime feed, Wanda's high-pitched laughter dominated the station. Wanda wore too-small jeans and a skintight T-shirt that said "Snake River College Grad" across the front, the words too curvy to read without some study.

"Put here by the good Lord to be humped," Lieutenant Allan said behind her back. When he addressed Wanda, Allan stared at her nipples instead of her smoky gray eyes. Wanda didn't seem to notice.

Trapping skinny Peter Daugherty alone in the watch office one afternoon, Wanda looped her arms around his neck and thrust her tongue deep into his mouth. Daugherty had been sucking a Cloret, and Wanda's tongue made him lose track of it so that he choked for ten minutes.

"Coulda killed ya," Fontana joked. "How'd you like that on your tombstone? 'Strangled by Wanda Sheridan's tongue'?" Pete turned red. His Adam's apple pistoned up and down. Despite the tomfoolery, he had dated only two women in his life—and he had married the second. He received such a high-voltage jolt flirting with Wanda, who was ten years older, that in a cold sweat he confessed his lust each week to his priest.

Lieutenant Allan interrogated Pete relentlessly. "She just grab you or did you make a move?" Even to guileless Daugherty it was obvious that given three wishes, Bobby Joe Allan would have squandered the first two deploying Wanda's tongue in his own mouth. But Pettigrew was deaf and blind to Wanda's coquettish forays.

Gil Cutty speculated that Claude and Wanda's relationship had not been consummated, that she was egging him along on gooses, wet kisses, and hand jobs. Often they parked in front of the fire station while a crowd gathered at the venetian blinds to watch Wanda screwing her tongue into Claude's ear in the front seat of his mother's Buick.

As fire chief, Fontana had set up shop in what used to be the sheriff's office. An unused holding cell lay directly oposite his desk. Behind him a rack of rifles and shotguns gathered dust. Fontana didn't much care for guns.

Nor did he care for Wanda Sheridan, who had been *dating* Claude Pettigrew for six weeks, all the while filching his money. Her latest swindle was the Northwest Soup Company.

"Clam chowder!" she announced. "Oysters in sauce! Fried prawns dipped in wine. My own shop!" She had wheedled the start-up capital from Claude, who immediately announced how much he'd shelled out. Two days earlier Fontana had watched him pen a thousand-dollar check to Wanda for a down payment on shop space in the Denny Regrade, then watched him send Wanda off with another man.

"Bye, baby. See ya later," said Claude.

"Oh, Claude, honey, sweetie." Hanging head, arms, and chest out the window of the car, she blew him a kiss. That afternoon at Longacres Randy Watkins spotted Wanda placing bets on the horses, guzzling beer, and groping her associate. Randy watched them drop six hundred bucks at the windows.

———

It was late Monday morning, and Warren Bounty, the former chief of Staircase's one-horse fire department, sat in the beanery, watching a hockey game on cable. Patiently awaiting Wanda's first yawn were Peter Daugherty, Lieutenant Bobby Joe Allan, Claude Pettigrew, Jim Caitlin, and two cotton-mouthed volunteers. Kingsley Pierpont, the only black in the department, had isolated himself in the game room on the other side of the apparatus floor, where he shot nine ball with a pearl-handled screw-together cue.

Fontana strode into the beanery and swigged down two glasses of cold water. "Afraid I'm out of the lunch clutch."

"Got plenty," Pettigrew said matter-of-factly, as he skinned carrots at the stainless steel sink.

"Not this time, Claude. Back in a couple of hours."

At the long table Bounty and Lieutenant Allan swapped war stories, Allan relating a house fire they'd had a week ago. "Firefighters are America's last heroes," he said as if he were a factor in making it so.

When he stepped out of the air-conditioned fire station, the dry August heat slammed into Fontana. Only a few wispy cirrus clouds outlined the horizon. He slipped on a pair of black-rimmed sunglasses to complement khaki patch-pocket shorts, a cotton T-shirt, two pairs of heavy socks, and light hiking boots.

For a week Staircase had been like the inside of a kiln. The hot breezes continued day and night. Not being used to such blistering weather, the citizenry wilted.

He shouldered a knapsack, fed Satan all the water he could drink, then led the 105-pound German shepherd to the fenced run behind the station.

Before he reached the truck, Wanda appeared, her words freighted with innuendo. "Mac? Stay. We were counting on you."

"Not all that hungry, Wanda."

Stepping close, Wanda spidered her fingertips along Fontana's bare arm. "Please, Mac? Please stay for lunch? Pretty please?"

"Wanda, I've asked you before not to talk to me like I'm an idiot."

"Oh, pooh."

"See ya later."

It was summer in the Snoqualmie Valley, and everyone had August on the brain. As he tooled through Staircase on Main Street in the rattletrap 1960 GMC Carryall he'd inherited from Warren Bounty's tenure in office, Fontana tuned the radio to KVI and hummed along to "Satisfaction" by the Stones. He'd hoodwinked the city into replacing the ancient tube radio with a thirty-watt model that could suck in the distant Seattle stations.

Fontana drove east across the ancient green bridge that spanned the Middle Fork and proceeded two miles up the Mount Gadd Road under a canopy of Douglas firs. In the parking lot along the base of Gadd forty cars baked in the noon sun.

After parking beside Rainy's red Jeep Cherokee, he climbed out and slung his knapsack. The Jeep's engine block crackled.

She wouldn't be far.

2

YOU STEAL MY HEART AWAY

Just shy of the two-mile marker, he sighted the familiar swing of her tanned legs. Minutes later under a haze of yellow sunlight he approached her in the thick trees.

"Yo," he said.

She swung her sun-streaked bronze-brown hair away from her eyes, and the somber look of her face eroded into a smile.

"Mac. Haven't seen you for a couple of days."

"Been hitting it early to avoid the heat."

"Walk with me?"

"That was my intention."

One of the most popular hikes in the state, the steep Mount Gadd trail was also one of the most grueling. Expeditioners to Mount Everest used it for conditioning. Switchbacks carried adventuresome hikers up forty-two hundred feet in four miles. Coming down could bruise even a conditioned athlete so that he was sore for a week.

At his tourist-killer pace, it was a rare day when Fontana didn't clock the peak in under sixty minutes. Yet his first ascent of the local landmark after moving to Washington State from the East had taken hours.

During tourist season chattering kids and weary parents scented the trail with pipe smoke, My Sin, body odor, Aqua Velva, suntan lotion, and Deep Woods Off. What few cigarette butts littered the trail ceased before the mile marker. Mac treasured the tang of dirt, pine needles, and the peculiar electrical odor which for some reason floated out of the forest floor on hot days.

"Nice to see you," she said. "I missed you."

He grinned at that. "You're looking good."

The facts of Rainy's life were unraveled only in anecdotal snippets. She had a husband who volunteered for Staircase, a son his own son's age, and prior to her second marriage she had worked for a car dealership. Aside from occasionally running into her at the grade school or Shop Rite he hadn't seen her anywhere but on the trail.

"You look glum," Rainy said after they'd hiked a few minutes at her pace, which was only one dead tourist slower than his.

"Figured fire chief of a small-town department was going to be a cakewalk. Not yet it ain't." He told her about Bobby Joe Allan's weak-kneed firefighting, about Wanda Sheridan, about the blow-ups he knew were coming. His. Claude's. Lieutenant Allan's when he canned him. The city council's.

He knew Rainy wouldn't relate the information to her husband, had discovered he could trust her in a roundabout manner one night during a first-aid drill, when it became obvious Jim Caitlin wasn't aware that his wife even knew Fontana. Without fully being aware of why, Fontana neglected to share the information. Neither he nor Rainy mentioned their mutual default.

"You want to boot him out?" asked Rainy. "The lieutenant?"

"His cousin is on the city council. Uncle used to be mayor. Mo thinks he's the cat's pajamas." Mo Costigan was the current mayor of Staircase.

16

When Rainy smiled, the sunbaked crow's-feet around her eyes intensified. She wore wire-rimmed sunglasses, the lenses only slightly larger than her pale blue eyes. Fontana and Rainy overtook a gaggle of tourists decked out in white Reeboks and Hawaiian shorts.

"But Allan's been here so long," Rainy said.

"The Dugan's going to get somebody killed."

"You'd think if something was going to happen . . ."

"We've had our share of close calls."

Dropping into silence, they tackled the last and hottest mile. Two inches shorter than Fontana's five-ten, Rainy was slender, her thin legs ropy with muscle. He watched a rivulet of sweat inch down the arch of her spine. Gray Hi-Tech boots, a coachman blue fanny pack, and a skimpy two-piece black swimming suit. He suspected her daring dress was some sort of compensation for her handicap, a topic they'd spoken of only once. He especially liked that she was all business, not the type to casually mention getting sloshed on sake on a train to Kyoto, even if she'd done it—nor the type to be impressed by such twaddle. Nor had she ever bluntly announced, "I'm a Christian," though she was.

From the bowels of his knapsack the department beeper squealed. On his portable RCA radio Fontana listened to the response dispatched from Control Ten in Issaquah. A house fire, flames visible. Confirmation from two separate callers.

"Some bimbo set fire to his house," Fontana said disgustedly.

Rainy turned and planted a foot on a rock pile. They were only three hundred feet below the last switchback, had already broken through the evergreens into the sunlight. A vampire wind was sucking them dry. For an instant the remoteness she displayed in public reemerged. "Going back?"

"Forty minutes if I run."

"They might need you."

He smiled grimly. "Damn thing'll be tapped before I get to it.

Out by the north fork near your place. We can see it from the saddle. If it looks bad, I'll head down."

Mount Gadd reigned over the flat landscape of the upper Snoqualmie Valley, sharp and jagged in the summer, dotted by mountain goats and capped by snow in winter. Steel-colored rock mixed with lighter browns, whites, and black crevices. Visitors seldom failed to grow solemn at the sight. Trees sprawled across the scree toward the base. Rotten, crumbling, the face was deemed dangerous and unclimbable even by experts. Every few years someone smarter than the experts got killed on it. Gadd bestowed an alpine feel to the town that some merchants amplified with Swiss scrollwork and shutters on their shops.

On top were scrub, brambles, and stumpy, windblown brush clothed in lichen. Blue-gray boulders were stippled with moss. Fontana crossed the first hump and settled onto a rock ledge overlooking the valley. To the west a rust-gray smudge of bad air strangled Seattle. Only the tops of five or six skyscrapers were visible in the distant sludge.

Even up here he could hear the siren atop the station house. A small-town tradition, it went off to rouse volunteers, even though all of them now carried beepers. Shopkeepers and gas jockeys trotted to the firehouse to man the rigs. Housewives peered out kitchen windows to see which direction the Seagrave headed. Aunt Marlene lived that way. Uncle Dan the other. A jolt of adrenaline to break up the workday.

Located up a long driveway off Dabney Road, the fire building overlooked the North Fork of the river. Through his field glasses he followed the first Staircase engine, then the second. Behind sped a green Pinto, Warren Bounty's car. Still rehabilitating, he wouldn't participate. In the past year he'd resurrected himself from alcoholism, the DTs, and near death. When the wind let up, Fontana heard the engines as they changed gears. Volunteers who hadn't made it in time to clamber onto a pumper zipped along behind in their own vehicles.

Rainy sat quietly beside him. The valley unfolded below in pastels of green, olive, wheat colors, and one small orange-flaming house.

"Hate to say it," said Rainy, "but from here it's beautiful."

"You ought to see one at night. This one's only an inch-and-a-half fire."

As unruffled as an embalmer, Lieutenant Allan gave a solid radio report. He'd admitted once he'd been practicing since he was a kid watching Broderick Crawford on *Highway Patrol*. No theatrical hysterics the way the movies did it. Firefighters ridiculed each other for displaying excitement on the air. Every professional tried to temper his voice.

Engine One dropped hose on the road and proceeded up the long driveway, the yellow supply line stretching out behind. If the evolution ran to form, Kingsley and Peter would mask up and haul the first line through the front door. A volunteer would man the pump on the Seagrave. Other volunteers would follow inside with a second line. They would break out windows with axes. They would ladder the building and cut a hole in the roof with a chain saw to vent hot gases. Until Fontana took over, they had never opened a roof.

Lieutenant Allan would stand in the yard, relishing his command. When someone suggested he venture inside, his eyes would glaze.

There were two basic theories of structure firefighting, often called aggressive and defensive. The first was to get inside and expunge the fire at the seat. This exposed firefighters to risk, but it always tapped a fire quickest, saved the most property, and was the best tactic to use when lives were at stake. The second theory advocated standing in the yard and dousing the flames from the sidewalk. Closed doors and interior walls often nullified these efforts. Lieutenant Allan subscribed wholeheartedly to the second theory, as had the entire department until Fontana arrived. Now they went inside when feasible. The trick was defining "feasible." Allan was on record. Never.

After a while Mac handed the binoculars to Rainy. As she perched her sunglasses on her head and rolled the focus knob with one finger, she said, "You called it an inch-and-a-half. Is that a little tiny thing?" Without looking at him, she put down the binoculars and held two fingers an inch apart.

"Doesn't Jim ever mention his work?"

"Not really."

Not ever, to judge by earlier conversations. Fontana found it puzzling, but then, he found a lot of things about Rainy's marriage puzzling.

"An inch-and-a-half hose puts out a hundred gallons a minute. A fire that can be handled by an inch-and-a-half line is called an inch-and-a-half fire."

"Oh."

3

PRELUDE TO A KISS

The first time he'd spoken to Rainy, she had been pointing out the landmarks below to a middle-aged couple who'd aged ten years trudging to the top. She'd patiently explained the layout of Staircase, Interstate 90, Fall City, the Tinkertoys spires of a distant Seattle and Bellevue, the three forks of the river, Mount Rainier to the south, Snoqualmie Falls.

After the florid-faced couple drifted off, he had been left alone with Rainy near the stone bench. Being stranded on a mountaintop with a stranger was not something she plotted. Not Rainy. He'd said, "They're going for recess in a minute. If you listen, you can hear the bell."

"Excuse me?" Eyes filled with a frosty, careful disdain, she made a show of brushing strands of hair from her face.

"Your boy is in my son's class. Name is MacKinley Fontana. The new fire chief. Call me Mac." Without hesitation he stretched out his hand, and they shook. Upon reflection, he'd thought that had been the ticket: sticking his paw out and gently grasping her as if it were nothing at all. He smiled broadly through his neatly cropped beard and never once took his blue eyes off her face.

"I've seen you on the trail before," she said.

Self-effacing, skittish, Rainy had few friends and didn't make new ones without a titanic struggle. Fontana realized this, and after he'd commandeered her loyalty, the feat sent a surge of vanity through him. Each time they sat on the windblown rocks after scaling Gadd there would come an intimate moment that in another relationship would have been a prelude to a kiss. Yet they never kissed.

The black smoke below turned white as water reached the fire. A few minutes later it was extinguished. All the fires in the valley were out. When criticism surfaced, Bobby Joe Allan was fond of pointing that out.

"See anything burning out there? Then I guess we're doing okay." They'd said the same thing in the East. Firemen all over the world said it.

Skimming the hot chinook, a red-tailed hawk soared several hundred yards off the mountain. Reclining on the rocks, they chatted for twenty minutes. As he stood and stretched, Fontana heard a call on the portable radio.

"Ah, this is, uh, Station One at Staircase. Give us a second medic unit. We've got some, uh, problems here." Chaotic shouting crisscrossed the airwaves in the background.

"Nature of the problem, Staircase?" asked the county dispatcher, all business.

"Firefighter down," Lieutenant Allan said, his words rushed. "Firefighter, sick, unknown. Ongoing CPR." The engines had long since returned from the fire.

"One of my guys is dying." Fontana slung his knapsack and jogged through the boulders toward the trail. Rainy watched until he disappeared over the rocky butte.

4

THE CAT'S HUBCAP

Fontana regarded it as a bad sign that he beat the first medic unit to the station. It meant the county unit and all Bellevue's medics were out of service on other alarms. The rapidly growing east side of the county lacked enough medic units to begin with. To make it worse, all of them were stationed at least twenty miles from Staircase.

He plowed through a spattering of mute onlookers. The patient was lying, apparently where he had dropped, on his back in the center of the watch office floor, arms limp, legs akimbo. His eyes were open and glassy as creek stones. Pete Daugherty.

He had been stripped to the waist. His skin was pallid. His heart had either stopped or was working erratically enough to necessitate mechanical assistance.

"Out!" commanded Fontana hoarsely. "Everybody who's not

doing anything, give us space!" The room cleared as people reluctantly gave up rubbernecking.

Barrel-chested Warren Bounty squatted on his knees, performing
chest compressions, elbows locked, fingers knitted together so as not
to curl around the patient's ribs. Rhythmic. An inch and a half deep.
He performed sixty compressions a minute, not realizing the new
drill was eighty. No matter. The medicos would switch back next
year. They doctored the resuscitation numbers incessantly.

Cocking his head to throw the perspiration off a whip of dark
hair, Bounty shot Mac a lugubrious look.

"What happened?"

"Nobody knows," said Bounty, breathing heavily. "He was sick a
few minutes and then this. Went stiff as a board before his heart
stopped."

Three years earlier Warren Bounty had enlisted Peter into the
Staircase Fire Department. Just that morning, before Pettigrew
showed up with her, Warren had been ribbing Peter about Wanda's tongue, and to Warren's delight, Pete had degenerated from
his is-there-something-icky-in-the-room smile to stuttering
speechlessness.

Jim Caitlin, Rainy's husband, had put a line into Daugherty's
thickly veined forearm, the clear bag of Ringer's held aloft by a
volunteer who worked down the street at the Chevy dealer.

Caitlin was a paramedic in the Seattle Fire Department. Having a paramedic respond with the volunteers was often a lifesaving
coup. Even when Staircase's aid car played scoop and run, meeting a Bellevue medic unit halfway, in Preston, say, or Issaquah,
it was a long haul to Overlake Hospital for a heart attack victim
or someone in the throes of major trauma.

Kingsley Pierpont knelt above Daugherty's head, grasping the
Laerdal bag mask, forcing 100 percent oxygen into Daugherty's
lungs. One squeeze every five seconds. Squashing the egg-shaped
green bulb against his thigh. Somebody had already hooked O_2
to the reservoir. Fontana checked the bottle to be sure the main

valve was open. They'd intubated him. His head was canted back at an angle that should have been painful.

Kingsley didn't glance up. Fontana didn't have to see his dark eyes to know tears were scumming them.

Small circular patches had been glued to Daugherty's bared chest, thin wire leads running to the Lifepak. The tiny green monitor exhibited a series of jittery heartbeats. Warren Bounty's clocklike rhythm, not Pete's heart, was prompting those. Daugherty's T-shirt and uniform had been scissored off. Bony ribs stood out on his pale white skin.

Caitlin's cold steel-colored eyes met Fontana's for an instant, but neither man let out even a glimmer of what he was thinking. Though a trifle battle-weary, Caitlin was regarded as one of the best medics around. All week Fontana had been thinking about having run into Caitlin outside the station. He didn't recall what they'd been talking about, but Caitlin had been stepping on ants, deliberately crippling them, then observing with an odd detachment as they dragged their mutilated parts around in circles. To Fontana it had seemed infantile, if not downright abnormal, especially from a professional healer.

"Clear," ordered Caitlin.

When everyone had removed his hands from the patient, Caitlin punched a switch on the Lifepak and Daugherty's gangly, motionless body jerked spasmodically. Caitlin repeated the process, watched the monitor in the silent room for what seemed like hours, then said calmly, "No change. Resume."

Paunchy and unfit, Warren Bounty was built like a shorter version of John Wayne. He even breathed in a raspy whir as Wayne had in his later years. His massive arms corded up with each compression. Wisps of steam cobra-danced off the sweat on his back and shoulders. Even in an air-conditioned room, CPR was uncommonly hard work, and Fontana could see that Zeke Brown, perspiring and fatigued also, had been rotating on compressions.

Fontana sent an onlooker outside to direct the medic unit to the proper door when it showed. "Why two medic units?" he asked. Zeke Brown pointed languidly toward the beanery. After the professional clutter and suppressed panic of the watch office, the beanery was strangely tranquil. Except for the TV.

Two patients.

Fat as a whale in a dingy, Claude Pettigrew swamped a black chair, one elbow propped on the armrest, head clutched in his hand. Eyes closed. Face colorless. Diaphoretic. In front of him on the table sat a quart container of milk, empty. Also a rack of raw eggs and six raggedy eggshells. An empty bottle of ipecac. Fontana laid a palm on Pettigrew's forehead. Cold and moist. Pulse rapid and thready. A wastebasket sat between his fat legs. It had been used.

"You guys know what caused this?"

"Food poisoning," said Bobby Joe Allan, charging his reply with the casual and irritating assurance of one who knew. Allan had a habit of knowing everything. He lay motionless on the long beanery table. "Salmonella. Botulism. Something."

Without rolling his head, Allan twitched one eye open, then closed it. He was forty-five pounds overweight, and his paunch pushed up at his white T-shirt. He had unbuttoned his navy uniform shirt. "You wash your hands before you cook, Claude?"

"Wasn't my food!" protested Claude weakly. "It wasn't my goddamned food!"

"Nobody else cooked anything!" said Allan.

"It wasn't my goddamned food!"

"Break it up," said Fontana. "I don't want either of you to get agitated. How do you feel?"

"How do you think I feel?" said Pettigrew. "My stomach's knotted up like there's a cow in there."

"Lord knows you got room for a cow in that thing," said Allan.

"Throat feels like I swallowed a batch of lye. I'm thirsty. I feel seasick." Fontana poured him a glass of water.

"You take ipecac?"

"Caitlin said to."

"How about you, Bobby Joe?"

"Just feel awful."

"Ipecac?"

Without opening his eyes, Bobby Joe made a distasteful face. "Didn't want it." Fontana noticed Allan wasn't doubled up, nor was he sweating.

"Food poisoning doesn't usually stop your heart," said Fontana. "What happened to Pete? He aspirate something?"

"Vomited at the goddamned fire," said Pettigrew.

"Yeah," said Allan. "Then, when he came back here, he ate more. Saw him chewing when he took the keys and opened the back doors."

"Wasn't none of my shit," said Pettigrew. "Got sick before any of us. When we was changing hose after the fire, he went across the bay to lay down."

"Pete's never shirked work," said Fontana. "Weren't you guys worried?"

"Said he was okay. Later Zeke went over there to get some paper towels and called us," continued Pettigrew. "Looked like hell. Wet all over. Clutching his gut. Said his throat was burning. He was crying, for godsakes, crying like a little baby."

"Your throat burning?" Fontana asked Lieutenant Allan. Savoring the attention, Allan took his time, swallowed, touched his neck. "It is or it isn't."

"Well, yeah, it is."

"Drink some of that milk. Swallow as many eggs as you can get down. I want you to take ipecac."

"Feel awful enough . . ."

"This isn't mayonnaise, Bobby Joe. You've been poisoned. Strychnine. Cyanide. I don't know what."

" 'Tater salad," said Allan. "Somebody left it out in the heat."

"Potato salad doesn't pop your ticker."

They canceled the second medic, sending Allan along with Peter Daugherty's rawboned, lifeless body in the Bellevue unit. Allan sat in front with a plastic garbage sack, waiting for the ipecac to produce. Fontana watched as Pete's bony arms flopped this way and that and got tangled between people's legs as they hoisted the spineboard through the rear doors of the vehicle. Fontana didn't want it to be his last memory of Pete, though he knew it would be.

Zeke Brown and Worthington rode with the medics to assist with chest compressions and the bag mask. Everybody knew it was hopeless. They'd shocked him until they all dreaded another call to "clear." Asystole. Straight line. Caitlin had pumped every chemical he had into the line, on doctor's phone orders injected twice directly into Pete's heart. They knew nothing was going to come of it just as they knew they weren't going to give up until a physician gave the order. Had he been a civilian, things would have been different. This was a comrade. If need be, they'd work on him until he was lowered into the grave.

Caitlin rode to Overlake Hospital, too. Pettigrew, whose condition had stabilized, waited for the manager of the Chevy dealership to give him a ride in a new Silverado. After the Bellevue medic unit peeled out, Fontana stood alone in the detritus of the resuscitation attempt: small white paper envelopes torn open; latex gloves turned inside out; needles; the brittle plastic wrappers Ringer's come in; white medical supply packages. A clump of volunteers and gossiping townspeople milled around outside. People who'd been there all along filled in newcomers with the cheap pride of earlier knowledge.

Mac stared blankly at Moses, the disreputable station mascot, who lay curled atop a cabinet in the watch office. Daugherty's cat. White originally, he'd streaked himself in dirt and grease until he was almost a cardboard brown. One ear was tattered. Only one of the cat's eyes was functional, the other whited over and oozing.

"Was his animal," said Warren Bounty.

Fontana looked up. Bounty stood beside him. Piercing blue

eyes that were every bit as hypnotic as a movie star's. Warren's nose had been flattened in bar fights, spidered like the drunk he had been. Now he was a dedicated member of AA. A raconteur. One of the most popular men in town. Hearing his gruff voice gave Fontana solace in a way he couldn't explain.

"Pete's damn cat," continued Bounty. "Moses. Found him out on Geisel's property, half starved. Damn cat was eating a slug. Pete picked him up. Took half an hour to coax him to the aid wagon. Trapped him in a cardboard box and hauled him back to the station. Tried to clean the damn thing up, but he naps on engine blocks. Peter loved that cat. One helluva fighter, that kitty. Being a longtime scrapper myself, I gotta admire that."

When Fontana failed to emerge from his trance, Bounty continued. "Pete couldn't talk the rest of us into using house dues for a nice bowl. Got all pissed. Grubbed around until he found a hubcap. Fed the cat out of that damn hubcap. Everybody was always accidentally kicking the damn thing. Allan tried to throw the hubcap away a couple of times, but Pete always scrounged it out of the Dumpster."

Last winter Moses had gotten into a screeching brawl with a rat out behind the station. It had lasted half an hour. Neighbors complained. Finally Moses had come limping in, tufts of fur missing from his face and shoulders. In his jaws he toted a fat rat, dead, plunked it down at Pete's feet for inspection, and casually licked a paw.

Ironically, he'd slumbered all through Pete's collapse.

"He's gone, you know," said Bounty.

"I know."

"Pete's gone. You been looking around the station much since you got back?"

"Hasn't been time, Warren."

"I got something you'll be interested in."

"Who the hell's going to tell Pete's wife?"

"Come here. This is good."

———

5

AIR-CONDITIONING MAYOR COSTIGAN'S SHOE

S tethoscope screwed into his ears, Bounty leaned over Claude
Pettigrew. "You know this was murder, don't you,
Mac?"

"Come again?" Even lethargic Pettigrew perked up.

"Use your noodle, man. Somebody tried to ice the whole
crew."

In his mid-fifties, Bounty was what one might call tough-
handsome, with a paunch, tufted eyebrows, and a shock of curly
black hair dramatized by a widow's peak. His stumpy legs were
too short for his freakishly long torso. When he was a young man,
baseball had been his passion, and his weathered face bore tes-
timony to assorted mishaps with balls, bats, and cleats. Once, in
a tavern fracas, the butt end of a pool cue had fractured his jaw.
His forearms were knotty with muscle, but the rest of him had
softened and bloated. Until recently he had smoked sixty unfil-

tered cigarettes a day. Before going on the wagon, he boasted his sweat was 4 percent alcohol.

A year ago, when he came down with the DTs, a mob of state patrolmen and King County deputies gang-tackled him, lumped his skull with billy clubs, and laced him into four-point restraints. Brandishing an Ithaca over-and-under shotgun, he'd been booming away at anything that could have been mistaken for the small toothy animals he believed were following him. Crows. Mailboxes. Doorknobs. Mo Costigan's shoe, which she had emptied as soon as she saw his intentions. He'd blown the ball off the firehouse flagpole while a bombed crowd from the Red Fern Tavern across the street alternately razzed and cheered—and Mo hobbled around, one foot bare, hollering at one and all.

Until three months ago he'd been living with his daughter in the Magnolia district in Seattle, but he'd gotten antsy, had moved back to Staircase to rent a small bungalow in the center of town. Thanks to the VA Hospital on Beacon Hill in Seattle, he was dry now.

For eight years he'd held the combined post of sheriff/fire chief in Staircase, knew everyone in town, all their secrets. Most of the dirt. He was a womanizer, teller of tall tales, eccentric, but a lifelong friend once he'd taken a shine to you. One had to look hard to find anybody who found fault with Warren Bounty. Few mentioned his former drinking habits. Or the fact that compared with Fontana's caring administration of the fire department, Bounty's reign was beginning to look slipshod.

Bounty's wardrobe rarely varied: cowboy boots, long-sleeved plaid shirts, and jeans that slipped lower and lower as he swaggered.

"Take a gander at this little booger," he said, poking the ham in a large cooking pan. Fontana slapped the off button on the Sony TV. "See them little lumps?"

"Mustard glaze?"

"Not bloody likely." Standing on tiptoe, he pointed across the top of the refrigerator to a small cardboard tray of the type designed to be left in the crawl space.

"Rat bait? What are you saying?"

"Burning in the throat, stomach cramps, nausea, extreme thirst, convulsions. Respiratory distress. Even the tonic stiffening. The eventual collapse. My guess is Pete ate some ham before the fire. Not enough to kill him, but enough to make him damned sick. D-CON is laced with arsenic."

"Ain't nobody ate my ham," barked Pettigrew. "Nobody touches the meat till I carve it. I mighta had a nibble, but no one else. What's the matter with you, Warren? You know better than that."

"You can see where somebody snipped off a couple of ears," said Bounty. "See here? My guess is they'll find traces of grease on Pete's Buck knife. Before the fire he musta snitched a little heel. Then, when he got back, he thought he'd settle his stomach by snitching some more. It's a wonder we didn't all swallow our fair shares and start stiffening."

"How'd you learn so much about arsenic?"

"Old man Phelan. We'd go up there to Barney's Grove and hold his hand and he'd gulp another brewski and nod off. Lung cancer. So we got a call up there one night around midnight and he had all these here symptoms. We sat like boobs watching him like we watched Pete this afternoon. By the time we called for help, he was dead."

"If you knew . . . ?"

"Goddammit," said Bounty. "I couldn't put my finger on it. Bobby Joe knew about Phelan, too. Why didn't he spit it out? Then Claude got sick. It got hectic. And Caitlin. When I finally told him, I think he panicked. We called poison control. They said if we weren't sure of the agent to dilute. But by that time Pete was convulsing."

"Why didn't they call for a medic sooner?"

"That damn Allan," said Pettigrew. "He kept phoning the dispatcher, trying to diagnose it between 'em."

"I thought Bobby Joe handled it," said Bounty, whose eyes were glistening.

"You ask me, Pete's wife has got a hell of a lawsuit," said Pettigrew.

"Maybe," said Fontana. "But Pete isn't going to make it no matter what. You don't come back from arsenic."

"Did you see this note?" Bounty stood in front of the bulletin board. Union announcements. A volunteer selling a '76 Dodge Dart. Business cards from a septic tank installer. A one-eyed horse for sale. Firewood. An elk-calling class at the local theater. "Was this up before you left?"

It was typed on a three-by-five card. Fontana read it aloud. " 'You took my affecktions—now you take this.' "

"Whoever wrote this tried to slaughter the whole lot of us. It was murder, Mac." Bounty shuffled across the room, breathing heavily. He snatched up a stack of neatly folded paper towels from the counter. Wanda Sheridan had decorated eight paper napkins, each with a name in crimped handwriting and a fleur-de-lis in the corner. Claude Pettigrew. Mac Fontana. Warren Bounty. Bobby Joe Allan. Kingsley Pierpont. Jim Caitlin. Peter Daugherty. And Wanda.

The Chevy dealer, Philip Breneman, walked into the room with two men to take Pettigrew to the hospital.

"Where is Wanda?" Fontana asked.

"Now you leave Wanda out of this here goddamned discussion!" Pettigrew's voice cracked. "Wanda didn't have nothing to do with nothin'. Wanda's a good kid. Ever since I brought her out here, you all been so goddamned jealous you could barely contain yerselves. Buncha hyenas in heat." Glowering from the doorway, Pettigrew waited while the accusation dried out. Then it occurred to him. "Fer christsakes! What if she ate some?"

"Been gone a good hour, Claude." Bounty glanced at his watch. "She ate any, she's gone."

"The hell." Pettigrew wrenched his bulk around in the doorway, knocking all three of his benefactors away. "I'm going after her. Wanda, honey!"

"Settle down, Claude." Fontana put his hands up. "Tell me where she lives and I'll do it."

"She ain't hurtin'," said Bounty.

"What the hell is that supposed to mean?" Pettigrew clenched his fists. Bounty was a big man, but Pettigrew had three inches of reach and eighty pounds on him.

"He doesn't mean anything, Claude," said Fontana. "Let's have her address."

Pettigrew looked dismally at the floor. "She thought they were going to be at the fire all day, so she give me a kiss good-bye and that little pinch she gives me and left. You're acting like she sneaked outa here."

"She eat any of the ham?" Bounty asked.

"I swear she didn't."

"You swore Pete didn't."

Breathing through his nostrils in a noisy whistle, Pettigrew penned Wanda's address on a notepad. It was on Yesler Way in central Seattle. The Ritz. Before leaving, he mumbled, "I'll tell you what. You're all so goddamned jealous is what you are. That's what."

"We'll check her," said Bounty. A surprising note of compassion dampered his smoky voice.

After Pettigrew left, Fontana dialed a Seattle cop he knew and asked him to have a patrol unit cruise Wanda Sheridan's place as soon as possible.

Behind the station Fontana unlocked the run and slapped his thighs. "Come on, Satan, you ugly lug. Get out. Work." Tail wagging, the dog followed Fontana into the fire station. He'd been police trained to search, track, apprehend suspects and to safeguard his handler. Massive even for a shepherd, he was dust-colored and raggedy, a spotty collar of black on his face and neck, a saddle of it splashed along his back. Scarred. Shaggy. He looked meaner than a moonshiner's hangover. He had bullet holes in his hide, an ear that had been half chewed off and sewn back. Mo called him the ugliest dog in America.

Other than the German shepherd, Fontana loved no dog. Never had. He didn't think a man on earth hated mongrels as much as he did. Yet he hauled Satan around everywhere. Held conversations with him when nobody was looking. Satan was different. Satan was more of a professional than ninety-nine out of a hundred cops. He'd saved Fontana's life. Fontana owed him.

"Satan. *Fuss!*" Instantly the animal trotted to Fontana's side. In the watch office Kingsley Pierpont stood in the chaos, gobbling a corn dog he'd purchased across the street at the Red Fern. A push broom was tilted against the wall beside him. Unnoticed on the wall above his head hung a charcoal sketch Pete Daugherty had executed, the Seagrave with five firefighters lined up beside it.

Standing at the open doorway in the warmth of the sun, Fontana said, "You'll be in charge. Maybe the rest of the week if Allan isn't back."

"He ain't sick," Kingsley said.

"Yeah, I know. Get somebody lined up for tonight to replace Pete. He was going to pull a sleeper. We'll talk in the morning. Anybody go out to his wife's?"

"Dempsey. They bein' friends and all. Mac? What happened?"

"Somebody poisoned him."

Bounty said, "King County'll be here awhile, Kingsley. Don't touch any food anywhere in the station, and don't let anybody else. County should be in your hair for a couple of hours. I'm going with Mac." The sour look on Fontana's face said, *Not really.* "Come on, Mac. What am I supposed to do? Give Sis a call to see why she's not in jail? I got a stake in this. I hired Pete. Goddammit, he was my kid."

"We'll take my truck."

Outside on the sidewalk a limousine pulled up in front of the station, blocking Fontana's path. The glossy black door opened, and Mo Costigan stepped out.

"Howdy, Mayor Mo," Fontana said. "Mayormo." It was only because he knew how vain she was about the title that he poked fun at it.

"Damn you, Mac. I told you never to call me that."

6

THE VANISHING SMILE

"I'm glad I caught you," said Mo.

A short woman, Mo Costigan wasn't fat, only solid. She gave the appearance of being chestier than she was because of hauteur. Full of fire and zip, she walked an hour in the evenings, always a different route through town, operated a successful CPA business in Bellevue, and held the politics of Staircase firmly in her iron grip.

In today's heat she wore a white skirt, a white blouse, stockings, bright blue pumps, and a necklace of matching blue beads. Her father, a druggist in Issaquah, let her poke through the damaged sunglasses on his racks. Mac and Brendan made a game of spotting the flaw in each pair. The limo belonged to Lars Ereckson, a real estate developer who, for the past several months, had been courting the town, the council, the planning commission, and, despite the fact that he was married, Maureen Costigan.

Prior to Fontana's appointment, though Mo had had scant training, she'd been in the habit of taking the reins at fire emergencies. It was a potentially disastrous habit, which Lieutenant Allan had failed to challenge during his brief tenure as ranking officer. Now with Fontana as chief, Mo's fitness to command at emergencies had become a bitter bone of contention.

She'd given faulty directions to the volunteers after a jumper went over the protective fence at Snoqualmie Falls. The metal-frame Stokes had gotten hung up in the rocks, an arm and leg of the suicide victim flapping free in a ghastly tango for the TV cameras to record. It took an hour to get the ropes untangled and the dead man back to the parking lot. All three networks rolled the videotapes repeatedly on their evening newscasts. Mo laughed uncomfortably after Fontana chewed her out for it but didn't show up on any more calls.

Everyone but Fontana was daunted by the mayor. Dragon Lady Mo, they called her—behind her back. It was common knowledge she'd slept with Fontana's predecessor, Warren Bounty. In a small town like Staircase, though, common knowledge was a dirty penny left on the sidewalk. Everybody knew it was there, but nobody bothered to examine it to see what it was worth.

After Mo cleared the car, one of Ereckson's lackeys, part of the legal staff, reached out and shut the door. Fontana caught a short blast of air-conditioned coolness, cologne, new-car smell, booze, and the taint of money packed into a wallet; caught a glimpse of an immaculately pressed two-thousand-dollar suit. In deference to the air conditioner, television, and stock market ticker, the chauffeur kept the motor chugging. It nettled Fontana, who preferred to breathe air that hadn't been used recently. He stepped upwind of the exhaust.

"What happened?" Mo stepped with him. "Mac? We heard there was trouble."

"Pete Daugherty's dead. I can't do it now, so I'd like you to visit his wife. Will you do that, Mo?"

"An accident? A fall? What?"

"We think he was poisoned," said Warren Bounty, jamming one hand into the front pocket of his jeans and rocking back on the heels of his lizard-skin cowboy boots. He sipped from a cold can of Sprite, then touched the dew-spotted aluminum to his brow. Mo appraised him, and he her. Bounty had a movie star élan about him that belied the relentless facts of his history. "Lookin' good, Mo."

"Why, thank you, Warren."

Fontana said, "We're in a hurry, Mo. Why don't you go inside and let Kingsley fill you in?"

"I'd rather talk to you or Lieutenant Allan."

"Sorry, sweetheart."

Mo goose-stepped across the sidewalk, blocked Fontana's path, and slammed her fists onto her hips. Knowing it intimidated people, she made a habit of standing too close. She smelled of Binaca, perfume, and hair spray. Fontana regarded her Ray-Bans. "I'm not talking to Kingsley. You're chief. Your primary obligation is to fill in the mayor when and if something of consequence happens."

"Don't get confused. My duty is to run the fire department. You don't pay me enough to kiss ass, darlin'. I can go across the street and pump gas for what you're paying."

Her face was flaming, but she kept her voice controlled. "The council will expect a report."

"Not in the next half hour, they won't."

"I've convened a special session. I want you up there in five minutes."

"Talk to Kingsley, and you can lay it out for the council yourself. Then you can all sip tea and gossip about which neighbor hasn't neutered her cat."

"I need you, dammit," said Mo. "Why do you do this to me? Warren was never like this, were you, Warren?"

Bounty smirked. "Nobody ever died when I was chief'n."

***

"Lars going to sit in on this council meeting?" Fontana asked.

Glancing at the opaque windows of the limo, Mo said, "Mr. Ereckson and I have been reconnoitering construction sites. I thought he might audit the session. You find anything improper in that?"

"Why not let's appoint him deputy mayor and hand him the key to the city? That way he can rip off all the land he wants. Let him put some golden arches out there by the highway so the whole world knows just how greedy Staircase can get."

Mo grew furious, her raspy voice dropping into the I've-been-to-hell-and-back tone Mac always admired. On the phone most people thought she was a man because of the low register of her voice. "He can hear you, for godsakes," she sputtered. "I've warned you about that kind of talk, Mac. You're a city official."

"City officials aren't supposed to think?"

"The least you can do is take this, you big galoot," said Mo, digging in her purse and thrusting a silver shield at him. "Take it, Mac. Damn your hide. You were the big shot fire investigator in the East. You cleaned up that Zajac murder last winter. I have a feeling we're going to need some law around here."

"You know Staircase has a contract with King County."

"I want *you*." Folding her arms under her breasts, Mo tapped a foot with machine-gun rapidity and stared at him. A gust of warm wind blew strands of her dark brown hair across her face, snagging strays in her mouth. "Warren's back. He could help."

"Anything you need," said Warren. Mo blushed.

"If the fishing's still slow, I'll give you a report at the end of the month." Fontana took the badge and strode across the street to the GMC.

" 'You big galoot'?" Bounty chuckled as he trotted to keep pace. "Are you kidding me? Hey, was it the lens?"

"The arm was bent."

"I thought it was the lens."

On the old highway the hot winds buffeted the truck. At the

Arco station rowdy teenagers in raggedy cutoffs and baseball caps inflated inner tubes for the river. Chinooks skidded down off the Cascades, baking the valley, dehydrating old men, killing lawns, and withering vegetable gardens. Staircase, thirty miles east of Seattle, was undergoing the worst drought in one hundred years. The Snoqualmie River was shallower than any old gummer remembered. Spawning salmon queued in the sound, waiting for sufficient water to swim upstream. Kayakers and canoeists waived the season. Logging operations were halted because of fire danger. Deer came out of the dry mountains and got zapped by trucks on the highway.

Seattle, Tacoma, and other cities imposed water rationing. Sprinkle lawns on odd days. Wash autos not at all. Brush your teeth out of cups. Stow bricks in your toilet tank.

In the prehistoric and rattly GMC the trip took forty minutes. Fontana hefted the badge and placed it in the ashtray.

Monday afternoon. The westbound highway was nearly empty, and Fontana appreciated the vast gray spaces. The Carryall eked only ten miles out of a gallon of gas. Mac's son called it the Destroyer. Burnt rose and white, it was the only vehicle Mac drove, and it belonged to the city. Mo had earned his everlasting ire by once calling it "titty pink."

During their drive Warren Bounty seeded their shock and disbelief with weeds of idle talk. Mac had known the man only a few months, but Bounty was half grizzly and half myth. His agile mind flitted from story to story. "A thing like that hits you so hard you think your kids'll be born dizzy, eh?" he said.

"I liked, Pete. His wife, too."

"Did what you told him. Kept his nose clean."

Fontana sat sullenly, their exchange generating the first and only silence on the trip. He admired Bounty's comeback from the bottle, and if Bounty hung around much longer, Fontana speculated he might have a best friend again for the first time in years. Below the sound of the wind flirting with their half-open

41

windows, Fontana hummed to himself. Roy Orbison. "Only the Lonely."

Bounty didn't seem to want his chief's job back. A California fire department he'd left ten years earlier mailed him a pension check each month. He had some savings. A few investments, including four shabby rental units in town. In a month he would move into one of them.

His daughter, Cheryl Briggs, drove out from her home in Seattle three times a week to keep tabs on him. Bounty scoffed at her mollycoddling, claimed he didn't need a baby-sitter in a Swedish sports car. He was pumping air, wasn't he? Yet, said Cheryl to anybody she managed to buttonhole, her dad's heart was bad. His lungs were shot. Liver barely functional. His kidneys needed replacement. He was taking eleven different prescription medications.

It was said he'd awakened in the middle of the night to take a leak and, losing his equilibrium because of the medications, had tumbled to the floor and split his head open on a piece of furniture. "Stitched up the little rascal myself. Just took a needle and thread and used the bathroom mirror. What? Ain't you boys ever sewed on a button? Nothin' to it." Despite a set of fresh railroad tracks crudely zigzagged across his brow, nobody but guileless Pete had believed it. "Talk about tough," Pete Daugherty said appreciatively.

"Poison is a woman's crime. You know that, don't you, Mac?"

"Seems like I heard it in one of my criminology classes."

"Women fix the food. It's something they think of."

"Let's hope Wanda's sick as a dog on a shrimp boat."

"Us showing up at her door might be the biggest surprise of her life." Bounty laughed uproariously. He segued into a story about his aunt who he said had died of spontaneous combustion. "Just lit up like a candle in a Boston rocker with a *Better Homes and Gardens* in her lap."

Bounty reminisced about his first wife, who, he said, had been missing one leg at the hip when he married her, then went on to lose an eye, a lung, all her teeth, and her kneecap before she lost the foot on her remaining leg. Most of that story Fontana knew to be hyperbole.

"Longer I stayed with that gal, the smaller she got. Wouldn't be nothin' left if we was still together. Just parts sitting in a jar on the mantel. She liked to save 'em. I'll always remember that one big old eye in pickle juice staring at me." Fontana had to laugh at the way Bounty said it, drawing out his words, spreading the lids away from his right eye with two fingers to demonstrate.

Bounty told of the time he spent ten days in an igloo with four Eskimo women. On the truck radio the Angels were singing "My Boyfriend's Back."

Bounty's voice dipped into a growl of angst. "Going to miss that kid. Never said an unkind word about no one. You told him something nasty about someone, why, Pete would be in the room with you still, but you could tell he wasn't listening. I 'member when he first signed on. We had a car wreck up towards the pass just beyond Truck Town. Some huge lady got drunk and drove her Datsun pickup into a guard rail.

"We got there, I thought it was too late, but you know how it is. Never know who we're going to bring back. Pete'd only been in maybe six months. Pete pulled her out of the car. He broke open her blouse and there was this brassiere the size of two airplane hangars. Everybody's ready to work on her and Pete's the closest so he's trying to figure out how to get this brassiere off without a winch. He fumbles around and finally he gets mad and he just digs his fingers under it, raises it up and hooks the thing around her neck. These two great big old titties roll out. Tattooed across one it says 'left.' Across the other, 'right.' We just all stopped and gaped. I mean, it was something.

"The medics showed up and said to stop CPR. So we're waiting for the Medical examiner's wagon and Pete sees what he's done to this woman, torn her bra all up and slung it around her neck like a noose, and kindhearted Pete, thinking it's a little indelicate, he tries to fit it back on. First he makes an effort to stuff one boob in, but it's so squishy he can't. Then he tries the other, doesn't have any better luck with that. They're bigger than both his hands can hold. We're starting to laugh. 'It was like watching a man trying to stuff a pillow into a condom,' said Gil Cutty. The more Pete works—the more frustrated he gets—and the harder we laugh. He's thinking he has to straighten things before they haul her away, like somebody in the morgue's going to say, 'Who the hell did this?' Took him five minutes, us all standing around in a circle busting our guts—and even then, he had em all cockeyed off in different directions. He could sure turn pink, though. That's what I remember about him most. He never talked shit about nobody, and he sure could turn pink. He had that funny little smile."

Fontana had always figured the smile came about because Pete's father had raised him roughly and he didn't have the confidence for a full grin. He'd smile, and then it would slowly begin to vanish. Unless he was around kids, Pete rarely gave you more than that fainthearted smile.

7

HOOKERS, NEEDLES, AND HIGH TIMES WHILE YOU WAIT

"**L**ookit," said Wanda as she paced in a sassy barefoot strut, "it's almost like you guys think I dumped the crap in the supper."

"The police were only here to check that you weren't poisoned," said Fontana. She stopped pacing and shot Fontana a look. Her smoky eyes looked astute enough that he realized she'd been faking stupidity for six weeks.

"Why'd ya take off, Wanda?" Bounty asked, straddling a creaky straight-backed chair. "You were keen on that ham clutch until you disappeared." He sucked iced orange juice through a plastic straw, cubes knocking around in the glass. Even without Staircase's parching chinook winds it was hot in Seattle. Humid. Windless. The city reeked of buses, cars, dogs, and the leftover ozone from electric trolleys. Occasionally Fontana sniffed seawater from the nearby sound. Yeast and the aroma of baking dough wafted from the Wonder Bread factory southeast of their location.

"Told ya why I left. Hadda meet my little brother. Gettin' sprung from King County lockup this afternoon. Lookit. Claude has his thing and I have mine."

"And yours is taking the big sap for every nickel in his sock?" Bounty grinned.

Accustomed to cheap-shot accusations, Wanda didn't flinch. "Claude's a big boy."

"With a brain the size of a peanut. And you're a big girl, right?"

"You know it."

"Cool off, Warren," Fontana said. "This isn't going anywhere."

"I had a boy die on me this afternoon, Mac. A boy I liked a whole heck of a lot."

"I liked him, too. We going to stand here and argue over who liked him most?"

"You and I both know there's only been one dog-and-pony act in Staircase."

"I ain't done nothin'!" she said.

"Everything's been runnin' normal out there for a hundred years, and suddenly Pocahontas here shows up and drops a spoon in the crapper. Now we got rat poison and dead boys and who knows what all else. We know you been cleaning out Claude's bank accounts. Watkins seen you at the racetrack the other day, blowing a couple of pockets full of Claude's loot."

"He's bankrolling the Northwest Soup Company. He'll get his money back. And plenty of return besides. What do you mean, *accounts*? He got more than one?"

"You know what I mean." Bounty gave Fontana an eye roll. "You ain't going to leave Claude nothing but a dime-store brass ring, and his biannual wet dream, are you?"

"Honey," said Wanda, "any little thing Claude wants to donate he does of his own free will." Wanda pigeonholed herself at the cracked window and studied the street three stories below.

She wore skimpy nylon maroon shorts and the Snake River T-shirt, the sleeves of which were loose. As she gesticulated, the funnels of the armholes revealed the edges of her white globes. The location of her apartment was an indictment, surrounded by lowlifes, hookers, needle freaks, pornographic graffiti, naked urchins, and welfare queens.

The Ritz. Trying to gain entry to the locked front door, they'd rapped at a basement apartment and through a chink in the water-spotted shades glimpsed six or seven people frantically stashing drug paraphernalia. Above them, a prostitute shambled out of the front door and down the steps in a tight leather skirt, walking as if her legs were made of lead. Mac grabbed the door before it closed behind her.

Crayoned scribblings disfigured the hallways. Apartment doors were fortified with padlocks. A battered pay phone stood guard near the stairs, a mouthful of garbage packed into the coin return. Plywood sheets were nailed across the fire escape where the original doors had been gorillaed off their hinges. Communal bathrooms. The smell of piss and wine. An empty whiskey bottle sat on the floor outside Wanda's apartment. A three-year-old Asian child with brown eyes deep enough to get lost in played stark naked on a scooter in the hall.

"My brother's comin' pretty soon." Elbows high, Wanda fluffed her hair. "He won't like you guys."

"Little brother gonna get pushy?" Bounty asked.

Wanda ran her hands through her short hair, which was shaved in the back like a man's and longer in the front and on the sides, an abused Dorothy Hamill look. It was the brown-blond color of stained pinewood.

"You and Claude have a fight?" Bounty asked.

"Course not. I got bored."

Peering out the window again, Wanda turned her back full on the two men, riding on her bare toes, flexing her calves, the arches of her feet going white and ridged.

47

A nurse's uniform swung on a hanger on the back of a bedroom door, a pair of white hose twisted around the neck. The couch was a war zone, dirty laundry and movie magazines. A pair of scuffed white work shoes lay on their sides.

"We can get the King County cops all over your ass," threatened Bounty. "They'd just love your ass."

"Don't feed me that crap," said Wanda, her face turning ugly.

Bounty sprang out of his chair and bulled across the small room. Instinctively Wanda slid behind Fontana. Her perfume smelled like bubble gum. He could feel the body heat from her breasts on his back, her fingers gouging his shoulders.

"Outside, Warren. I'll do the rest."

"She did it, Mac. Look at her face. Claude probably put her in his will and she wanted to off him."

"Ha!" shrieked Wanda.

"Out!" said Fontana.

"Look at her!" hollered Bounty.

"Ha!"

"Look!"

"Ha!"

"You were seeing her mug instead of that little rump you'd know she's got guilt written all over her," said Warren.

Satan sat in the corner, watching his current and former handlers bicker. Inured by the rowdy goings-on at the fire station, the dog rarely displayed more than perfunctory interest in shouting matches. His one good ear pointed at the ceiling.

After Bounty left, the room lapsed into silence. Wanda crossed to the kitchen table, picked up his drinking glass, scrubbed, rinsed, toweled, then set it carefully in the cupboard. It was the only clean glass in the apartment.

"Got a phone I can borrow?" Fontana asked.

"In the bedroom. You been here a long time, though."

"Leaving in a minute."

"I ain't." She fixed him with her gray eyes, held the look for several long beats. The interrogation had cemented them into a certain intimacy. "I ain't lyin' neither."

"See anybody tack a note up on the bulletin board?"

"Didn't pay attention."

"Claude been himself lately?"

"Three hundred pounds of sugar."

In the bedroom Fontana sat of the edge of the unmade swaybacked double bed, picked the phone up off the floor, and dialed Overlake Hospital in Bellevue. After he announced who he was, they told him Pete was dead. The confirmation was like a hammerblow. Lieutenant Bobby Joe Allan had been treated and discharged. He dialed Charles Dummelow, a King County detective he'd worked with last winter. A soft-spoken cop answered and gave him a second number.

"Chuck."

"MacKinley? How's it hanging?"

"Surprised you recognized my voice after all this time."

"You do things makes you stick in a body's mind."

"Want you to run a name through the computer. NCIC and then the local stuff. See what you come up with."

Fontana found Wanda's purse on the floor next to the closet door and rummaged through the clutter. He pulled her driver's license. For a few months, a year if they were unlucky, the Ritz was the sort of seedy place students, drunks, and recent Southeast Asian immigrants called home while they organized their finances, flattened cockroaches, and got their acts together. According to the address on the license, Wanda had languished here three years. "Wanda Cynthia Sheridan. Got it?"

"Sure. What's going on?"

"Had an unexplained death in Staircase this afternoon. One of my men. Your people are up there snapping Polaroids as we speak."

"You looking into it?"

"I'm hoping you guys solve it. I'm not ready for this."

"How's the fishing?"

"Water's so low if the bears quit pissing, we won't have any rivers at all."

"I'll get ahold of your neighbor or the station. I've got the number still."

In the other room Wanda had switched on the radio and tuned in an FM station. A sultry melody: jazz. Lots of sax and keyboard. Mellow. Her closet was better organized than the rest of the apartment. Fontana pulled the door wide and flipped through her clothes. Sandwiched between a pair of gaudy party dresses studded with sequins he discoverd a white paramedic smock. The name tag was what put the heat in his face. James Caitlin. Now why would Rainy's husband hang his shirts in Wanda's closet?

8

THE DEVIL WINKS
AND NUDGES

Before leaving the bedroom Fontana peeked under the bed:
unmated shoes, a detumescent sock, a ball point pen, dusty
coins, and August's dog-eared *Playboy*. The odor of Wanda's
perfume. She slept here but not alone. Maybe not every night,
but some nights a man bedded with her. He gave the pillow to
Satan. "Just tell me how tall the guy is and what size shoe he
wears," said Fontana. "Yale or Harvard?" Satan cocked his head
at Fontana.

In the main room he found Wanda dancing to the radio, eel-
like, sinuous. She moved as if she'd had professional training:
ballet; modern jazz; assorted bar tops.

Seated at the kitchen table with his back to Fontana, a long-
haired man maybe twenty years old wore tattered blue jeans and
a faded ebony T-shirt. Across the back of the shirt it said, "Hit
me—I need the money." He manipulated a bent spoon, ignited

a candle, and fussed with the fixings. He hadn't noticed Fontana.

Lost in the rhythm of the music, Wanda danced slowly. Fontana dropped a hand and absently scratched Satan behind the ears.

"Pete liked you, didn't he?"

She didn't stop, only chinked her eyes open sleepily, and let the lids clunk closed again. "Pete was just a kid."

The man at the table jerked, eyeballed Fontana, then made a sprinter's move toward the door. So did Satan. They both stopped in mid-flight, taking each other's measure.

"He'll get your legs out from under you before you hit the hall," said Fontana. Eyes glued to the black-faced German shepherd, the man backed up and sat.

He resembled Wanda. His long black hair was swept straight back and held in place with a chartreuse headband. He was tall and striking, pale skin, a hawk nose, and dark brown eyes set too close together. Maybe six-five. And thin. He had a delicate mouth, same as Wanda's, drawn and turned down naturally at the ends.

"Harold Glass," said Wanda. "Mac Fontana. The fire chief in Staircase."

Holding aloft a small packet, Harold said, "Just got out, man. Thirty days for public indecency. You ain't gonna bust me?" He was about to swallow the packet.

"Kill yourself, buddy."

"Thanks, man."

Fontana watched Harold add water to the gray powder and heat the product over the candle, using the bent spoon as a cooking utensil. Watched him wrap his arm with Penrose tubing, tug it tight with his teeth. Watched him fill the hypodermic syringe, zero in on the vein, insert, and ooze some juice in, then back off, drawing blood back into the cylinder, squirting more of the mixture into himself, then siphoning off more blood. The plunger filled with a pinkish backwash.

Smiling sheepishly, he said, "Called jackin' off. Makes it last longer."

"Maybe you could go around to day-cares and give lessons." To Wanda, who was still dancing, he said, "You kissed Pete."

"Kiss a lot of people. Warren. I kissed him. Even thought about kissing you. You got beautiful eyes."

"Do anything else with Pete?"

"Like what?" Wanda operated under the assumption that all men desired her.

"Ever see him alone?"

"Like I said, Pete was a kid."

"How long have you been screwing Caitlin?"

The question aborted her dance. She opened her eyes. "Jimmy? What makes you think I been dating Jimmy?"

"How long?"

"I dunno. Five weeks."

"You've only been with Claude five."

"Six."

"I get it. You've got scruples. You date a guy seven days before you start two-timing him."

"Very funny."

Fontana got an idea and had her write the words across the margin of a week-old Seattle *PI*. One line. He waited to see how she spelled "affections." He had a feeling in school she hadn't gotten A's in anything but gym and boys. She spelled it "afektions" the first time, lined that out, and tried "affecshons."

"This your brother?"

"Little brother. Harold Glass. My maiden name was Glass. Works in the theater up the street. Gonna be a star."

"Not if he kills himself first."

"You should hear him sing." She surveyed the paraphernalia scattered across the table. "It's not my bag, you know? Haven't touched shit in six years. Too many friends died on it."

"Who pays for little brother?"

53

She thought before answering. "Harold's got a boyfriend on Capitol Hill. Works for Royer—mayor of Seattle, in case you didn't know."

"How'd you meet Claude?"

"He come in to Virginia Mason to get his ulcer operated on. I was his night nurse. Used to give me money to smuggle Johnnie Walker to his room, then have me stick around and take a snoot."

Fontana walked to the door, snapped his fingers for the dog. "*Fuss!*" he said. Wanda sidled around the beast and stood close, grasping Fontana's bare forearm. He remembered that first day Claude Pettigrew showed her off at the station. She'd been duded up in a tight blue dress. Fontana had thought of that old rock and roll song "Devil with a Blue Dress on" by Mitch Ryder and the Detroit Wheels.

Not that Wanda was the personification of evil.

Just cheesy. And a bit thrilling. The way a firecracker going off in your hand was a bit thrilling.

He thought she was going to say something like, "Now you know where I live, come back when you're not in such a rush," but she didn't.

"Satan."

On the drive home they got embroiled in the afternoon commute out of the city. Parked on the I-90 bridge, waiting for the infinite line of idling cars to start moving, Bounty panned across the haze at the south end of Lake Washington. The water was like molten glass. "Why'd you throw me out?"

"You were acting like an ass."

"I can get out right here."

"Don't be like that. I know what's going on with you."

Warren faced Fontana. "Do you?"

"Same as me. You don't lose a man off your crew and keep your poise. All I did was remove you from a situation that was getting unhealthy."

"You acted like you were going to hit me."

"Wasn't going to let you maul Wanda."

On I-90, almost to Staircase, the crosswinds ripped at the tree-tops. "You didn't really spend ten days with four Eskimo women, did you?"

"You know what a goddamn liar I am, Mac."

"Didn't think so."

"Six days. Three women." For a half mile they guffawed. The tension released itself in waves of laughter. Fontana liked listening to Bounty's booming laugh. When they'd settled down, Bounty said, " 'Sides my eight years' sheriffin' in Staircase, I put in a couple as an MP. Just a lunkhead kid out of high school. Seen the Philippines. Japan. Been around the block. I got experience, too, Mac. Wanda's hidin' something."

"Hiding and killing are different animals. We're all hiding things."

"You gonna follow this to the end?"

"I think I am."

"Thought you weren't going to let Mo push you around."

"Doesn't have anything to do with Mo."

Warren slumped, dropped his head onto the back of the seat, and crossed his arms. "Damn, I wish I was sheriff." Fontana took one hand from the wheel, removed the badge from the ashtray, and tossed it onto his lap. "No, I don't mean it like that. I wish I hadn't made such a muddle of my life. Like I still had something left of the first fifty-six years except fog. A daughter who fusses over me but really can't forgive me. A lousy pension from California. Me, I'm starting almost from scratch."

"You've got a hundred good friends."

"Like who?"

"Me."

"Trouble is a guy can't spend friends."

"Take back the sheriff's job. I don't want it." Fontana grinned. In the three months since Bounty had returned this was the first time the subject had come up.

"I'm past that. Too broke down. Them DTs. Three-D video hell with sound effects. Chair arms turning into pythons that wrap around my hands. People's faces falling off while I'm talking to them. Hobgoblins with razors for teeth. Then my mother came back. I don't have the constitution. 'Sides, I braced Mo about being sheriff." He gave Fontana a look, swiping at his cheek and jaw with one large hand. "She won't let me have it. Tried to sweet-talk her, but . . . Hell, eight years ago she was just a kid. Sleepy little town. We'd drill the volunteers Thursday evenings and Saturday mornings. When somebody got burgled, I'd drive around with Satan. Usually neighbor kids. We'd track 'em right up to their front porch; they'd hear him barking and confess. Bikers'd sweep through town, I'd give 'em a chaw, chugalug a few beers. Everythin' was peaceful as a museum in Tacoma. Then I near ta drank myself to death."

As they crossed the South Fork on the old highway, the limousine passed them heading west.

"Ereckson," said Warren. "Half the town thinks he's a saint passing out free dollar bills, and the other half thinks he smells of sulfur and brimstone. What dya know about that guy?"

"He built the lodge down on the river in the lower valley," said Fontana. " 'Bout six months ago. He's been using it as his base of operations. Rube Wilkerson, since he sells real estate, did some investigating and learned Ereckson's been snapping up every piece of land he can get his hands on. Using different names. He wants to put in about a million houses. And a shopping center out on the floodplain where nobody's got any business putting up a pup tent. He's a scary guy."

"Ha! Didn't think you were scared of nothin', Mac."

"Progress. I'm afraid of what these sorry Dugans call progress."

9

OOOOOOOOOOO!
I LOVE IT!

The Westside Savings revolving sign said it was eighty-eight degrees in the upper valley. *Cinderella* was splashed across the reader board at the tiny Staircase theater. Abby's Furniture had advertised its summer sale, though everybody in town knew the prices hadn't been lowered. Video rentals kept the furniture store afloat. At the hardware store the clerks were switching off the popcorn machine and rolling the lawn mowers inside for the night.

The banners were strung up for the annual Cascade Days fireworks and Grand Torchlight Parade with the Timber Queen riding a logging truck. He would keep himself upwind away from the soot and diesel exhaust nobody else seemed to mind. Logging trucks out the kazoo. In this boondock town even Santa showed up riding a Kenworth.

At the fire station Bounty decamped the GMC. "You and me are going to work on this, Mac."

57

"Let's hope the county comes up with something lickety-split."

"If they don't?"

Fontana mentally rehearsed the bollixed scene in Wanda's apartment. "Sure, we'll work together."

"Realize I ain't no big-city arson investigator like you was. And I ain't ever solved a murder. But it means a lot to me. Pete was just . . ." Fontana had a feeling as soon as Warren was alone, he would sit down and have a good cry. "Pete was always so compassionate to our aid victims. Pete hugged people I wouldn't even kick."

Fontana spoke softly. "One little thing, Warren."

"Yeah?"

"You screw Wanda?"

Warren stopped breathing and gave Mac a beleaguered stare. He inhaled deeply. "Me? Hell, no. Well . . . maybe played around a time or two. Never dicked her. Why?"

Fontana shrugged. After Warren Bounty sped off in his battered green Pinto, he fed the dog a snack, gave him a large bowl of cool water. It was after six. King County had finished scouring the crime scene. In his office he found a dusty ticket book in the bottom drawer.

Outside, Fontana plodded across the street and began writing. Wilber Humphries had been bellyaching that the council members and firemen had been leaving their cars in his vacant lot. Humphries had tried to fence it, but the council passed an ordinance barring fences within two blocks of the fire station. He wrote six parking tickets, one of which he slipped under the wiper of Mo Costigan's red Porsche.

In the air-conditioned station house Fontana took Pierpont into his office and shut the door. "Thanks for staying, Kingsley."

"No prob." Kingsley was the first black many people in town had had a chance to observe up close. He reveled in fulfilling their expectations. Mac was certain the pink Cadillac, the mink-lined mirror, the gold jewelry, and a lot of things Kingsley said were part of an elaborate mocking tap dance.

Pierpont, who had a tendency to put on weight, was in the midst of yet another diet and jogging program. His hair was combed straight back, wet and slick-looking. His skin was coffee-colored, lots of cream. He was a good-looking man with a tidy mustache. Vanity kept his fingernails as long as a woman's, groomed weekly by a lady he called "da nail bitch."

He wore two gold rings impregnated with diamonds. More than once, Allan, behind his back, had accused him of pimping. Fontana had put an angry stop to the trumped-up charges. Fontana sank into the swivel chair behind the desk. "Have any runs?"

"Kid cut his foot on a broken bottle down by the river. Off Jacobsen? Sent him to Snoqualmie in his mom's car."

"Allan come back?"

"He was here."

Allan had bitterly opposed Pierpont's recruitment eight years earlier. In order to be democratic about it, the city had given an open exam, coded the written section, and graded the physical agility test by number. Pierpont had earned the highest total composite score. Because so many volunteers wanted the position, the civil service board had publicly made a production of the testing process. The city was committed to hiring the highest scoring applicant: Pierpont. Since then Bobby Joe Allan, who'd obtained his job years earlier through a cousin on the city council, had been sniping.

"Din't say nothin' to me. Filled out his disability papers and left."

"He'll be off tomorrow then. You don't have to come in either. Take a couple of days. With pay."

"What am I gonna do? Sit home and watch Oprah? I'll be here."

"What happened at the fire today?"

"If you're askin' if Allan went inside, you're wasting your breath. Me and Pete masked up and took an inch-and-a-half. I never saw Allan."

"Room fire?"

"Closet fire, really. Don't think we used ten gallons. Another couple minutes, though, and it woulda flashed over and taken the whole upstairs. Pete broke out the window, took his facepiece off, and threw up. I thought he'd taken some smoke, but I guess he was sick."

"And back here?"

"You pretty much heard that. Allan fucked around getting a medic unit."

"Got any theories?"

Pierpont's voice went into a high, scornful whine. "Heeeellll, nooo! All I know is Bobby Joe comes in here throwing things around, filling his paper work out, and mumblin' some shit about why was I da only one din't get a tummyache." Kingsley's eyes widened. Kingsley could say a lot of things by raising his eyebrows and showing white. Right now he was saying he wouldn't tolerate Bobby Joe's innuendo.

"Forget it. Allan doesn't run the show. What about Wanda? She been sleepin' with more than just Claude?"

"I know what you know."

"What about Bounty?"

"Warren? Now a year ago I wouldn't have put anything past him. He's different today. I don't know how to explain it. More serious, or somethin'. Maybe that comes of knowing you're gonna die. I don't mean he's gonna die, but you know. After that trouble, he hadda be thinkin' about it. Whooo. He was something in the old days. Know old Doc Mendenhall? Used to be the department doctor? Had these big old knuckles on him. You look, next time you see him, and see if he don't got knuckles like the knob on a baseball bat. He'd do our yearlies and we'd all sweat bullets waiting for him to put on the rubber gloves for the annual prostate hunt.

"One year Warren's had about enough, and when the doc starts his probing, Warren yells out loud as he can, 'Oooooooo, Doc!

60

Don't stop! Don't stop! I love it! I love it! Ooooooooooo!' People in the waitin' room like ta went crazy. But he sure stopped Mendenhall. 'Oooooo, Doc. I love it!' " Fontana smiled. He'd heard the story before.

Pierpont launched off the edge of Fontana's desk in a controlled glide and moved to the window. He winked open the blinds with two fingers, then let them snap shut. "Wanda still kickin'?"

"She's kickin'. What'd County tell you before they left?"

"Guy named Hebert was in charge. He wasn't talkin' to no brother."

The night men were already in the beanery, scrubbing walls, counters, tabletops. The local Northwest news was on the TV. Fontana might have stayed to see if the excitement in Staircase was getting coverage, but he didn't much care. He said good-bye to Kingsley and tramped around the station. He didn't know what he was looking for.

It was a three-bay station in the west end of a huge modern building erected fifteen years earlier. Constructed of brick, tile, glass, and aluminum, it was contemporary and serviceable. In front were two roll-up glass-paneled doors. The long double door opened on the main bay, where both pumpers were kept. Behind the first pumper the three-thousand-gallon tanker was parked. In the sticks it was sometimes an unforgiving trip to water and many a house fire wasn't tapped until the tanker arrived. A drive-through station, it had identical doors in back on the alley. The smaller door served the aid car.

On the east side of the bay a bunk room was situated, along with a weight room, a large bathroom with showers, and a cubbyhole big enough for a pool table. On the west side of the bay were the offices, the beanery, and, down a long corridor off the side of the building, isolated, the tiny unused jail cell and Fontana's office.

The station abutted the two-story municipal building. On the first floor in a corner was a set of offices used by the King County police. Staircase paid the county a monthly fee for police protection.

In the watch office Satan was curled up, asleep, Moses on top of him. Fontana leaned over and glared into Satan's face. "How many times have I told you? Don't be letting that cat sleep on you. Makes you look like a wimp!" The chagrined dog flattened his ears.

Fontana loaded Satan into the truck and drove home. He lived with his son on a dogleg at the end of a long macadam road that led directly to the river. They had two acres, a buffer of trees lying between them and the North Fork Road. There were four other houses on the dogleg. His landlord, Mary Gilliam, lived next door. Mary baby-sat when Mac was away. She'd adopted Mac and his son, spoiled them: cupcakes, pies, roast beef, and the cheapest rent in the upper valley.

When they got home, Satan jumped out of the GMC and stretched while Mac traipsed along the trail to Mary's house. He could hear Brendan cutting up in the yard with a couple of other boys. Timmy and Reeves. When Brendan spotted Fontana, he sprinted and performed a flying leap into his arms. " Mac! You're home. You're late."

"I had a bad day. How about you? How you been, Brendan?" He nuzzled the seven-year-old's neck.

"Fine."

"What do you want for dinner?"

"Chocolate pie, orange pop, and potato chips."

"Let's see. I think I can manage salmon and baked potatoes."

"Ah, Mac."

10

SET A PLACE
FOR THE DEAD WOMAN

It was almost seven-thirty when Mary made her way up the well-worn trail through a hundred yards of alders, briars, bright purple thistles, and ragtag wild rhodies.

Mac had gulped a single beer, showered, then cooked dinner. After they ate, he and Brendan washed and dried the dishes. Three place settings, as had been their habit for the year and a half since Linda's funeral. A couple of weeks ago Mac had gently urged Brendan to set for two, but Brendan insisted on a place for his late mother.

Too short to reach the drying rack on the counter, the boy had knelt precariously on a stool and wielded a dishrag almost as long as he was tall. Now the two of them were flopped on cushions on the floor in the family room. Checkers. The nightly tournament. According to the weekly log they kept on a piece of cardboard, Mac was trailing, 27 to 4.

"Yoo-hoo?"

"In here, Mary," yelled Brendan. He was thin. Healthy. A head that seemed twice as large as it should have been, the way children's heads always look too big. Knobby knees. Gray-eyed with a mop of hair the exact deep chestnut color his mother's had been. A thin wash of freckles. Chin cradled in his small hands, he lay on his stomach, thumping his bottom with his bare heels. He resembled Linda so much that when Mac looked at him, it was often with a blend of bliss and agony.

"What are my two gentlemen up to?" Mary asked.

"The final championship," Brendan said, without glancing up from his hard-eyed strategies.

"You boys are always playing the final championship."

"This is really it, though." Brendan found a double jump, clicking his piece loudly on the wooden board. "I'm slaughtering Mac."

"I can see that," said Mary. "What do you need, Mac? Couple hours? You know me. Just as well be over here with company as rattle around my lonely old shack with Mother. Lord, you'd think a woman would plan for retirement. Thirty-two years I been taking care of her. Hasn't got a blessed cent to her name."

Mary Gilliam looked like a Raggedy Ann doll the dog had been chewing. Fat as a fairy-tale toad, she wore off-pink slacks and a sleeveless button-up blouse thinned with age. Bifocals dangled on a cord from her neck. Innumerable handkerchiefs peeked from pockets and waistband. Her hair was white-gray, chopped short and jutting out in all directions. She wore bright lipstick that could have been better applied with a boot. Her lips always seemed slick with saliva. Norman Rockwell would have posed her smiling face helicoptered over a tray of steaming cookies.

Falling heavily onto the sofa, Mary said, "Whole town's buzzing. This is the grimmest thing to land on Staircase since the flood of '61, when the movie theater took on three feet of water."

Brendan frowned. "Mac? What you guys talking about?"

"There was an accident at the fire station, Brendan. Peter Daugherty died." Brendan's gray eyes began watering over. "Got sick and died before we could help him."

Brendan mulled that over while Mary sat very still. Mac rose to his knees on the carpet and hugged Brendan. Too independent for this sorry comfort, the boy went rigid and shrugged. "Why don't you go out and throw a stick for Satan?" said Fontana.

After he'd trotted out of the room in a jerky gait, and they could hear the dog barking in front, Mary said, "It's a sad thing, Mac. Anyway, he's too young to understand."

"Lost his mother less than two years ago, darlin'. He understands."

"What's going on down at that station of yours? I thought Mayor Costigan said she'd rot in hell before she let you take over again as sheriff."

"I twisted her arm."

"There's hardly a soul in this town doesn't think you should be wearin' that badge permanent. People been pesterin' Mo about it."

"A lot of folks around here didn't get enough O-two at birth," said Fontana, stacking the checkers and putting them away.

"Just so's I get the exclusive."

"Same agreement as before." For three decades Mary had tried and failed to scoop the national rags on local atrocities. The closest she'd come so far was an article entitled "Man from Outer Space Robs Service Station: attendant to bear his baby," written after a man in costume stuck up the Chevron station, kidnapped the female attendant, and wheeled around the countryside with her locked in the trunk of his Pontiac for sixteen hours before she kicked the back seat out and escaped not two miles from where they started. "Bounty suspects Claude Pettigrew's girl friend. There was a note on the bulletin board. It's really the only thing makes this look deliberate. Said, 'You took my affections—now you take this.' County took my typewriter for a comparison. Had Wanda scribble a sentence with 'affections' in it. She spelled it wrong. Was all botched in the note, too. But different."

"People can spell things wrong on purpose." Mary pursed her lips, tented her plump fingers in her lap. The August heat had been putting her through hoops. "Half the town figures the Mafia sneaked into the valley to assassinate you."

"When was the last time the Mafia used rat poison? Or had me on their hit list?"

"Who would want you dead, Mac?"

"I spent eighteen years making friends and a few enemies in the East. I worked in operations as a firefighter, then a lieutenant, and then eight years in Fire Investigations. Captain right before I quit. If somebody wanted me, they would have come long ago. From here? I'm planning to terminate one of the firefighters. I find it hard to think he'd murder over it."

"Why *planning*? You're chief."

"We're talking civil service. You need a trail of paper work longer than a White House guest list. It's easier to make your first million than it is to fire a guy. Documentation."

11

TEEN ANGEL

Outside, Fontana found his son by the river. Brendan would throw a stick. Satan would lumber after it, knowing this wasn't real work, carry it back, drop it. As if patronizing the boy with that dog look in his eyes.

Each time he picked it up, Brendan searched for a dry part, and now he peered up at his father. Wide-spaced gray eyes. The stick was wet with slobber. Fontana scrounged up a new one and flicked it underhanded toward the water. Satan raced after it, gravel and dirt spurting from his hind feet.

"He runs for you."

"It's hot, son. He's wearing that heavy coat. He was saving himself."

"Stupid dog."

"Sorry I didn't tell you about Pete before." Brendan picked up a rock and hurled it toward the water. It fell short. A second missile plunked into the river with a musical boink. "When I get back, we'll talk about it."

"Don't want to talk about it."

Fontana could hear the freeway rush of the river, the breeze riffling the alders above their heads. One had to walk to the east end of the property to absorb the sweeping panorama of half a mile of tumbling river, rounded gray rocks, dead falls, white water, and emerald pools. In the spring one could hear the ominous thunder of boulders being bulldozed along the bottom by the current.

He remembered his amazement when he'd begun touring real estate in the area. Emigrating from a smoggy, rain-sodden city in the East, where a view was a clean shot of a panhandler sleeping at the bus stop, he had found it incomprehensible.

Thirty miles east of Seattle, where the AM radio signals needed to be coaxed, where the local paper came out every Thursday, where the television signals were nonexistent except via cable and satellite, Staircase lay smack in the center of a small dead-flat valley dominated by rolling foothills. To the west was a gradual gradient. Logged-out low hills to the north. To the east, the steep Cascades. To the northeast, Mount Gadd, sixty million years older than the Cascades. Three separate forks of the river drained through the valley, merging just before the falls.

A house with a view? Every home in the valley had one. The garbage dump had a beaut. Photographers trekked to Moon Valley to take postcard shots. One of the local real estate jokes was to advertise in the Seattle papers with the word "view."

Fontana's rented two-bedroom pine-walled house lay directly under Gadd. Separated by the middle fork of the river, a rock and debris scree angled steeply into the steel- and mustard-colored rocks. Between the scree and the river a band of fir trees girdled the mountain. He couldn't see quite to the top of the mountain, he was so close, and it took awhile for the morning sun to scramble over the crest and burn the mist off his property.

They'd spotted ospreys, bald eagles, one small black bear fishing in the river, beaver, deer, and two runaway horses being chased by a tall, hippy woman with a bunch of carrots. The mares whinnied mockingly as they trotted along a hundred yards in front of her. Brendan had laughed uncontrollably at the sight.

Fontana let Satan into the truck and drove up the graveled rocky drive, through the woods, along the river, past Armistead's pasture. The heart of town was a mile distant by road, three quarters of a mile by path. Three trips out of four he and Brendan hiked, Brendan donning a backpack to tote his share of groceries. Tonight Mark Dinning's original "Teen Angel" came on the radio, setting Satan off. The dog rolled his head back and bayed, his flattened canines bared. Because of his enormous jaw power, his original trainer had had a vet flatten the teeth so that he wouldn't be so likely to injure a suspect. It was common practice for police dogs.

At the sheriff's office he let himself in the side door, unlocked the gun rack, took down a Remington pump shotgun, and worked the action. Through the walls he could hear the muffled television in the beanery.

Empty, the weapon smelled of Hoppe's Nitro Powder Solvent #9. Twelve-gauge. No choke. He shoved in a slug, then six magnum rounds of double-aught buckshot. He secured the rack and pocketed two boxes of cartridges. Federal. Hi-power. Twenty-five shells per box. He mixed the slugs with shot shells. In the truck he fitted the shotgun into the rack Warren Bounty had had built. The dog whined and clambered in.

"Take it easy, big guy. You know something's up, don't you?" Fontana went back inside and packed up Pete Daugherty's bunking coat, helmet, bunking pants, and boots, red suspenders looped around the neck of each boot.

12

THE ANGER

R eedy arms flashing in the evening sunshine, broad rump monitoring the road, Jane Daugherty was propped on hands and knees, weeding viciously.

Staircase consisted of a central township that contained the Chevy dealership, movie theater, firehouse, a strip of real estate offices and small businesses, the lone stoplight, and a small contingent of older housing. The rest of the community consisted of isolated neighborhoods, some many miles from the heart of town. Daugherty's makeshift neighborhood was just shy of Truck Town under the southern ridge of Mount Gadd. Two lots removed from the seldom-used railroad tracks, the Daugherty family lived in a house trailer. The lot next to them bore a vacant run-down shanty. The next, another trailer.

A black Labrador retriever Daugherty had nursed back to health from a nasty accident with a logging truck slumbered on his side in the russet weeds in the crawl space. Fontana spotted three more dogs on the property. Parking the GMC in the shade, next to the Daughertys' gray Toyota Tercel wagon, a purchase Pete had agonized over for months, Fontana left Satan inside. He didn't need a dog fight.

"Jane."

She hardly glanced up. At the trailer door a gray-haired woman with faded blue eyes stood behind the torn screen with the two-year-old on her hip. Fontana heard the boy behind the trailer. Pete had set the backyard up with a jungle jim, a sandbox, and a pair of huge wooden electrical spools for his kids, who tended to be a little wild.

A pretty brown-haired woman with dimples that deepened when she smiled, Jane Daugherty hadn't fully recuperated from either pregnancy. She was twenty-two. In high school she'd been a stick. Now her arms were the only part of her that was slim. As was her custom, she wore baggy sweat pants to cover the weight she'd put on. On top she wore one of Pete's white T-shirts. Huge clumps of uprooted grass and weeds lay beside her.

"How are you doing tonight, Chief Fontana?"

"Making out. I brought Pete's bunking stuff. I thought you'd want it."

"Thanks."

"Tell me if there's anything I can do. Money. Arrangements. Baby-sitting."

She didn't stop weeding, gave only an occasional wayward glance at Fontana's knees. He squatted beside her and felt inhumanly powerful. He decided it was because he was alive and half of her wasn't.

"Don't expect I'll be needing anything."

"You'll get his pension. I'll have the exact figures later in the week. He had some accident insurance. And there's a federal grant of a hundred thousand to the family of any firefighter in the country killed in the line of duty. We should get Gilhausen or somebody to help you invest it prudently."

"Uh-huh."

"You need help with the funeral?"

"Dad's doing it."

When Fontana rose, his knees cracked. A crow squawked on a phone pole. Across the street fifty feet back from the road stood a patchwork house in which a silver-haired man watched him from behind a plastic storm window.

"Chief?"

"Call me Mac."

"Mayor Costigan was here. She was very kind. They're sayin' maybe somebody was after you. Or Wanda tryin' to kill Claude."

"Nobody's proved anything." He outlined what County was doing on the investigation. He glossed over Wanda and the intrigue with Claude. He wasn't going to pour gasoline onto the campfires of local gossip. When he finished, she was still weeding. He assumed the compulsive activity was a result of suppressed anger and grief.

Without a word she stood slowly and, legs stiff from stooping, limped into the house. The screen clapped shut behind her. Fontana waited a decent interval, then headed for the truck. Before he reached it, Jane emerged with a sheet of foolscap in her hands, carrying it by the corners, hobbling over to him. It was a pencil drawing of Mac and Brendan in front of a slash of river.

"Wasn't very good," she said apologetically. "Pete was planning to redo it in ink and give it to you for your boy's birthday. Last picture he drew."

"You're too kind, Jane."

"No. Pete would have wanted you to have it."

It was on the drive to Caitlin's that the anger embraced Fontana. It wasn't a normal anger over flat tires or road hogs. This rage had sputtered inside since he was a boy. Eighteen years in the East wallowing in the depravity firefighters are subjected to had amplified it. Pundits talked about cops seeing the downside of life, and they saw their share—dead children, rapes, murders, grizzly accidents—yet often, when a cop saw something, a fire-fighter was in front of him on his knees, blood to his elbows.

Fontana had been one of the walking wounded. In fact, it had taken him a lot of careful thought to put in an application for chief of Staircase. It was only the rural character of the department that swayed him. The twenty grand it paid was just about what he needed to scrape by.

The summer of Mac's fourteenth birthday Tommy Simpson challenged him to a fistfight late one evening. He had knocked Tommy to the ground three times and bloodied his nose before Tommy ran home in a maniacal funk and came back lugging a hatchet from his father's garage. If Mac had had any common sense, he would have called his own father. Instead, a curious rage took hold of him. Calmly he slipped inside Tommy's first wild swing with the hatchet and knocked two of his front teeth onto the grass. Even as a kid he'd had a rep.

Over the years he'd come to the conclusion his anger was a minor form of insanity, something to be ashamed of. He had tried every ploy he could think of to nudge it out of his persona. Now, ignited by Jane Daugherty's almost transcendental complacency, he felt the slow eruption within. He'd nail this Dugan. He'd nail him so it hurt.

13

THE VERY, VERY
SCARY HAND

When Rainy Caitlin answered the door, he sensed he'd strayed into forbidden provinces. She appeared almost to be a different person, the way people look incongruous when you've seen them out of context. Hair knotted in a ponytail, she wore cotton slacks, yellow rubber-soled thongs, and a simple peach blouse. When she spoke, it was with rebuke and disappointment. "What are you doing here?"

"To see Jim about Pete's death."

"I guess Jim was lucky to escape, huh?"

"Yeah. He here?"

She stared at Fontana, blank-eyed, her pale blue eyes set far apart in her tan face. She had a deadpan look about her this evening. "I don't know what he has to say about it."

"Suppose we find out."

The Caitlins lived midway out the North Fork Road under the

---

shadow of the rocky west face. Almost directly under the steep cliffs, their house was in an area so close to the mountain that weatherworn boulders were lodged alongside the road like fallen meteorites. In one place a huge moss-shrouded rock obstructed the roadway so that the one-lane road zig-zagged around it. Jarred from the top of the mountain by some ancient cataclysm, it had tumbled thirty-five hundred feet. Several boulders, one as large as a gymnasium, hunkered in the woods, barely visible through the forest of birch and maple. Home buyers touring the region in the back seat of a chatty real estate agent's Lincoln often grumbled they would be afraid to sleep out here. Something might drop out of the sky.

Warren Bounty told a tale about responding out here to investigate an alleged gunshot. A stone had dislodged from the top of the mountain, bounced down, and boomed through Sam Winnamaker's roof, leaving a fist-size hole in the attic, the ceiling, the bed, and subsequently the floor of his mother-in-law's room in the basement. Bounty claimed it sucked all the bedding off the bed and buried it so deeply in the cellar floor they had been unable to recover it with picks and shovels.

The lots were all heavily treed. It was a narrow three-mile strip of land between the rocky base of the mountain and the wild North Fork of the river, a cranny you couldn't find without a map. The Caitlins lived off the Moon Valley Road on three acres, their backyard butted up against the North Fork.

This would be the first time Fontana had seen the two of them together. He was curious how it would make him feel. But then, a lot had happened today for him to get butterflies over this.

It was a modern two-story house painted gray with white trim. Rainy's red Jeep Cherokee sat on one side of the wide driveway; a spotless 1967 blue-gray Jaguar, on the other. A four-wheel-drive pickup was inside the open garage. It had high wooden rails around the sides for transporting sawn logs. A stack of split wood was ricked up near the side of the house. Another stack in the garage. Everybody burned wood out here. Summer was the season to stock up.

"Gonna let me in, or we just gonna look at each other?"

Rainy blinked, clicked the brass knob in her hand, swung the door to and fro. "Course."

He grinned, but she was scanning the immaculate room over her shoulder, as if to dash around and hide evidence of some domestic felony. "I wish you'd called."

"Next time I will."

She didn't open the door wide enough, so that as he entered, he brushed it with his shoulder. Then, standing off from him, she didn't close the door. The wind slammed it into the stopper. Sunlight refracting off the yellow kitchen walls at the other end of the living room blinded him for a moment.

In shorts Benny stood in the doorway, the brightness from the kitchen backlighting his bare legs. He was Brendan's age. His hair stuck straight up like a brush.

"Nice do." Fontana caught Benny's eye. "How do ya keep it like that?" Out of the corner of his eye he saw Mom relax for a moment.

"First I wash it. No. First I take a shower. Then, when it's all wet, then I comb it straight up. Then I look in the mirror and I spray it with this stuff. And then it just stays."

"Neat," said Fontana.

Off the kitchen was an open door leading into the garage. Fluorescent light mixed with shafts of softer, slanting sunlight. Not a speck of grit or grease sullied the garage floor. Bicycles were suspended from the ceiling, skis nocked into a handmade rack. Under an overhang outside another door to the garage he glimpsed the shiny maroon rear end of a '52 Ford. Jim Caitlin restored automobiles and sold them, a hobby he'd pursued since before his first driver's license.

"Looks like you're getting ready to go out," said Fontana.

"Yes."

"I didn't mean to bust in."

"No bother."

"Going to the movie?" In the summer the films commenced at eight-thirty. Every evening except Wednesdays, when the theater was closed, there would be a flurry of local traffic at eight-twenty.

"Benny and I were getting ready for soccer practice."

"Was gonna sign up Brendan. He didn't want to."

"I don't know that I buy into team sports at this age myself. It seems to rob them of time to goof off and use their imaginations. They have enough structure. But Benny insists. Wait. I'll find Jim." She exited through the garage.

She spoke as if they were virtual strangers. Over the months he'd known her, he'd wanted her family to be idyllic, the kind he could not have.

During their conversation Benny had been underfoot, zipping around the room. Now he lost him. Fontana heard voices in the backyard. The chirring of a drill. More voices.

A Chagall print hung on one wall. A couple of western prints by an artist he didn't recognize. Numbered and signed. The other wall was strewn with family portraits, baby photos of Benny, pictures of Jim in an Army uniform, in a Seattle firefighter's uniform, and stiff-necked and thick-headed at his high school graduation. Jim had been a football player in high school, a time he spoke of often and fondly. After he'd observed the bank of photos thirty seconds, Fontana realized there were no pictures of Rainy alone.

A shadow wiggled in the patch of bright sunshine on the carpet at Fontana's feet.

It was the distorted shadow of a hand, revolving around and around inhumanly, as if the elbow were on a ball bearing. Benny's wavering voice mooed from the kitchen. The hand projected out from behind the corner.

"This is the very scary hand," he said in the gruffest voice he could muster. "This is a very, very scary hand!" His little fingers came out too far with the prosthesis, so Mac saw him operating it.

"Too scary," said Fontana. "Stop! Stop!"

No smile, Benny stepped out from behind the corner, lugging the prosthesis, walking toward Fontana. He handled it as a treasured toy. This was serious business. It was heavy for him, almost the length of a flesh-and-blood forearm. At the wrist was a serration where the hand clicked in and out, replaceable with a hook or another hand. The plastic forearm was built like a vase so that the stump of the wearer fitted inside. A pair of straps designed to attach to the elbow dangled.

"I know it's scary," said Benny.

"Course it is."

The hand had nail polish on it. Berry-colored. He'd seen the same on Rainy's toes a minute ago. "Some kids get very scared when they see this."

"I'll bet."

"I don't."

Mac's eyes widened. "You don't?"

"My cousin Marsha cried when I scared her. Boy, did I get it." Benny pulled on a wire inside the sleeve and held it up so Fontana could watch the thumb and fingers closing. He worked the contraption to pick up a *National Geographic* off the coffee table.

Hands black past the wrists, wearing grease-stained jeans and a plaid work shirt, Caitlin sauntered into the room behind the boy. Smudges creased his brow and one side of the blued stubble on his jaw.

"Chief? Nice to see ya." His smile was slow and warm. Man to man.

Benny jumped at the sound of his stepfather's voice.

Fontana said, "Jim. Thought I'd stop by and see what happened at the hospital. Talked to the doctor in charge of the emergency room at Overlake."

"Autopsy's what they're waiting for," said Caitlin. "Ramstad is a good doctor. Real good." Rainy came in softly behind him, thongs slapping at her bare heels. When Caitlin looked down at Benny holding the plastic hand, Caitlin's steel-colored eyes iced. "You know you're not to touch that."

"Sorry, sir." As delicately as a bomb disposal officer, the boy placed the prosthesis on the magazine, then marched outside through the garage. Fontana heard the Cherokee door open and close.

Rainy stepped around her husband and picked up the prosthesis. "It was my fault, Jim."

"I hate it when you leave that around."

"It was my fault."

"Towels."

Without a word she left the room, returned a moment later with a handful of paper towels, waited while he wiped his blackened hands, then carted the crumpled towels away. He hadn't looked at her during the exchange. They spoke as if they'd been in the throes of a bitter argument before Fontana's arrival and now were pretending nothing was awry. Fontana suspected that they always talked this way, that the house was full of domestic transgressions. Caitlin's arrival had siphoned the warmth out of the house.

Fontana watched Rainy behind Caitlin in the kitchen as she fiddled with the hand. It looked real enough. On the trail she'd always worn a hook or just the smooth stump. He'd never seen the hand before. One would think she would never be without it. Using her flesh-and-blood left hand, she inserted the stump into the long plastic cup at the end of the prosthesis, tugged a strap up around the elbow, and fastened another strap around her forearm. Oddly, strapping on the prosthesis was the least self-conscious move she'd executed since his arrival.

"Chief Fontana. Met the wife?" In the kitchen Rainy looked up with a start and rapidly shook her head. Because of the sunlight bracketing her, he couldn't see her eyes, only the corona around her ponytail.

———

Fontana said, "We've met." Caitlin turned to face her. She looked for a moment like something caught in the high beams on a midnight highway. "Met at school," said Fontana. "Brendan and Benny were both in Mrs. Swofford's class last year."

Caitlin turned back to Fontana and said nothing. He looked down at his powerful hands. He was a big man, six feet, two hundred pounds, heavily built, though he didn't keep himself in shape. He'd been a Ranger in the Army, and it was said around town he was a capable person. They meant he was no one to fool with. He had styled hair, almost black, and heavy cheeks.

"Thought you were leaving," Caitlin shouted over his shoulder. They heard the jingle of keys, a door closing, then the Cherokee motor purring.

"You'll have to excuse her," Caitlin said.

"For what?"

Caitlin shot him a scowl that slowly dissolved against Fontana's mirrored look. Fontana had never noticed before, but Caitlin was cloaked in a thin charisma the Lord usually reserved for politicians. His cheeks drooped. "Look, I'm frazzled. I been working on that car since I got home. I need a shower before I touch anything. You wait a few minutes?"

"Sure."

"Just be a few minutes." Caitlin loped out of the room. Fontana sat on the flowered davenport in front of a couple of art books and a family album. He picked up the album and started to sweat.

14

THE FIRST GATE OF HELL

A hot wind soughed through the front door and suffocated the rooms. At the back of the house the dim susurrus of the shower competed with the wind in the trees outside. In the corner a fern in a pot rustled. A bead of perspiration pussyfooted down his temple into his trim beard. Splayed open on his lap, the album's cool vinyl cover stuck to his legs.

Ancestors and other things.

Black-and-white photos cluttered the first three pages. Immigrants in wedding poses. Clear-eyed, sober boy children dressed in the old-fashioned manner: dresses and caps. World War II photos of square-jawed chaps in flying helmets. A cheeky young man standing rib-deep in the compartment of a light tank in the desert. Scrawled beside it: "Teddy—died 1943, Egypt."

School pictures of Rainy. From the look of her she'd been a cheerful, though timid, student, both hands intact. The only time they'd spoken of it, she confessed the accident had been "almost too long ago to remember." She had used a tone that colored it in unemotional pastels. "It happened. I live with it. No big deal."

He skipped quickly through to the middle of the book, found himself with an inexplicable and voracious appetite for her history. To a remarkable degree her first husband resembled Jim Caitlin, tall, muscular, dark. As if she'd purposely ferreted out a look-alike the second time around. According to Rainy, number one spouse had been a boob, notorious for punching out bosses and getting into late-night car accidents.

The baby photos of Benny. He'd resembled a turtle with the overbite upper lip. Placid. More so than most babies. Fontana chuckled. Her infant pleased him more than he thought fitting. Photos of her second wedding. The newspaper announcements. Rainy Johansen weds Jim Caitlin. Jim had become Benny's stepfather.

Obligatory hunting photos took up a lot of space. Caitlin in the mountains, one leg up on an elk, standing beside his father. Caitlin sitting in some sort of primitive mountain camp with Gil Cutty. Another photo of Cutty, Claude Pettigrew, and Caitlin, all holding rifles against their hips, cans of beer in their off hands. This was news to Fontana. If the three of them were still hunting together, he didn't know anything about it.

They'd lived in a double-wide trailer at first. Three pages of album chronicled Jim's construction of their house. Benny's second birthday; the three of them smiling. Benny with cupcake smeared around his mouth, frosting stiffening his wispy hair. Splashing in a green pool in the river—Benny about four. Jim and Benny in the snow, though Benny, for some reason, didn't look too thrilled.

Rainy in a two-piece bathing suit, bashfully batting at the camera. Laughter sparking in her eyes. Don't take this one, dear. Her near nudity robbed Mac of breath. She had both hands! It was the first time he'd noticed her hands in a photo since the childhood pictures. From the bulk of photographs taken around the same time—same hairstyle in each—it had been shot in Staircase, the background a blur of green.

On the next page her hands were artfully concealed behind her back. And the next. In her pockets. Under another birthday cake. Out of sight.

He flipped back through the album.

When did she lose the hand? He was curious because if he was reading the pictures correctly, she'd lied when she told him it happened a long time ago, and until this evening's cold reception, the subtle theater with Jim, he'd believed her incapable of deceit.

The river and two-piece bathing suit was the last photo with both hands intact. "Almost too long ago to remember," she had said. He skimmed the remainder of the album. The later sections were sprinkled with the occasional photo or entirely empty. He went back and looked at the bathing suit picture.

When Caitlin came out, Fontana was in the front doorway.

Drying his hair with a towel, Caitlin wore jogging shorts and leather sandals, walked slowly. In one hand he held a tall tumbler of lemonade and ice. Outside Satan hung his head half out the GMC window, tongue lolling. Fontana felt the wind brushing his backside as he stepped outside.

"So, Mac. I don't know what to tell you about Daugherty. Arsenic can work too damn fast. I'm just glad he took enough so the rest of us didn't chow down. You imagine the mess you would have found then? If we'd all eaten?"

"Uh, yeah. That would have been something."

15

FIREMEN ARE LIKE COWS

"We'll know for sure in the morning after the medical examiner runs his tests," said Caitlin, strolling past Fontana into the front yard. "Had one of those drugstore poisonings in Seattle about three years ago. Some middle-aged two-twenty was getting his heehaws dumping cyanide into Ex-Lax on the store shelves. Gawd, I hated to see Pete go like that. Basically, Pete was a pretty regular guy."

Caitlin sat heavily on the front lawn, wriggled his squarish toes in the grass. The lawn was green and cool-looking. Caitlin gave his dark head of hair one last scrubbing before he pitched the towel into the house through the doorway. Rainy would pick it up.

"He suffer?" Fontana asked. Caitlin looked at him queerly. "I know what we saw. But did he?"

"Hell, yes."

Fontana thought back to the first time he'd seen the paramedic. He had just taken over as chief, had responded with the volunteers on a Saturday morning to Bryant's Grove. A goofy-looking elderly man writhed on the sod in his backyard, an apparent epileptic seizure. Caitlin gripped Joe Hourihan by the shoulders and jerked him away just as the patient kicked at Hourihan's testicles. No Dilantin for him. Clay Salts was a full-fledged nut case who took out volunteers by faking seizures and then aiming a brogan at the family jewels. Caitlin was street-smart. It made him a valuable addition to the department.

"So what do you believe happened?"

"At the station?" said Caitlin. "You asking me?"

"Asking everybody."

"Pete did something to get somebody riled. That's what."

"Doesn't make a whole lot of sense, does it?"

"He was a nice kid, but kind of a wimp. I figure it was something on the job. Something he did without realizing he'd even done it."

"And how were they going to ensure Pete was the only one who ate? Seems more like somebody wanted a whole bunch of people sick."

"Dead, you mean."

"Dead."

"Nobody saw any strangers in the station."

"In this town, tell me who's a stranger?"

Standing and bending vigorously from the waist, Caitlin performed a series of toe touches. Nobody except a driver of the rare car traveling the dead-end road through Moon Valley could peer into the yard. The only people with business on it would be the five or six residents who lived closer to the end than Caitlin.

The paramedic's legs were thick, hirsute. He was thirty-four. His chest was heavy, arms bulging with muscle, all with a blanket of smooth fat over it. "Maybe somebody was holding a grudge because Pete and the crew let a relative die. Or they thought they let a relative die. It happened to a doc at the View a couple of years ago. A guy lost his wife, thought the doc caused it, and tried to kidnap the doc's girl friend from a Capitol Hill condo. The guy strong-armed the cleaning girl, and she ended up beating him half to death with a telephone receiver, then tying him up with the cord. She broke four of his fingers and blinded him in one eye."

Firefighters were like cows, Fontana thought; their experience was the seven stomachs from which they could regurgitate station house war stories from fifteen, twenty years ago. They never forgot an alarm, and you never knew when they'd cough it up. Fontana was the same, in his head and in conversation. A brotherhood.

"When did you show up?" Fontana asked. "You weren't there when I left for my hike."

"Went hiking, did you?" As he sipped lemonade, something rolled around behind Caitlin's steel-colored eyes, a thought, an unspoken conjecture. "Up Gadd?"

"Saw the house fire from up there. Interesting perspective."

"Lot of people on the trail?"

"It's summer." Caitlin didn't look up, resumed his toe touches. After another half dozen he stopped and dropped to the grass on the palms of his hands, pumped off ten ponderous push-ups next to the tumbler in the warm grass. "What do you know about Wanda and Claude?"

"Claude and Wanda Sheridan aren't the best match in town. But each to his own."

"How long you been sleeping with her?"

Caitlin stopped at the top of a push-up, rolled over, and sat with his knuckly hands clasped around one white knee with a star-shaped scar on it. He laughed. "Me and Wanda?"

"You and Wanda."

"Who finked?"

Fontana didn't reply.

"I gored Wanda a couple of times. So what? She was born with a blue stamp on her ass. Grade A. Bet you want a piece of it yourself."

"Claude know about you two?"

"Claude's retarded."

"Maybe so. Maybe not. He's still a human being."

Caitlin squinted as a gust picked up a smattering of sawdust from the rose beds and whisked it around the yard. "You saying Claude tried to poison the lot of us to get at me?"

"I'm asking if Claude knew you were sleeping with his girl friend."

"Frankly, I don't much care. Claude's scared of me."

He looked hard at Fontana, his mouth chipped into an impish grin. Dimples darkening. It was as if he were trying to imply Fontana should be scared, too. Caitlin was constantly polishing his image, always aware whether his actions were adding to or detracting from it. Toughness was the adhesive that held it together.

"Where'd you get acquainted with Wanda?"

"In the station, same as you. One night Claude got potted over at the Bedouin, and she asked for a ride home. I drove her up the hill to the winery past Snoqualmie, parked on a logging road, and had at her in the back seat of the Cherokee. Lives in Seattle. Drive by once in a while on duty and buzz her. Seein' me in that uniform with that page on my belt pulls her chain. Hell, she's a groupie."

"So what's she doing with Claude? You've been around both of them. You must have some idea."

"Damned if I know. She's got a husband in the Navy. You know that? And some faggot brother lives with her off and on." Caitlin's watch beeped the hour. Nine o'clock. Fontana often said he wanted to find the man who'd invented those watches and drag him a hundred miles in the desert behind a mule.

The colors of the setting sun imprinted themselves onto the crags above: pink; a fuzzy purple; shades of ocher and red.

Caitlin continued. "You know Claude and Wanda screwed in the hospital the first night they met? Don't think Pettigrew's naive. He's going to get some for his money. Bet on it. But she's a little loopy, too. Before Claude, she bunked with some paratrooper from Fort Lewis. Then a cop. Then a Bothell firefighter. She tells Claude everything. He doesn't seem to mind. In fact, despite all this, I bet he still thinks Wanda was a virgin when he met her. Guys in uniform. Some women are nuts for 'em. She tells me her mother was a German war bride. Maybe that's why she likes uniforms. Maybe it's in the blood."

As Fontana walked to the GMC in the driveway, he turned and said, "How'd Rainy lose her hand?"

Pausing a moment, Caitlin plucked at some grass, tossed it into the air. "Car wreck. She's very touchy about it. Almost mental."

"I'd say she's handling it pretty well."

"You have to know her. You don't know her."

"How long ago?"

"Three years. If I hadn't been right there, she probably would have bled out. She owes me her life."

"Lucky."

It wasn't until he'd driven out the Moon Valley road from under the shadow of the mountain that the radio came in again. Roy Orbison sang "Crying." Fumbling the falsetto trills, Fontana sang along. It had been one of Linda's favorites. In the East he hadn't listened to music unless Linda was in the car or unless she switched on the stereo in their town house. He had been too busy chasing down a career to relish moments one at a time. His wife had been addicted to the oldies, knew all the words to songs he'd never even heard and could wheel into a falsetto better than Frankie Valli. After her death he'd inherited the addiction. A loving tribute. Like the third plate at the table.

16

THE BEST SEASON TO
PICKLE YOUR GRANDMOTHER

"**T**his Wanda Sheridan is a yakker," said Charles Dummelow.

Fontana was on the phone at Mary's house. "Thanks for getting
back to me."

"Poisoning's bad. Somebody gets away with yours and we'll
have copycats all over the county. Thought they could skate,
there's a ton of bimbos would crawl out from under rocks to pickle
their grandmothers. In salt, arsenic, you name it."

"What'd you find out about the woman?"

"Most people clam up when they get their tit in a wringer.
Want to know Sheridan's shoe size or just all her marks in pre-
school?"

"I knew she had a mouth. She got a record?"

"Prostitution in Seattle. Worked the Sea-Tac strip and, according to reports, the escort services. Never been picked up from

a service. Worked the circuit ten years ago. Seattle. Tacoma. Portland. San Francisco. Alaska. Spring a year ago she spent a hundred and eighty days in the calaboose for theft. She shoplifts. Couple of old drug charges. According to one FIR, she lives with a young stud bisexual prostitute name of Harold Glass. Calls himself her brother, but there ain't any brother to it. She bails him out. He bails her out. He pimps her. Dropped out of high school in Tennessee when she was fifteen, married a minister, if you can believe that."

"You sure about the field incident report? The guy I saw looked like he could have been her brother."

"Ain't never met the lady. I'm just reading. One of the detectives works vice used to know her pretty good. Talked to him a couple hours ago. She been rode hard and put away wet. Seems like she's trying to get out of the life. Maybe bag an insurance settlement. Something of that nature."

"What else?"

"Last time she was arrested was early July. She and some big turkey busted up Maxi's out by the airport. I guess her date got drunk and went haywire. Got into a pushing match with some guy there."

"Names?"

"Right here, I think. Let me check. Marshal Rood. George Pettigrew? Know either of 'em?"

"Pettigrew's a fire buff out here. Goes by his middle name. Claude. Hangs around the station. Knows more about the equipment and history of the department than anybody alive. He's almost an institution. People like to say he's mildly retarded, but I can't really vouch for that."

"Charges dropped. This Sheridan gal sounds like a fireball."

"She's hot, all right."

17

PHONE CALLS
TO THE DEAD

From his bedroom Brendan was sighing in his sleep in catchy whirs. The Everly Brothers' "Bird Dog" was on the stereo. Fontana had been sitting in the dark an hour, listening to Brendan and the woofers and tweeters. In a misguided effort to let the wind off the mountain chill the house, he had propped all the doors wide. He'd snuffed the lights to sidestep bugs, though the breeze manhandled most insects into the wild blue yonder before they became a nuisance. Ten-thirty. The temperature had soared to over a hundred.

If the dog hadn't pricked up his ears and sat erect, Mac wouldn't have heard the visitor. The faint knocking came a second time. He clicked on a lamp next to the sofa, and the light caught the blond, brown, and banana yellow tones in the pinewood walls. Beside him Satan let out a soft whine. "*Platz!*" said Mac, giving the German command for lay down. "Come in."

She pushed the front door wide open with her fingertips. "Rainy."

"Don't get up on my account. I just wanted to explain something." She glanced around the room. He knew she was estimating the house's market value, she, who, despite her deep religious bent, had turned into a diehard state lottery gamester. Rainy had a penchant for the prestige brand. To Fontana, who believed the more religious people were, the less material possessions should mean to them, the two strains in her never seemed to gel. "Somebody at soccer practice told me where you lived."

Fontana walked to the door in his moccasins. "Brendan's asleep."

They stepped out into the darkness.

"I haven't heard the Everly Brothers for a long time. Kind of sweet." He could tell from her tone her mind was cluttered, her words perfunctory; what she wanted to throw down between them was going to become an event. As they strolled side by side into the yard, the music dimmed.

Though concealed by a ridge, the moon whitewashed the sky. When the light rose, a newspaper could be perused under it. Without the city lights to bewilder the night the upper valley was the perfect spot for a boy with a telescope. He was mulling over one for Brendan's birthday but wondered whether he was old enough. Linda had done the shopping, most of it. He ached to speak to her and ask just the one question: What should we get Brendan for his eighth birthday? If some AT&T gimmick could only plug him through to the beyond.

Rainy stopped and looked at him, her eyes wet and bright. In one of those unspoken pacts they seemed to make at every meeting, they turned in unison and moved across the yard toward the river. Monitoring his every move, Satan sat behind in the doorway. "You've got so much going for you, Mac. You could make something of yourself. Get a nice house on Mercer Island, Redmond, someplace. Launch another career. Bank some savings."

"You don't approve of the way I live?"

"You know what I mean. That old truck. That scruffy dog looks like somebody took sheep shears to him. Who flattened the tires on your ambition?"

Fontana shrugged.

"You're forty years old. You don't even own your house."

"Had a house. Career. Bucks in the stock market. Drove a BMW with all the bells and whistles. Was well on my way to a battalion chief's job back east."

"What happened?"

"They say the surest way to put a man in hell is to give him what he asks for."

"That's no explanation."

"It's all I've got."

"I just don't see how anybody in your circumstances could be content."

"Darlin', an easy job I do well. Friends. Time with my son. Surrounded by this." He gestured. "You think there's something else? What'd you really come for?"

She sucked in a deep breath and gazed through the trees at the river. "I've never seen it this dry. Not in twelve years."

They strolled along the hard-packed dirt path through the rustling trees, to the twenty-foot-wide levee that ran alongside the Middle Fork. Fifteen feet above the water level, the levee was constructed of dirt and crushed rock, boulders below that. Cars used it infrequently since it led nowhere. Canoeists. Kayakers. Elderly blackberry pickers. Fly fisherman. Most of the riverbed was exposed rocks, rounded and looking in the starlight like skulls of various sizes.

"How'd you meet Caitlin?"

She wore the sandals, slacks, and blouse she'd had on earlier. Still had on the hand. Her words were clipped and cool. "Jim and I met at church."

"After your divorce?"

"I'd rather not talk about Jim and me."

"I'm interested."

"I know you are. He doesn't know I'm here. I should get back." When she turned to square her body up with his, the starlight caught the bronze-brown strands that angled across her face. Her voice vacillated. "I came to tell you to leave us alone."

"For some reason, I thought that was why you were here."

"And?"

"The all-American family. I'm not going to bother you any."

"I don't want you at the house again." When he didn't answer, she continued. "Families are all different. Ours with Jim and me and Benny, it's different from my first marriage, and they're both different from the home I was raised in. Look, Mac, I know you try to do what you think is right. I just don't want you out there. It's bound to cause trouble. Understand?"

"Clear as a bell."

"I don't mean to be brusque. Every relationship has its peculiarities. Sometimes people who aren't involved don't appreciate them."

"I think you're not very happy, Rainy."

She was getting sullen and testy. "What you saw . . . maybe it didn't look like the ideal marriage, but Jim's really a very good father. A wonderful provider."

"Maybe I'm reading too much between the lines, but when they start talking about what a good provider he is, you know things have gone rancid."

The insolence of his remark put color into her face. Even in the darkness he could see it. She averted her eyes. "I love Jim."

"Yeah. Me too. I was only there a few minutes, but I wanted to put a boot up his ass."

"What an ugly thing to say."

"What you're trying to tell me, Rainy, is you like being abused."

"I don't. He wasn't abusing me."

———

"I'd treat a slug in my garden better than he treats you."

She slapped him.

It came so quickly he almost didn't see it in the darkness.

Instinctively she'd used the prosthesis instead of her left hand, and it knocked his head around in a looping circle, came close to rendering him unconscious. The prosthesis felt like a pipe loaded with shot. Behind his eyes he saw a brilliant flash. He might have ducked, but for some nonsensical reason he wanted to play this out.

She gave him a contrite look. Rainy had a habit of swallowing him with her eyes as if she'd never looked upon a man before. He wasn't fool enough to think she looked only at him that way, though in the dark he wished it were true.

"Mac. I'm terribly sorry. I have this temper. I guess it's because I hold too much in and then, when I'm not ready, it explodes. Forgive me? I've never hit anybody before. I won't sleep until you say you don't hate me."

"Nobody could hate you."

"Look, Mac. No man can appreciate the vulnerability a woman feels every day of her life. God, I'm sorry I did that." She stepped forward as if to touch his face but didn't.

She said, "I guess you're smart enough to figure out I wouldn't have slapped you if you hadn't been getting close to the truth."

"What about your boy?"

"Jim's a good father!"

"You say it like a catechism."

"He *is* a good father."

"I'm glad."

If she caught his sarcasm, she didn't let on. She wasn't going to strike him again, and part of that was letting things slide. Her voice subsided into a whisper. "I think, sometimes, that if people knew certain things, perhaps I'd rather not even be here. If people knew all about me. Every tiny little riddle." Her voice caved in again. "I just wouldn't want to be here."

———

"You mean, you might kill yourself?"

"I'd just be gone."

She was staunch, almost pigheaded, and when he fused that to her confession, it frightened him. The unpredictability of her. And yet there was a gentle nobility, a self-possessed, suffering woman who seemed capable of enduring almost any hardship for the sake of others, her child, her family. He picked up her left hand. "Rainy, I want us to stay friends."

Dead silence.

Tears spasmed in her eyes.

He'd been thinking about her a lot during the past month, and tonight's events had extracted nothing but guilt.

"Mac?"

"I won't interfere."

"I'm really sorry."

"Nothing happened, Rainy. Forget it. Go home. Live happy."

"Mac?"

"Good night, Rainy." He turned and walked east on the levee. Several minutes later he heard her Cherokee fire up. When the moon finally rose over the lip of the Cascades, it looked scandalous. He sat on the riverbank, watching the light bounce off the river in soft, milky needles. Satan sat next to him. The warm chinook whistled down the pass, rustled the firs across the river, and tickled the birches above his head.

It was after midnight when he pushed off on his knees and walked into the house. Brendan had tugged a blanket over his small shoulders, his brow hot, perspiring. Mac peeled the cover back, leaving only the sheet noodled up around his neck. He kissed the boy.

18

CRAWL

The siren squalled as Engine One careened around the corner onto Main. Unexpectedly returned from disability that morning, Lieutenant Allan rode in the officer's seat. Kingsley Pierpont drove.

On the way out the door they'd shanghaied a volunteer, Hank Walford. The best pump operator in town, Hank had been crippled years ago over a dispute between a tree and a chain saw.

With Fontana following in his GMC, they had a quorum.

As they rolled, Fontana spotted a smudge of wind-tossed black smoke to the west. Two fires in two days. Always in bunches. Six months without the taste of smoke and then suddenly you couldn't wash it out of your hair. Fontana worked the blue electronic siren box under the dash of the GMC. He picked up the microphone.

"Chief Eighteen-ninety to Control Ten. We have a walk-in

alarm on Hilltop Road between the old highway and the new highway. Reported house fire. Smoke visible. We're responding with Engine One-six-one. Give us a first response. We'll need the tanker from Staircase."

"Chief Eighteen-ninety. Reported house fire on Hilltop?"

"Hilltop between I-Ninety and the old highway."

"Okay, Chief Eighteen-ninety."

In a minute the District Ten dispatchers would signal every volunteer in the upper valley. Fontana had worked eighteen years in an all-professional department back East, and volunteerism was new to him. He was impressed. Several weeks ago Bert Puckett had hurdled out of the dentist's chair, a rubber dam in his mouth and half a hypo of Novocain in his jaw, to respond to a brush fire in Clyde Gatton's back pasture.

It was a two-and-half-story farmhouse isolated at the end of Hilltop Road off its own eighty-yard driveway. Behind lay a screen of firs, and above that to the south a logged-off ridge a thousand feet above the valley.

Kingsley slewed Engine One around the corner at the inter-section of Hilltop and the old highway. In the back seat of the GMC, Satan howled in tune with the siren, pacing from one window to the other.

"Shut up back there," Mac said.

The burning farmhouse sat in the center of a large green field with a broken-down fence crisscrossing it. Shielding it from the new highway was a lineup of Douglas firs. The smoke was being carried almost horizontally by the winds.

Kicking up a mushroom cloud of dust, Engine One turned onto the rutted gravel road that led up to the house. Fontana rolled his window up. To his disgust, the engine stopped in the middle of the spiraling smoke. By the time they realized their mistake and relocated, Fontana had driven past and gotten a look at three sides of the fire building. A volunteer who must have spotted it early had parked near the barn and was hurriedly climbing into bunking gear. One pump operator and four men. It took him several seconds to figure out how he wanted to work it.

"Eighteen-ninety at Hilltop Road," said Fontana. "We have a two-story wood frame structure approximately forty by forty. No exposures. Flame showing from three windows on the west side. We're laying a preconnect."

The dispatcher repeated his report.

Apparatus 161 carried a thousand gallons in its booster tank, in most cases enough to put out a farmhouse. He would lay lines and order tankers anyway. One learned to set up for the worst-case scenario.

As he stepped to the rear of the GMC, Fontana scanned the road and highway. It would be a few minutes before help arrived. He'd leave the volunteer and Lieutenant Allan outside. The volunteer could man the extra hose. Allan could direct incoming units. It was that or send Allan inside with Pierpont, and for a variety of reasons he nixed that.

The flames had lapped vertically up the side of the building from broken-out windows. Tar and composition shingles were burning lazily. The white paint outside the gable on the second story was charcoal now, blistered. In the lower windows flames erupted like a blowtorch.

After stepping out of his shoes and into his bunking boots with the bunking pants down around the ankles, Fontana pulled everything up, hooked the red suspenders over his shoulders. "*Bleib!*" he said to Satan, who sat. He swung the coat onto one arm and grabbed his portable radio. Allan was supervising Hank Walford at the pump panel, Hank, who clearly needed no supervision.

"Bunk up, Lieutenant. What are you waiting for?" Fontana smoothed the Velcro and Nomex flap over the metal snaps on his heavy coat. By rights, Lieutenant Allan should have scrambled into his bunkers at the station. Kingsley hadn't because Kingsley had been at the wheel, and almost every driver of fire apparatus drove in shirt sleeves for better maneuverability. Fontana slung a mask backpack from the compartment on the side of 161, slipping an arm into either strap of the thirty-pound pack, fastened the belt buckle, and cinched the shoulder straps. "Allan, take that volunteer and dust off the side of the house. Don't hit anything inside. Kingsley and I are going in the front."

"Gotcha, Chief."

"Remember, don't hit anything inside."

"Gotcha." It was so like Allan. Instead of saying "yes, sir." Or "sure." Gotcha. He strove so hard to be one of the boys, never quite made it. Fontana could see the relief on his face that he wasn't being directed inside. He'd returned from disability this morning, Fontana was certain, only because with Daugherty dead, he feared an impromptu reorganization of the one-horse department might short-change him. Because other people ceased to exist the moment they walked out of Allan's eyesight, he assumed the same thing happened when he walked out of theirs.

"Lieutentant Allan. Get Engine Two to lay a line to that hydrant on the road. Have somebody overhaul hose out to meet them. When you get some more men, send a pair in behind us with another inch-and-a-half." Lieutenant Allan gave Fontana an upraised thumb, a wink, and the wrong part of a smile, the grimace part. He was too nervous to spit.

The fire seemed to be centered in the rear of the house, although it had made its way upstairs, possibly into the attic. If they went in through the kitchen, they would be hitting the seat first, but they would also be pushing it into the rest of the building.

They would enter in the relatively unscathed front room at the north end so that the only place they could push the fire would be out the kitchen windows. Kingsley had slung his mask and was already stretching one of the two-hundred-foot preconnected lines from the rear hose slots of Engine One. Fontana heard Hank priming the pump, the powerful engine transferring its horses from the rear wheels to a dual-stage Hale pump, the roaring-calf bellow of the priming gears kicking in.

When they got around to the front of the house, they found an old man with a garden hose squirting ineffectually at a smoky bedroom window. "Anybody inside?" Fontana asked.

"Just me. Damned teapot fired up. Got to gabbing on the phone and forgot it."

On the radio Fontana reported the building clear, tugged the blue rubber facepiece across his face, snugged up two straps at each side, tested the seal, and pulled his helmet up onto his head. Kingsley kicked at the door twice, but it didn't open. At their feet the inch-and-a-half line was filling rapidly, kinks popping with a sound like cardboard boxes being crushed as the water pressure made the line tumescent.

Kingsley booted the door again. Fontana picked up the line, pulled the bale to let the air seep out the end of the Wooster nozzle, closed it again, then reached in front of Pierpont, twisted the knob, and let the door waft open. From inside the bubble of his facepiece Pierpont gave him a dirty look. Fontana had managed to snitch the pipe from the department's ace pipe snitch. He could feel Kingsley behind like a second skin, ready to back him up or take over if he faltered. To Kingsley, fires were a ritual of manhood, though he was having a bad day. First he'd parked in the smoke, and then he'd tried to boot open an unlocked door.

Visibility was marginal for the first four or five feet, and then it blacked out entirely. Hot, roiling smoke pushed into them. Midway through the room they were forced from a stoop into a low crouch by the gases banking down from the ceiling. At head height, it was probably eight hundred degrees. Farther inside, it would increase another thousand. By the time they fumbled their way to the hallway that ran to the rear of the house they were crawling on hands and knees and still hadn't seen any flame. Fontana's face and ears, the only exposed portions of his body, were beginning to warm up.

Very few house fires presented a scenario where an unmasked individual, especially early on, couldn't snake out of the place on his belly. The only good air in the house sank to the floor, maybe three inches of cool oxygen, maybe one inch. The trick was knowing about it. People woke up in the middle of the night smelling smoke, leaped out of bed, and took a deep breath at head height. The superheated gases surged into their lungs and cauterized the works. Hugging the floor, they might have bellied out the front door.

The first room on the right backdrafted and burst into flame when they opened the door. Moving the Wooster in a circular pattern, Fontana aimed at the orange on the ceiling. A cloud of steam engulfed them. A gallon of water became seventeen hundred cubic feet of deadly steam.

Twenty feet down the hallway they found another room fire. It took a minute to tap that one. The kitchen at the end of the hallway was rolling, yet he couldn't violate the basic precept of putting it out as you came to it. When he backed into the corridor, he found a furnace of heat and flame roaring down the ceiling, lighting up everything in sight. His face prickled in the heat.

Bracing himself, Fontana opened the nozzle wide and screwed the tip almost to straight stream. Gradually, as the heat lessened and the orange began to disperse, he widened the pattern. He wasn't coming anywhere close to the seat of the fire. That was the problem. The seat was in the kitchen at the end of the corridor. All he was doing was chasing the tail on this fiery demon. They scuttled forward two feet, three, feeling as if they were crawling through an oven. They scooted to the kitchen doorway and pulled more hose in behind.

Fontana heard the drumming of hose streams on the outside of the building, then felt a brilliant hot burst in his face. Instinctively he opened his nozzle to protect himself, widening the spray into a heavy fog pattern. His hose stream acted as a shield. An inverted umbrella.

"What the hell's going on?" Pierpont shouted, his words garbled in the bubble of his face mask.

"They're shooting through the goddamned windows," said Fontana.

Two lines outside shoved the fire at them from different directions. Flame continued to penetrate the fog pattern. Pierpont grabbed Fontana's backpack and dragged him back.

"Too close."

"Gonna get that bastard," Fontana yelled, taking advantage of a respite in the rolling fireball to crawl forward and splash the ceiling. He opened it wide on straight stream and plunged into the room on his knees. Seconds later he had most of it tapped. He could hear the hose lines outside doing their mischief upstairs now.

By the time they got into the kitchen Fontana could feel the perspiration inside his heavy bunking coat, the straps of the air mask cutting into his shoulders. The equipment he was wearing, bunkers, mask, ax, and portable radio, weighed a little over fifty pounds. The coat was bulky, awkward, waterproof, didn't breathe. On a hot August day a man could break into a sweat simply donning it.

Long, tall, and shaped oddly, the kitchen had a ceiling that was clearly much higher than in the bedrooms. It was free-burning up there, had found an orifice into the room above. Balloon construction. No fire stops in the walls. Once inside a wall, flame could gallop unimpeded from basement to attic.

He directed the Wooster up and jerked the bale backward. They were standing taller now, and the heat and steam came down on them immediately. When he shut the pipe for a second to get his bearings and search for orange in the blindness, he could hear Bobby Joe's hose streams drumming the outside of the house.

Suddenly a straight stream smashed Mac in the face, knocked him into a crouch. Kingsley snatched the pipe and hollered into the bubble of his facepiece, "What da fuck are you doing, Allan?"

Fontana keyed the portable radio in his chest pocket. "Chief Eighteen-ninety to Engine One."

When the reply came, it was Hank Walford. "Engine One."

"Shut down your outside lines."

"Engine One, okay."

Ten seconds later the torrent of water inside stopped, but only for a moment. Outside, Fontana could hear hundreds of gallons beating against the shingles of the house, thumping on the walls upstairs. He didn't have any way to judge how much flame was upstairs, but he doubted it warranted the deluge. The ceiling was drenching them from a dozen spots. Wasn't anybody listening? He'd ordered them to shut down. He keyed the mike again but got no answer this time.

One night Fontana's first captain in the East had been trapped in a burning hallway, another crew pushing fire gases at him from the opposite end. He'd bellowed and, when that had no effect, had gotten so enraged he'd stood up and thrown a service ax end over end. One of the first things you learned in the fire service was not to push fire into people. You never attacked a fire from opposite sides.

In a limbo of steam and smoke they felt their way about like blind men. Fontana wiped the moisture and grit from the outside of his facepiece with his gloved hand.

When the waterlogged ceiling caved in, Kingsley and Fontana were hitting the last hot spots in the kitchen. For a moment neither of them realized what the cracking sound was. The ceiling kayoed Kingsley, who flopped onto his back in two feet of sloshing water and hot coals and broken lathe and wet plaster. Fontana climbed to his feet and reached down and grabbed the backpack of Kingsley's Survivair, lifting his lolling head above water so he wouldn't drown. It was still coming down. Like a frigging waterfall.

19

BARE-CHESTED MEN

"I am not happy with that performance," said Fontana.

Pierpont wiped his brow. "Allan been a window firefighter all along."

"I am not happy."

"What you're tryin' to say is, you thinking about shovin' a baby ladder up our 'lustrous lieutenant's ass until you see aluminum in his teeth."

Rolling his eyes was the only answer Fontana would allow himself. They were stripped to the waist, both of them, bottles, facepieces, low-pressure hoses, regulators, soggy gloves, wet shirts, coats, helmets, all of it exploded around them on the grass like spent shrapnel.

"That was distinctly not the easiest fire I been in," said Kingsley, gulping Gatorade from a paper cup. It was almost comical the way Kingsley's hair was molded into a ducktail from his helmet. A string of black sooty phlegm adhered to his front teeth. Fontana knew he was equally dismal.

Beads of sweat snaked down Fontana's neck and bare chest as he swallowed ice water from a thermos. They wore nothing but soot-stained yellow bunking pants and black rubber boots, suspenders dislodged from their shoulders and drying in red loops in the sun-warmed grass. A pair of men upstairs chased down sparks with a jiffy hose. Lieutenant Allan had failed to ensure they were wearing masks, but that was a minor miscue.

Two engines, a tanker, and six or seven private vehicles clogged the farmyard. The blue sky was a brilliant contrast with the slender ribbons of white smoke trickling out of the house. On the other side of the courtyard next to the burnt-off kitchen door Lieutenant Allan stood with a knot of men in bunking coats. Their chitchat and laughter exposed a contagious postfire excitement.

"Had a duplex fire last year when we was between chiefs," said Kingsley, leaning back on his elbows so that his hairless black chest gleamed. "Allan was ridin' high them days, thinkin' they were going to make *him* da chief. Afterwards, we's outside talkin' 'bout the same as he is over there. Reminds you of a little kid, don't he? The way that big old lick of hair hangs off to the side. *Leave It to Beaver.*"

"The chubby sidekick on *Lassie.*"

"It was a good fire, burnt up half this flat. It was a duplex with each half stuck onto the other half so it was one long building, right? And we're all standing outside heehawing and chewing tobacco and Allan's full of hisself 'cause we didn't burn down half the county this time. 'Cept nobody'd stuck their head up the cockloft. One of those common attics? The fire gets on one side, it's on both sides.

"We out there talking, and all of a sudden we hear this whaaaoomph. Everybody turns around, and we got fire comin' outa every crack on that roof. Allan says, 'Oh, shit.' He can hear his chief's job slipping away. Now we go from a tapped fire to a fully involved duplex. Lost most of the other side. I shoulda had a chain saw and got up there and opened the bugger. Least I wasn't runnin' around afterward flapping lips, saying there wasn't anything I coulda done."

"That what Allan said?"

Kingsley gave out a high-pitched cackle. "Just one of those things, he says. It happens. What are ya gonna do? Nobody there realized how bad we blew it."

"You tell 'em?"

"You jokin', right? You want me to tell a buncha honky volunteers with deer rifles in their pickups they fucked up?"

"Yeah, I'm jokin'."

A red Porsche drove into the farmyard and pulled up in front of them. Mayor Mo in a red dress with a white scarf around her neck. He thought she looked rather fetching. But then, as he slumped in the grass with the sun and hot winds drying him off, a plucked chicken would have looked fetching.

"I can always count on you, Mac. That's one thing, we get a fire out here and I know we're in good hands," said Mo. Kingsley and Fontana looked at each other for a couple of long beats, then burst into laughter, mirth their narcotic. "What is it? What did I say?"

"Nothing," said Fontana. "Except I was just on my way over there to fire Lieutenant Allan."

"Say again?"

"Fire or suspend. I haven't decided."

"Sorry to say, Mac, but you can't fire him."

"Why not?"

"For one thing, he makes more money than you do."

"Nice reasoning. We have to have a knock-down, drag-out over this, I'm ready. But he's not working here while I'm in charge. He almost got the two of us killed. You want to squabble, fine. I'll write my charges, you write your reasoning, and we'll go before the town council. You're going to look bad, Mo, darlin'."

"I can handle the council, Mac." Grunting, Kingsley climbed to his feet, picked up his equipment, and made tracks. "Chief Fontana, if you want to dismiss anyone, you come through me."

"That's not how it's written, Mo. You know it. I run the department. You don't like it, you fire me. That's how it's always been."

"The chief has never fired anybody!"

"Then this'll be a first."

"Let's work it this way. I'll join up with the volunteers. I'll go to some fires, and that way I can see firsthand. If somebody needs to be dismissed, there will be two of us attesting to the fact. You'll have a stronger case before the council."

"Bullshit."

"I've been thinking about joining the volunteers for a long time."

"You were *running* the volunteers when I got here."

"And doing a capable job, I was told."

"Had your ass hanging out a mile. You don't know the difference between a backdraft and an SOB. I don't want you in the volunteer ranks, and I'm not holding off. Hold off any longer, I'll end up strangling the bastard."

She dropped her voice into her sexiest register. For just a minute it stymied Fontana. "I want to volunteer. I'm strong enough to wear an oxygen tank and carry all that stuff you guys carry. I work out at the high school four nights a week. You'd be surprised."

"Compressed air, Mo. Nobody would take oxygen into a fire. Hell, you put oxygen into dirt and it burns. Being strong enough isn't why you wouldn't make it, Mo. You're squeamish."

"Me?"

The fact was Bobby Joe Allan had an in with Mo Costigan and was friends with or related to many of the volunteers. He had a cousin on the town council. He'd been buddies with Warren Bounty. He'd served the town for eighteen years. Firing the man was going to create a stink. When Fontana publicly accused him of incompetence, it was going to create a scandal. Still, though he'd lived here less than a year, Fontana had his own notorious celebrity. He just might pull it off.

He got up and walked towards Lieutenant Allan.

"Mac?"

When he turned back, Mo was staring at his bare chest. "Mo?"

"Don't you dare leave me standing here."

"Later."

"You gave me a goddamned traffic ticket!"

"Parked on private property."

"I appoint you sheriff and three hours later you give me a sixty-dollar parking ticket. Do you know what that says about our working relationship?"

20

PUSHING FIRE

"We ever have another fire together," said Fontana, "I'm putting you in charge of the water cooler."

Scanning Fontana's face for signs of a joke, Allan bared his large teeth. "The cooler, huh? Sure. I can handle that. With all the rest of it, I s'pose."

"The water cooler."

"Somebody been talking about me?" Without an ounce of assishtance from his apprehensive blue eyes, Bobby Joe Allan smiled.

A few years younger than Fontana, he managed to shave ten more off because his was so boyishly plump. The shock of long brown hair had hung in the same horse bangs sweep since high school. With his fair skin, coarse lips, and large nose, he resembled an overgrown ten-year-old. Kingsley had once kiddingly told a volunteer not ever to throw pennies at Allan's shirt, which was so tight against his belly a penny might ricochet and put your eye out.

His bunkers were as bright and yellow as the day the city purchased them. It was a common firefighter's conceit to gauge others by how grimy their equipment was, by how much heat and scoring their helmets had taken. Not wishing to contest a sport he could never win, Allan feigned disinterest. He made a point of polishing his helmet with Turtle wax.

"I told you to dust off the building but not to throw streams inside."

"That's not what you told me, Chief."

"What?"

"Said I was in charge outside. Said to dust off the house."

"And not to throw any streams through the windows."

"No. You never said that." Fontana was going to be lucky if he got through this without coldcocking him. It wasn't the misstatements that galled Fontana so much as the certitude with which Allan asserted them. His performance would have destroyed any polygraph.

"I told you not to shoot through the window."

"Never said anything like that."

"Guess I'm a damn fool for not recording all our conversations, Bobby Joe." It wasn't the first time Allan denied what they both knew was true. Nor was it the first time he denied receiving an order. "What did you think you were doing?"

Lieutenant Allan blew air into his cheeks. He'd played tuba in his high school band, and the fishy faces he was making reminded Fontana of it. Recently remarried after a devastating divorce, Bobby Joe had just finished several years of catting about. Fontana disliked firing anyone, even for cowardice and lying. He had been thinking perhaps they could make Allan the permanent city inspector, keep him off the active roster yet not deprive him of his pension or salary. After all, he had only seven years until retirement. But the blithe lies and puff-chested cockiness destroyed the remnants of Fontana's charity.

"What was I doing?" said Allan. "We tapped the fire. We saved your ass."

———

"Cripple that and run it past me again."

"We saved your ass."

"How do you figure that?" Fontana had rarely seen anybody throw sand across his tracks so expertly.

"That kitchen was out of control. We waited for you guys to come in and get it, but you never showed. So we hit it from out here. The whole house would have fallen down around your ears."

"The whole house did fall around our ears. You filled up the second story until the floor gave way. You might have killed us with either of those stupid stunts."

"Without me," said Allan, "you wouldn't have escaped. I got witnesses. We *saved* your ass."

"You didn't save anything, Bobby Joe," said Fontana in a whisper. "*We* would have tapped that kitchen if you'd done what I told you. Which was to keep your streams on the outside of the building. You threw the fire in our faces. Understand? You came close to burning us. You roasted Kingsley's ears. Didn't you see our hose stream coming back out the window?"

Allan was finally beginning to take the measure of Fontana's fury. "Nothing came out the window. We saw some steam."

"All I can think of, Bobby Joe—and this matches everything else I know about you—is that even standing outside where you were safe, you got so scared you couldn't stand not to hit it. Surely you know about pushing fire into people's faces. We drilled the volunteers on it. You know everything in theory. I can't tell you a thing in theory. We get out in the field and you become a nincompoop."

"I get it," said Allan, grasping the overall conspiracy. Gone was the uncertainty. "The nigger set me up."

"Say that again."

"You heard me."

"How you got into the fire service is beyond me. Why you want to stay is beyond me. You must stain your shorts every time the bell hits. I'm suspending you. With pay. You can keep quiet about why and we can try to work something out with your pension. Or you can blab it around and I'll make my reasons public. I'm dying to tell everyone you're scared of fire."

"You're not giving me a chance to defend myself?"

"Make an appointment. Bring a lawyer, your union rep, the mayor over there. Whatever. You're not going on any more alarms."

"They don't know anything. These are volunteers."

"That's why we owe it to them to be professionals."

"I'm fired?"

"Suspended."

"You're kidding?" Allan's smirk had straight-lined. This was the first clue he had that he was in real trouble.

"I'm not kidding."

"Never had any problems with Bounty."

"Maybe you didn't come as close to killing Bounty as you came to killing me."

Across the yard Mo Costigan leaned against the front fender of her Porsche and observed. At the other end of her car Satan lifted a leg and oiled a tire.

Lieutenant Allan pivoted, stumped across the yard, spoke to Gil Cutty, and slid into Gil's Roadrunner, drove with him past Mo Costigan. Inside, Fontana could see Allan staring straight ahead, speaking quickly. He wouldn't have been able to read his lips if he hadn't heard the same words a few minutes earlier. "The nigger set me up."

"That seemed to go well," said Mo snidely as Fontana lugged his equipment back to the GMC. He stroked the dog, who'd sat calmly through the fire. Balancing on one heel, Mo stood next to him, hands behind her. The left lens of her tortoise-shell sunglasses had a scratch across it.

"Kingsley!" Fontana shouted.

"Yeah, boss."

"You're in charge. Go easy. There's going to be a sticky period here."

"He fired?"

"Taking a little sabbatical."

"Sure, boss." Twenty minutes ago they had been pals. Now people were being axed. Now it was time to duck into the foxhole and count fingers and toes.

"Sticky period?" said Mo. "That's what you think this is going to be?"

"Mo?"

"You're going to be up to your eyeballs in angry citizens, Mac. The first thing Bobby Joe's going to do is buttonhole his cousin on the town council. They'll hold a special meeting. You're going to explain this."

"I don't know that he's going to buttonhole anybody. I don't imagine he'd want everybody knowing what I said about him. Especially since it's true."

"And what was that?"

"Ask him."

"I have a right to know why you've suspended our only lieutenant, Mac."

"Yeah, you do. And I'm going to write it all up the minute I get a chance."

"Small-town politics is a nasty little snake with nasty little fangs, Mac. You could end up losing your position."

"That'd be tough, Mo."

"You want me to give Bounty back his job as chief?"

"Don't threaten me."

Her tone grew theatrically contrite. "I'm sorry. I didn't mean that. The council would never agree anyway. Even if they felt like giving him charity. Poor Warren. Did you know when he went off to the sanitarium somebody broke into his place and trashed everything? Smashed his walls open. Never caught the culprits. Wait a minute. This doesn't have anything to do with

114

Kingsley, does it? Pierpont and Bobby Joe have been at each other's throats since Pierpont came to work here. I hope you didn't get yourself in the middle of something racial."

"Allan might try to flip-flop it into that. For a smoke screen."

Fontana was in the truck now, had loaded the dog and his equipment. "Mac, one last thing." Mo draped herself across his windowsill, her face close enough to kiss. He'd always had a soft spot for brash females. "Would you meet with Lars and me and his attorneys sometime this week? Just as a favor."

"You flatter me, Mo. I talk out about Lars being a land-grabber, and all of a sudden we're going to have a power lunch. Have Lars's secretary call my secretary."

"You don't have a secretary," she said, but he was already driving off the property. Mo was always a step behind. Once he'd told her his answer phone was in the shop and wouldn't be back for two years. She'd offered to lend him one of hers. For reasons he couldn't fathom, her obtuseness made him feel protective in the manner of an older brother. But Mo Costigan could take care of herself, formed alliances in the most unlikely places, and had a reputation for hardball politicking.

She had the town under her thumb. And she didn't have a hint what Fontana was joking about. Ever.

21

FAT ENOUGH TO
GAG A MAGGOT

Fontana typed his letter to the city council.

He found it difficult not to disparage Bobby Joe. The biggest gamble Allan had taken in his life was a vasectomy he'd had on the sly while his first wife, desperate for a baby, was experimenting with everything from thermometers to voodoo. It was shortly after she uncovered his deception that she divorced him. He claimed she robbed him of everything. Bobby Joe had a new wife who made more money than he did, a fact that dismayed him when he wasn't gloating over it.

Allan had been raised not by his fanatically religious mother and father, who tented around the country, putting on revival shows, but by relatives, most of whom didn't care a peck for the chubby child. As an inducement to board the boy, his folks left a console color TV with him. In the days when only the affluent and trendy had color, the family that kept the kid kept the TV.

"Just me and that damned Motorola shipped all over the state," Allan griped. "The family'd get their own tube, and I'd be off to live with Uncle Benito."

While Fontana sometimes felt empathy for him, more often he wanted to push him out of an airplane with a Kleenex on a ripcord. Smug and smarmy, Allan made a practice of belittling volunteers in ways that were difficult to put into words but easy to feel. He would listen to you if you made him, but it was always clear from his vacant eyes that Bobby Joe didn't care a hoot. Despite the fact that he'd known everyone in town most of his adult life, nobody really liked him; he was one of those people you tolerated because you thought the other guy liked him.

Shortly after Fontana took over as chief, Bobby Joe Allan bought a new Ford van. Each morning at the beanery table he would meticulously calculate the mileage. Day after day he bored everyone with how far he could go on a gallon of gas.

After two weeks Gil Cutty and several others began skulking out each noontime to pour an extra gallon into the gas tank. Bobby Joe couldn't stop crowing. He explained to everyone how careful he was about accelerating, that he used his brakes less than any driver in the valley, that he coasted down hills. He penned a letter to the president of General Motors suggesting he write a booklet for them on gas-saving tips. Pierpont, who didn't approve of Allan's junk-food diet, accused him of running the engine on farts.

After two weeks Gil and the boys began siphoning gas instead of adding it, hacking Allan's figures down into single digits.

"Whatcha gettin' in that new van this week?" Gil Cutty would ask. Everyone laughed, especially Claude Pettigrew, who had engineered the scam. It was only after Allan had bitched to the dealer and threatened to hire a lawyer that they confessed. Everybody thought the prank hilarious except Allan, who rarely laughed, never at a joke on himself, and rarely at one he hadn't told. Mostly Polish jokes. Watermelon jokes about blacks whispered behind Pierpont's back.

Six months later a sure way to light Allan's fuse was to ask about his mileage. Pierpont told him if he ate more beans, he'd do better.

*　　　*　　　*

"They said you were back here."

Fontana looked up from his typing and smiled. "Haven't seen you in six months."

Charles Dummelow, a paunchy King County detective, had a bushy head of faded red hair, fingernails bitten to the quick, and a complexion so delicate his face burned under a sixty-watt bulb. He'd worked with Fontana on a case the previous winter and harbored an enormous respect for Mac, most of it based on the fact that Fontana had given a dirtball named Max Draper a third eye with a .38 slug. Charles would have paid anything to see it happen.

Sitting heavily on the edge of the desk, Dummelow wore slacks, a pink dress shirt, and a brown tie loosened at the neck and ruffled by the heat. His pockets were bulging with loose change, keys, pens.

"Gawd, it's hot out. That wind ever stop howling?"

"Cleans the air. I like it."

Dummelow had a disconcerting habit of rolling his tongue backward between his teeth, showing only a snatch of the pores on the back side between his incisors. It was only one of a dozen nervous mannerisms.

"First thing is that note from the bulletin board was pecked out on the machine we confiscated from your office. No prints except for a thumb belonging to our deputy. Second, we dusted the kitchen. Collected prints from eighty some individuals. No telling at this date when any of them were laid down. Third, the meat was poisoned, and there's no way it could have been accidental. Somebody laced it good. Your man died of arsenic ingestion.

Way I understand it, there's some sort of lover boy relationship going on between this Wanda and Pettigrew?"

"I interviewed her yesterday afternoon right after it happened."

"And?"

Fontana shrugged. "Claude Pettigrew met Wanda Sheridan when he was in the hospital a few months back. A part-time nurse. Him? He's kind of a gofer. I think you'll understand when you meet him."

"Where is Pettigrew?"

"Works at the mill over by Snoqualmie. Let me call his mother's house and see if he went to work today." Fontana phoned. He had. "I'll drive you."

On the way Fontana briefed Dummelow on the affair between Pettigrew and Wanda, leaving out her extramarital trysts with Jim Caitlin. Sending a county detective to Rainy's house wasn't on his list of chivalrous things to do.

"One thing you gotta know about Pettigrew. He looks slow. He acts slow. Maybe in a lot of ways he is. People keep telling me he's mildly retarded. But he's stashed more money in the bank than you or I are likely to see in our lifetimes. Won two different insurance settlements that I know of. One at the service station here in town where a car fell on him. He lives with his mama, and he wears pants that are fifteen years old. Resoles his shoes. Saves his chewing gum overnight. They don't build 'em like that anymore."

North of the small, depressed town of Snoqualmie, the mill abutted a huge pond the Vancouver Lumber Company used for sorting logs. A one-man tug powered across the surface. Stacks across the still water spewed plumes of white smoke into the hot wind.

When they flashed their shields at the woman guard in the shack, she said, "You investigating the fire station catastrophe? Hell of a deal. Who do you think would do such a thing?"

Fontana smiled weakly and waited for her to give directions to a large parking lot beside some office windows. Fontana left Satan in the shade of the GMC. Inside, a grimy man with warts on his knuckles and a hard hat on his skull handed them each a helmet, grunted, "Regulations," and left without waiting to see if they followed.

Pettigrew worked in a noisy tin-walled building near the pond, one of the few sit-down jobs in the plant. The concrete floor was frosted with black muck and sawdust mush. Wet logs came into one end of the building on a jagged-toothed conveyor. Pettigrew scanned them and pulled levers to divert them in three different directions. Scrap one way. Prime logs another. Medium and small logs another. The place reeked of wood, sweat, coffee, and cigarettes.

"Claude," shouted Fontana. "This is Charles Dummelow. Detective with King County. Working on Daugherty's case."

Pettigrew looked up, his dark brown eyes set deep under his shoe-brush brows. The man with warts hung around until Fontana gave him a grim look. Then he turned and left. Pettigrew reached low on his control panel and pushed a button. The conveyor stopped, and the noise level dropped forty decibels. Unscrewing a pair of orange rubber plugs from his ears, Pettigrew began thoughtlessly balling up ear wax from the plugs between his fingertips.

"What the hell you mean, Daugherty's case? They poisoned me, too, you know."

"Yeah, well, he's working on the whole case."

"Guess I got a few minutes," Pettigrew grumbled. He was acting peeved, but Fontana knew he was tickled to be important enough for a King County detective to visit. For a few beats Pettigrew and Dummelow took each other's measure. Pettigrew's helmet was plastered with decals. Chiquita Banana. KSEA radio. Read the Word. Mess with me, we'll bury you at sea.

The county detective said, "You see anybody fooling with that chow?"

"I told your people yesterday at the hospital. I'll tell you. I didn't see nothin'. I don't know who did it. If I did, I'd take a piece of pipe and give 'em a good rap on the noggin.''

"Understand one of the people in the station at the time of the poisoning was a friend of yours?"

"Whyn't you call her what she is? A girl friend. She ain't the first neither."

"Her name?"

Pettigrew's voice grew whiny. "You know her goddamned name. What are you playing?"

"Wanda Sheridan," said Fontana, trying to ease the interview along. "Sure you should be at work, Claude? You took a good dose yesterday."

"Hell, no, I shouldn't be at work. They called me. Been short-handed all summer. Won't hire nobody. Cheap bastards."

"What I want to know is," said Dummelow, "did you see anything yesterday?"

"I mighta."

"Feel free to amplify that."

"I mighta. I mighta seen somethin'. I mighta done somethin'." Pettigrew closed his mouth and moved his lips around in a circle as if his nose itched.

Dummelow addressed a questioning look at Fontana, who rolled his eyes and kicked a piece of bark into an oily puddle. Across the way a large water-pressure debarking machine made a racket. Fontana spotted a rat in the shadows.

The county detective said, "You want to confess or something?"

Pettigrew's laugh was jittery, his smile sour. "Hell, no, I don't want to confess."

"How'd you like to walk out of here in handcuffs?"

"You asked me about Wanda. What do you need to know? And listen. You can't talk to me like that. Got me a lawyer."

"You two have a fight recently?"

"Hell, no, we ain't had no fight. We ain't never had no fights."

"She's got a record."

"Bull. What sorta record?"

"How long you been going with her?"

"I dunno. Six, seven weeks. What do you mean, *record*?"

"Got into a jam at Maxi's."

"Hell, I caused that beef myself. Had one too many martinis."

Claude assumed that every male in the county lusted obscenely after Wanda Sheridan. He stretched his heavy legs, shimmed a hand down the front of his pants under his bulging belly, as if to readjust the goods, sipped from a Diet Coke can in a row of identical cans on the arm of his machine, and wiped the perspiration off his brow with the back of a filthy glove.

"She climbed in my bunk the first night," said Pettigrew.

"What?" Dummelow glanced at Fontana.

"The first night."

"That's nice."

"Didn't even pay her nothin'."

"She must really love you," said Dummelow.

Ten minutes later, riding along a hot country tarmac road in the GMC, passing a blue handkerchief across his face, Charles said, "Jeez, he's a squirrelly piece of work. Fat enough to gag a maggot."

"Watching you question him was like watching a man in boxing gloves trying to floss his teeth."

"Think he could have poisoned you all?"

"With Claude, there's no telling."

22

THE BIGGEST HEROES
ARE THE DEADEST

In the half-dry riverbed Fontana could feel the heat from the sunbaked rocks. Pumped through Snoqualmie Pass from the desert country of eastern Washington, the chinook blew hot and malignant. It was late afternoon. Blistered skin, browned vegetation, and parched landscape greeted him wherever he looked.

Staircase overflowed with pickup trucks towing boat trailers, cars with inner tubes strapped to their roofs, hikers with peeling noses, a Plymouth Voyager crammed with children sucking purple Popsicles. Young girls rode tall horses clippety-clop down the country roads. Bike racers in glossy skintight shorts and clunky helmets whirred through town. Two parachutists launched off the mountain, their orange and white nylon chutes milking the thermals high above town.

Brendan wore black-rimmed sunglasses, shorts, and a faded black T-shirt that said, "I love New York." On top of it all was a child's faded orange life vest borrowed from one of the volunteers. An hour earlier Mac had parked the Destroyer three miles downstream, hitching a ride back in Mary's air-conditioned Dodge. Before launching their journey thirty yards from their back door, Fontana had swabbed his son down with sunscreeen and put on a pair of black-rimmed sunglasses identical to Brendan's.

"Sure isn't very deep," said Brendan, touching the bottom with his hands.

With their rumps in the holes, they floated on car inner tubes. In the sargasso spots where the water movement was almost nonexistent they paddled. Twice they chose shallow channels and had to stand up and portage, tubes for tutus.

Fontana had promised Brendan this trip, and he was determined to forget that one of his men had died yesterday, that he'd suspended another this morning. He tried to disregard the fact that he'd have to confront the town council. Mo still hadn't committed herself. If she took the offensive, he could lose his job, a prospect he was beginning to find disagreeable. He was fond of the job. The town. The mountain. Even combative Mo Costigan.

They drifted along the winding river, pastureland alternating with deciduous woods, here and there a swamp full of dried-up cattails. After the bridge they came upon a vast sandy area known locally as Unemployment Beach, staffed, as it always was on hot summer days, with families, mothers and children, and a few women in pairs.

She was on the sandy beach in a lawn chair, pretending not to see them. After paddling over in the lazy current, Fontana beached his craft without climbing out of the black rubber doughnut. He realized he must look inane.

"Afternoon."

Her children were digging on the beach behind her, sand stuck to their wet bodies like sugar on doughnuts. "Chief Fontana?"

From her reclining position Jane Daugherty shielded her eyes with one hand and peered over her fat knees. Behind, Brendan ran aground on a sandbar in the middle of the stream and clambered out of his inner tube. The river stalled and swelled into a cove here. Eight or ten families had spread blankets and nylon mesh lawn chairs on the flat sandy banks. Fontana counted six dogs running amok. Three belonged to the woman in front of him.

"Just out taking some sun?"

"The kids begged. I'd already promised we'd go to the beach today, and I didn't have the heart to back down. They don't really know what's happened. I don't mind. At home the phone keeps ringing. People keep coming by. This is the only place I can forget for a few minutes.

"It can get like that."

She looked frayed. She was plump in all the wrong places, and her skin was chalky enough that he knew this was the first time all year she'd wriggled into a bathing suit. He noted a bruise the size and color of an eggplant on her left thigh. Her hair was greasy and tangled.

"You're looking good," he said.

"Thank you." Nearly capsizing the lawn chair, she patted her hair and sat upright. She'd been a looker in high school, which hadn't been too many years ago. "I'm glad you came by. I've been thinking about what happened. I was kind of in shock yesterday, but I was awake all night thinking. Pete was going through a crisis. He was going through this thing where he believed he was either in big trouble or he would sit around planning to buy a Porsche."

"I don't understand."

"Dollars," said Jane Daugherty. "I thought about it all night. Pete was worried about something. Maybe the past couple of weeks. At the same time he thought he might be coming into a lot of money. Something nobody was supposed to know about. And afterwards we might get a ski condo up in the mountains. We might fly to Maui on his vacation. Silly stuff like that."

"He made it sound illicit?"

"I told him he better not be doing anything illegal. He had a good job now, and we were almost through paying my medical bills. I didn't want him spoiling it all over something stupid."

"What'd he say?"

"Said he didn't have to do anything. That it had already been done."

"Say what it was?"

"I wish he had. I went through all his belongings last night, but there wasn't a thing. More I think about it, the more I know it has something to do with yesterday."

Brendan was rolling a large rock across the sandbar, laying the foundation for a dam on the far side of the bar where the divided river was a mere trickle.

"Thanks for telling me, Jane. I liked Pete a lot. You know that." Jane peered at him over her sunglasses, saluting with both hands. A dagger of sunlight lanced off her thin gold wedding band. "Pete had the same point of view I started out with. He was bashful about it, but he told me once, when we were alone, he wanted to win a medal for rescuing someone. I never heard him say it again, but that was the fire service for Pete. Fighting fires and saving lives. I felt that way once."

"I was proud of Pete," Jane said, tears appearing in her already swollen eyes.

"With good reason."

Fontana collected Brendan, and they bobbed downstream.

"Hey, Mac?"

"Yeah."

Floating behind, Brendan had discovered a deeper section of the river, greenish blue. The water was cooler. They could still make out the oiled sunbathers in the distance on Unemployment Beach. Here the high banks were laced with ripening blackberries and wild blueberries. To the south was a rolling pasture threaded with birch.

"Hey, Mac. Look." Brendan was churning around and around in a miniature whirlpool. "Mac. Come on over here and try this. This is great fun."

23

A DOG THIS DIABOLICAL

"You got here faster than I thought you would."

"Hundred miles an hour all the way," Fontana lied. They both knew the old truck would never make eighty, much less a hundred. He glanced up the street. It was midnight. No traffic. "You sounded scared."

"Yeah, well," said Kingsley, "dat was on the phone. I'm feelin' better."

"Police?"

"Been and gone."

"They bring a dog?"

"Said their animals were being used up north somewhere. A double murder."

"Your visitor had good timing."

"Not that good," said Kingsley.

"Why do you say that?"

"I'm still here, ain't I?" Kingsley scratched his head. His nails, long and manicured like a woman's, annoyed the bejesus out of Bobby Joe Allan.

City light and the moon combined to brighten the street. Most of the neighbors had their windows propped open, though Seattle seemed cool compared with the Upper Snoqualmie Valley.

Ever alert, Satan trotted along the porch behind his master, picking up random scents. "Bad guys, Satan," Fontana had said, loading him up in Staircase. He'd drummed his palms on his thighs. "Bad guys. Let's go catch us some bad guys." Satan perked up. Ears straight, tail high.

Pierpont resided in the heart of the Central District in Seattle on Jefferson Street. The CD was the primary black neighborhood in the city, the state. When Kingsley first got on the Staircase FD, it had been a bone of contention, his living in Seattle, since most of those who'd applied lived in the valley, but he battled and won the right to reside anywhere he wanted.

Fontana patted Satan's side. "When? About an hour ago?"

Kingsley glanced at a squarish gold-plated watch. "Hour and fifteen minutes."

"Cops got here fast."

"Seattle's finest."

Garfield High School sat at the east end of Jefferson a few blocks away on Twenty-third Avenue. To the west was Providence Hospital. Cherry Street, where half the drug deals in the city went down, was less than half a mile distant. These houses had once been the tiara of old Seattle, owned by political mavens and society families. Now, interspersed with run-down apartment buildings, plagued by owners who didn't keep up their properties, the region had atrophied into a hodgepodge.

Pierpont's was one of two upgraded and recently renovated residences on the block. Three stories. Fenced. Painted light tan with blue shutters and trim. Inside, the floors were polished hardwood. Fontana recognized a Tiffany lamp, or a good imitation of one.

"What'd the cops say?" Pierpont was escorting him to the rear of the house.

"Said they'd be by my crib every hour. Said to call, I had any more prowlers. They wasn't takin' it lightly, but then again, they didn't come up with shit."

"A dog would've helped."

"Satan gonna be any good?"

"It's his handler doesn't know what he's doing. Bounty's been giving me tips the past couple of weeks, but it's been so hot I haven't wanted to work the mutt."

"Been hot."

Kingsley wore a royal blue robe trimmed in gold piping. His lanky shins flashed as he walked. Canted against a doorway in the back of the house stood an Asian woman in a matching robe.

Kingsley said, "Oh, yeah. This is May. Stays here sometimes."

"Interesting to finally meet you, Mr. Mac Fontana. I've heard lots of stories."

"All lies," said Mac grimly.

"I hope not. He said you were the best thing to hit Staircase since he joined."

"Thanks, May," said Kingsley. She'd embarrassed him. Maybe that's why she stayed in the hall when Pierpont took him into a kitchen. It was festooned with brass cooking utensils. Yellow patterned wallpaper. A fancy gas range fit for a chef. He'd obviously paid a decorator. "Right here."

Though the lights were on, Fontana drew a flashlight out of his jeans pocket and examined the two holes in the doorframe. Across the room shattered glass had already been swept up. "Maybe a twenty-two. The cops were neat digging 'em out. May shook up?"

"Was sitting at the table. I walked into the room, and the window shattered. I thought a bird was behind it. Then I saw him and flipped off the lights. Think that's what saved us. He was definitely gunning me."

"Sure it was a him?"

"Had a ski mask. I hit the floor. Told May to hit the floor, but she walked to the back door and looked out. But it was me they was after."

"Two shots?"

"That's what I counted."

"See them running?"

"May said he jumped over that low fence by the garage, hung a right, and booked."

"You get a look at the way he moved? Sometimes you can recognize people."

"Think this was somebody I know?"

"If it'd come out of the blue, I'd say no."

Kingsley thought about that, used one of his fingernails to scratch his temple with a rasping sound. "I don't know who'd wanta cap me. Unless it was Allan. I heard from a couple of the guys he was plenty pissed. But even with all that blowhard talk about his three-fifty-seven and how if a burglar broke into his crib, he blow his brains away, Allan ain't shit. Allan wouldn't cap a squirrel."

"Think about the figure you saw."

"I hit the floor pretty fast. By the time May spotted him out the window he was already running."

"Police look for shell casings?"

"Footprints, too. Big zeros."

Fontana patted the dog's side and led Satan onto the back porch. "Neighbors got any dogs?"

"Just across the way there. A dachshund."

"Maybe Satan won't kill him. *Suche!*" he commanded.

The Alsatian began tracking up and down the porch. There would be a lot of scents now. The gunman. May. Kingsley. At least two policemen. Fontana was hoping Satan would sort out the odors the way Bounty claimed he could.

"Get the bad guy," said Fontana. "Out here somewhere. *Suche!* Go get 'em!"

Standing back quietly, Fontana let the dog work. Humans have 5 million olfactory cells; dogs, which live in a world of scent, anywhere from 125 to 200 million. In addition, in humans there are 6 to 8 cilia per receptor cell; in dogs, between 100 and 150. That is why dogs can sometimes smell odors in parts as minute as one part per trillion. The animal hopped off the porch and trotted into the yard twice, sniffing back up onto the porch that ran the width of the house. He seemed confused. Once he looked up at Fontana, as if for instructions.

"*Suche!*" repeated Fontana. It was important he did not lead the dog. In the backyard under a dogwood Satan rooted out a screeching cat, paid it no heed. He vaulted over the three-foot fence, nuzzled around the base, and headed past the garage. Fontana switched on his flashlight and followed. He was counting on the flashlight and a gray T-shirt that said "Police" to keep him from getting gunned by a spooked citizen.

Twice Satan followed track back to the fence, leaped the pickets, and meandered toward Kingsley's porch. Kingsley had gone inside. Finally the dog proceeded up the alley and around to the street. The gunman had canvassed the house from the front. Probably not anybody who'd been here before.

Plodding through the sodden grass, Satan led him through a yard that had had sprinklers running until recently. Despite popular opinion, the wet held a trail, kept it fresh. Now, half a block from Kingsley's, Fontana knew the cops wouldn't have ventured this far.

A year ago the evil-looking shepherd had been Bounty's, obedient only to him. Ofttimes the transference of allegiance from one owner to another with these one-man animals wasn't successful. Realizing the confusion his return might have instilled, Bounty rarely petted him, never offered commands. The dog seemed to understand.

Warren had laid out the drill for Fontana, taught him how to order the big police dog to search, obey, track; taught him what the limits of the dog's capabilities were; taught him the German commands as well as the English. Even taught him his secret code word for "sic 'em," though Bounty had never had occasion to use it: *Eis!* German for "ice."

Trained in Germany in a *Schutzhund klub*, Satan had graduated with honors from the association to which only 1 in 150 candidates qualified for initial selection. The animals the club produced were overpriced, sleek, and flawless in their professional capacities. Satan had spent a couple of years working with the police in a small town in the south of the state, where he'd been involved in more than one rumpus—enough to convince his owners his useful professional life had been expended.

He was eight now, getting long in the tooth for a shepherd. He looked as if he'd been through a hay baler. Twice. Knife wounds had just about dismantled one ear, laid scars across the top of the dog's skull, and barely missed taking out an eye. He'd been shot. He'd saved Mac's life last winter. Technically the township owned him, but nobody could handle the pooch but Fontana. Or Warren.

Two blocks away on an avenue the trail went cold.

The prowler hadn't taken any chances. He'd parked here. Fontana had done exercises with Satan, one of which involved a friend making a trail and then climbing into his car and driving off. Satan was acting the same now as he had then.

The dog whined, sat, looked up at him, curled in a circle as if asking a question, and whined again. He stared at Fontana quizzically.

"This it? This as far as we're going?"

A young black man coasted up the avenue on a ten-speed, regarding Fontana suspiciously. Men who talked to their dogs.

Kneeling, Fontana scanned the shadowy pavement with his flashlight. He found two fresh oil spots. They might or might not have been laid down in the past two hours. They might or might not have anything to do with the shooting. The streets were full of oil spots. Satan nosed them. Fontana took a plastic evidence bag out of his rear jeans pocket and blotted up the oil with a tissue, then put it in the bag and sealed it. The spots resembled small stars, one slightly larger than the other.

24

THE ALMOST HUNG MAN

"I don't want you telling anybody around Staircase," said Fontana.

"Ain't you bitchin'?" Kingsley thought he was joking.

May said, "Why on earth not?"

"Things like this can get contagious."

The three of them were sitting at the kitchen table, sipping herbal tea that tasted to Fontana like weeds. He smiled stoically and said the flavor was subtle. A medium-height, sleek woman, May had long black hair that hung in waves, an exotic rather than pretty face. Satan sat in the corner on his haunches, panting loudly.

Kingsley said, "You think this is a racial deal?"

"If it is, I don't want everybody and his brother knowing the details. Copycats come out of the woodwork at times like this."

"How many copycats you expectin'?"

"That's something I'd rather not find out."

"What about the county cops?"

"They're not going to blab it."

Kingsley brought his left hand out of his robe pocket and laid a small blued automatic on the table. "Next sucker messes with me gonna end up on Q Street."

"Honey," said May, dropping her hand across his, "let the police handle this. Let Mr. Fontana work on it."

"I ain't going out to look for it," said Kingsley. "I'm just sayin' next sucker messes with me is in for a jolt. I know one thing. I won't get any sleep behind this."

"I've been thinking," said Fontana. "What if this whole thing *is* racial?"

"What are you saying?"

"What if the ham had been meant for you?"

"How do you single me out with a hunk of meat for eight?"

"I'm not saying it makes sense. Just what if."

"Ain't never had that much trouble of a racial nature in Staircase. Sure, I tease the folks. I tell Allan my clarinet is two feet long and he believes me. But I don't think there's any deep-down hard feelings."

"Allan's been on your case for eight years."

"Yes and no. He was pretty obnoxious when I first showed up. Bounty was chief and Allan just made lieutenant. Bounty didn't have much control over the troops."

"Drinking?"

"And bitches. He was hell on bitches until he got so boozy he couldn't get it up. Was a legend up in the valley."

"What about Allan?"

"He just plain didn't like me. Tried to jam me up behind damaging the rig and not telling anybody—that was when we had a '68 Mack. Turned out one of the volunteers 'fessed to it. Bobby Joe wanted to turn me out for that one. You want the truth." Kingsley pronounced it 'troof.' "Truth is there's racists in Staircase, don't get me wrong. I just don't think Allan is one of 'em. He's had black friends. Not too many, but he had one in the Naval Reserve. Thing about Allan. He thinks I'm a pimp. That's what jams him up."

"And you throw fuel on the fire every chance you get."

"I like a good time as much as the next dude."

"I never have thought that was funny," said May.

They sipped tea and pondered the situation.

Kingsley said, "Maybe you don't know all there is to know about me and Allan. When I first came in, he wanted my ass. Then I proved myself in a couple of rippers, and I think I kinda took the pressure off him. We kinda got into an arrangement. I tapped 'em. He talked big. And if I complained, I was the black guy."

"So you didn't complain?"

"I bitched when the occasion called for it. Then I got divorced, and about a year later Bobby Joe broke up with his wife. It stung him. You know how settled he is. That's not it." Kingsley snapped his fingers, trying to dredge up a word.

"Complacent," said Fontana.

"There you go. You know how complacent that dude is. I mean, that's why people don't like him. Somebody that complacent just comes off arrogant. When his wife upped and threw him out, it sorta turned him upside down for a while. We had some long talks, see, 'cause I could sorta see where he was comin' from, having been through it myself. D'you know Allan almost hung himself behind it? He told me one night he got so low he had the rope tied to the rafters in the garage."

"That's pretty low," said May.

"Allan an' me's had our ups and downs, but underneath it all, he respects me and I don't bother him much." Fontana wondered if it was a breach of friendship not to tell him what Allan really thought.

25

MY FATHER DANCED
WITH NUNS

Friday night the Bedouin opened its spacious hardwood dance floor. Velma switched on the rotating mirrored spheres, the jukebox, and the orange, violet, yellow, and blue neon lights. People trucked in from as far away as Tacoma and Enumclaw. Couples in jeans and cowboy shirts came from the valley. In wintertime, skiers and snowmobilers. In summer, hikers. Loggers. Housewives. Millworkers. Boeing engineers. Dress was informal, and the milieu included everything from jeans and cowboy boots to business suits and high-top basketball shoes. Lots of cowboy hats.

Any valley resident going out on the town put in an appearance at the Bedouin—the slow-dancing capital of the Northwest. Log walls and an antler motif inside, an alpine look with frosted shutters and gingerbread roof outside, the building had been inappropriately tagged the Bedouin sixty years earlier by Velma's grandmother. A diehard fan of Rudolph Valentino, she'd made a pilgrimage to his grave once a year until her hip replacement.

"Me? I'm a dancing fool," said Velma. " 'Member watching Mama and Big Jack Daddy on that floor forty years ago. Hell, Mac. She had a date with Merlin Cummins, and Big Jack kept cutting in. Couldn't keep his eyes off Mama. I live for Friday nights and Johnny Mathis. I'd stock the box with nothing but Johnny, 'cept if I did, Hal would spit blood and die. Thinks Johnny's a fag."

Tonight the floor was bristling with the penny loafer crowd from Issaquah and several groups of backpackers who'd been attracted by the sandwich board on the sidewalk. In the past hookers from Seattle had given twenty-dollar blow jobs in the parking lot, but a furious Velma learned of it and stamped out the practice by turning a garden hose on several couplings.

Three nights had passed since Kingsley's ambuscade.

Signaling Mac, Mo, in a slinky green dress, had thumbed a nickel into the jukebox slot and made the first selection. The lights were low. The dancing was just getting started. Little Anthony sang "Going Out of My Head." Across the room Mo chatted and drank with a contingent of developers, including Lars Ereckson.

Warren Bounty and Mac sat at a table in the north end of the sweltering building, Mac sipping Rainier beer, Warren 7-Up from a tall beer stein. Brendan was staying overnight with a friend from school. In the dim light Bounty watched the first hoofers pair off. "Pete's funeral was a hell of a deal."

Fontana said, "Somebody had stood up and sung 'Danny Boy,' I would've started bawling." As in a lot of friendships, Bounty and Fontana avoided emotional topics; grief was not something Mac could expatiate upon.

"I'd just like to get my hands on that slime. Five minutes."

Fontana recognized ten or twelve volunteers. Sometimes Pierpont showed with a date, always different—always Caucasian and usually painted like a streetwalker. Fontana was convinced he hired them from an acting class to distress the locals. Before his second marriage Bobby Joe Allan had been a Friday night fixture, but not tonight. Claude Pettigrew was across the room on a high barstool, gulping martinis, next to a fidgety Wanda, who kicked her crossed legs in a thigh-high black leather skirt and flirted with the man on the other side of her.

"Been all over this valley asking questions," said Bounty. "Nobody knows beans. You talk to Allan?"

"Haven't been able to find him. I figure he's holed up somewhere, licking his wounds and trying to find a cheap lawyer. The King County police have come up with zilch."

Bounty wore slacks and a dress shirt sans tie, the sleeves rolled on his thick forearms. It was hot in the building, even though Velma had had the air conditioner cranking all afternoon. Warren unbuttoned another button to expose his chest. He sipped his soda pop.

"Me?" Warren said out of the blue. "I'm not like you. Never killed anyone in my life. Been in bar fights. Goin' into the rest room to finish it off with a guy once but decided he wasn't worth it. Ten minutes later some other guy went in the can to duke it out with this clown, and the clown slipped on the floor and cracked his skull on the commode. Guy got sent up for manslaughter. Coulda been me. I always think about that."

"Kingsley called me Tuesday night. Somebody took a couple of potshots at him through his kitchen window."

"You're shitting me." Fontana gave him the details, including why he'd neglected to make the information public. "The dog get you anything?"

"Found where the Dugan took off in a car. Went back a day later at dinnertime and talked to the neighbors. Nobody saw diddly."

"The dog's not that good. Don't put your trust in that animal."

"He got agitated, was all."

"You gotta work a dog; else he loses his skills. There she is," said Bounty, glancing across the jammed room. "My second suspect. Wanda and her."

As far as Mac knew, Rainy had never been to the Bedouin. She was with her husband. Rainy in tight, dressy jeans. Caitlin in slacks. They searched for a table.

"What makes you think she had anything to do with it?"

"Her husband was fooling around with Wanda. You knew that, didn't you?" Bounty winked, making Fontana laugh. "She could have been so teed off she didn't care who else she nailed along with him."

"She has an alibi," said Fontana.

"She does?"

"I was with her."

"You don't say?" Bounty's face contorted crookedly, half dubious, half surprised.

"We're friends. Nothing else."

"Sure, sure."

"Caitlin doesn't know, does he?" Fontana shook his head. "You realize she dropped by the station that afternoon right before it happened? You were in your room. She came with Jim. In and out. Everybody looking the other way for a second. Dump the d-CON into the ham and kiss hubby good-bye. Eh?"

"No way."

Fontana sipped beer and watched the Caitlins meander around until they found a table along the wall. Their boy was in Tacoma for a week at grandma's. Rainy looked devilishly attractive tonight, chopped bronze-brown hair swinging across her face. She glanced around at the crowd; failed to spot him.

As Warren trudged off to the washroom, the Righteous Brothers came on the jukebox with "You've Lost That Lovin' Feeling." Mo Costigan snaked through the crowd, eyes glued to Mac.

He rarely missed a Friday night at the Bedouin and, even though she was much shorter than he was, frequently paired up with Mo, who was the smoothest dancer he'd ever met. They would move half an hour together without saying a word. His father had once laughingly told of having danced with nuns in college, a tale that prompted Mac to claim it was hereditary. The mechanics of his relationship with Mo had always been baffling. Their Friday evenings at the Bedouin were as silky as their business relationship was tempestuous. But then, all of Mo's business dealings were stormy.

"Mac, I need to talk. Everything's been so hectic. The funeral and all the newspeople hassling me."

"You loved every minute of it, Mo. You had your way somebody'd be murdered in Staircase once a week."

"What a horrible thing to say."

"It's true. You're a publicity hound."

"I resent you saying that. How's the investigation going?"

"Not well."

She scooted into Warren Bounty's chair, pressed both bare elbows onto the table, cupped her chin in her hands, and stared at him. "We have things to talk about."

"Such as?"

"Bobby Joe Allan. I've got a deal for you."

"I was afraid of this."

"You know as well as I do you've got yourself into a rather sticky wicket. You've suspended him, and I admit you wrote a rather persuasive letter. Trouble is you've got to make it stick in front of the city council. And the civil service board."

"And?"

"I might help."

"In exchange for a gallon of blood from my veins?"

"You know I've been trying to get this town on the map. It just happens that I have a couple of men with me tonight who might help us. They have a solid track record, and they want to do something for Staircase. The town hasn't had any significant growth in ten years."

"That's why I moved here, Mo, darlin'. I figured Staircase was last in line for that little old hobo with the body odor you call progress. When he arrives, I'll pick up my marbles and leave."

"You don't want this town on the map?"

"Nope."

"Nobody's against progress, Mac. Nobody."

He smiled and slowly swallowed the rest of his beer. "I am."

"Staircase is going to expand whether you want it to or not. Why not have some say in the nature of the growth?"

"Just had my say."

"Damn you. You're just not thinking clearly."

"Go to the East Coast sometime if you want to see progress. Maybe we should all subdivide our lots and put condominiums in our backyards. I could get three in mine. We can end up looking like New Jersey. We don't need franchised greasy spoons and slipshod mall jobs. This town has businesses that've been in the same families for fifty years. The Bedouin here. You're going to knock that all to hell. You might as well take half a mile of strip malls in Federal Way or Lynnwood and dump it in our laps.

"Drive into Seattle during the commute you'll know what I'm talking about. The streets are full of madmen. You're afraid you're getting left behind, but it's the best thing that ever happened. We've got something once destroyed, never comes back. Like killing a baby."

"Mac, that's just absolutely about the sickest analogy I've ever heard."

He laughed, a booming, raucous bellow. When he saw how much it nettled Mo, he laughed until tears tracked his cheeks.

"That's really how you feel? You're not just putting on an act to annoy me?"

"It's really how I feel."

"I feel sorry for you. I wanted to cut a deal. You come over to meet Lars and his friends and I'd get behind you on this Bobby Joe Allan termination. You know I could make all this brouhaha into something easy or I could stay on the other side of the fence and make your life rather unpleasant."

"For some reason, that doesn't worry me."

"Listen. You endorse the development out by the highway, and I endorse you on Allan. It's called politics. Don't you understand how things are run?"

"Here's how things run. Someday your house will be on fire and the first to show will be Bobby Joe and you'll be trapped on the second floor and Bobby Joe will look at you and you will look at Bobby Joe and then he'll pretend he never saw you. You get out alive, he'll deny it. When that happens, you'll know what I'm talking about."

"It couldn't be that bad, Mac."

"It is."

"Well, whatever. But the perception is that your suspension of Bobby Joe has something to do with Pete's death. Also, we don't get that many fires around here. So what real difference does it make? This is going to be a real political hot potato. Can't you leave him on?"

"You don't understand, Mo. Maybe we get a lot of fires; maybe we don't. Firefighters fight fires. That's what we do. We're not going to sit around and hope we don't get one."

"You like trouble, don't you?"

"Yeah, I think I do." Fontana stood. People were shuffling around the dance floor now, between tunes. Grabbing tables and manhandling extra chairs. Swigging drinks. Switching partners. Gossiping.

"Don't turn your back on me when I'm talking business!"

"Watch close, darlin'. You see me getting smaller, that means I'm leaving."

Elvis Presley came on the jukebox as Fontana crossed the busy floor. He passed Gil Cutty and his partner, a mannish little woman he'd been dating for years. Waved to Pettigrew at the bar. Then nodded at Jim Caitlin and Rainy, who had just finished the last part of the last dance and were standing among the couples as if trying to make a decision. "Fontana," said Caitlin, a half smirk on his face, "Rainy here needs a partner. We got some people meeting us here, and I'm afraid they got lost or something. You mind dancing with the little woman till I get back?"

Stepping away from her husband, Rainy gave Jim a distressed look. "Of course," said Fontana. "Would you care to dance?"

Stunned, she looked away from her husband, who had already started to wander off. "Me?"

Fontana smiled. So did Rainy, tentative, timid. She presented her plastic and steel hand and slipped into his arms.

26

VENUS IN BLUE JEANS

Elvis belted out "Can't Help Falling in Love," and Rainy squeezed Mac's hand, a mechanical squeeze administered through wires and steel and plastic. With expectation, he thought. Or was all the expectation on his part? He had some peculiar feelings about the Caitlins these days. It wasn't until Rainy had visited him in the middle of the night that he recalled something Jim had said long ago. "I ever caught my woman cheating on me, I'd gut-shoot her." It had been an offhand remark, hyperbole perhaps. As if it were one of those ignoble feelings most people were afraid to allude to but he could because they were all men and they all knew he didn't exactly mean it.

"I wish he hadn't set this up," she said.

"Thank you."

"I didn't mean it like that. You know I didn't. It's just that . . . with Jim you never know what his ulterior motives are."

"So what do you think they are?"

"I love Jim, Mac."

"You didn't answer my question."

"It's just that he gets these ideas."

They had moved into the mob and wended their slow way out of sight of her table. Fontana glanced back once, but when he did, Jim Caitlin was with a staid middle-aged pair, he in a suit, she in a dinner dress.

It surprised him that she didn't dance as well as Mo. A better match physically than the short, chesty Mo, but she didn't flow the way Mo did. Still, it did something to his insides. In her heels she was half an inch taller than his five-ten. It was stifling in the pack, body heat intermingling with the hot outside summer air from the constantly opening and closing main doors. Her real hand felt warm on his shoulder; the prosthesis alighted like dust in his palm.

"You dance quite well," Rainy said, her cheek nudging his.

"It's hereditary. My father danced with nuns."

"I guess you come here a lot? I'd like to, but Jim's not keen on it."

"What makes tonight special?"

"The Muhlhausers. She gets a little boring with all that talk about their new Mercedes and her dynamite aerobics instructor. He's into triathlons, the bond market, and signed prints. Jim wants to show them some of the local sights. They'd heard about this place. Jim's mixed up in some humongous investment he's trying to egg Muhlhauser into."

"I didn't know Jim invested."

"Mostly he dabbles."

"You know where he was Tuesday night?"

"This past Tuesday? At work in Seattle. Twenty-four-hour shift. He leaves at maybe six-thirty in the morning and doesn't get home until nine the next morning." Her words were clipped.

"You sound upset."

"I'm not angry. Not at you. I just can't figure out why Jim did this. And you didn't have to come over here. You didn't have to walk past us like that. You know I want you to stay away."

"I was just walking across the room, minding my own business."

"Were you?"

"You didn't have to say yes."

"That was my mistake."

"I hope not."

"I didn't know what else to do."

"Things must be bad between you two."

"Look, Mac. I know lives are at stake. I know everybody in town is spooked that this is going to happen again. Business in all the restaurants is negligible. Everybody's double-checking the produce at the markets before they take it home. I'll tell you anything if you think it'll help. Just don't ask about us. Me and Jim."

"Just tell me how he's been lately?"

"Edgy. Isn't everyone?"

"He say anything about the poisoning?"

"Jim and I don't talk much."

"About the Staircase Fire Department?"

She shook her head.

As they danced, their movements became an eloquent statement of what their relationship was and was not. It was not platonic. No, it was certainly not that. On both sides there was an undercurrent. As he danced with Rainy Caitlin, he strained to think of the proper word for what he felt.

"Rainy. Is there some way for me to smooth this over for you?"

"What? Dancing?"

"Yeah."

She tipped her head back and stared at him in the darkness. "You might hold me a little looser. Jim sees this, he'll go over the bend."

"From your table Jim can't see." Fontana pulled her closer. It was ruder and bolder than anything in their previous dealings, and he fully expected her to twist away from him. He could feel her smiling against his cheek, melting against him. Then she laughed, airy and so close to his ear it pained him. They didn't speak again. Just danced.

27

WAR STORIES
NOT FOR THE SQUEAMISH

"Sheriff of Staircase," said Mo. "And former sheriff of Staircase."

Lars Ereckson stood uneasily over the table where Fontana and Bounty had blatantly refused to make room for him, stolid looks on their faces. Neither bothered to stand, Fontana slouching, legs spraddled under the table. Mo Costigan had towed the developer across the room, straining to smooth over what she perceived as Fontana's misconception about the beneficence that would shortly bless the upper valley if Lars had his way. Fontana sensed she was so smitten with Ereckson's regal bearing, money, and unctuous highborn manner that she artlessly assumed Mac would be, too.

Lars was the kind of natural man who had his teeth capped again and again. His hair was brushed straight back, silver and unusually thick for a man his age—late fifties—as precise as polyester. Sunlight hadn't graced him in years. He had a sunken look. A turkey gobble under his chin added to the impression. He moved the way a man in pajamas walked a hospital corridor.

"Splendid to meet you both," said Lars. His voice was the best thing about him, deep, resonant.

Fontana nodded but did not speak.

"I've heard many good things about the job you're doing here in Staircase, Chief Fontana. There's wonderful potential in this town. This whole area. You've got what? Three people working for you now? The way I envision it, in ten years' time you'll have many more." His smile was bright and glacial.

"That'd be a shame," said Fontana, staring hard. Mo stood beside Ereckson and gazed up at him.

"I take it then you belong to the faction opposing the Green Valley Mall project south of town?"

"Don't belong to any faction."

"But you oppose the development?"

"Hell, yes."

"On what grounds?"

"All grounds."

"Mo here tells me your opinion sways a lot of people. I'd very much like a chance to change your mind. If you could see things from my perspective, you might think differently."

"I doubt it."

Lars Ereckson's face stiffened. Some pundits speculated Mafia affiliations. Dated news photographs of Lars arm in arm with Frank Sinatra didn't help. It was common knowledge there had been questionable circumstances and unexplained events during the construction of his apartment complexes in Issaquah. One of Ereckson's principal detractors had suffered a nasty car accident. Charges were hurled back and forth. Nothing was proved.

Mayor Costigan led Lars Ereckson away and returned a few minutes later alone.

"Go on, Mo," said Warren Bounty. He was acting drunk,

beaming at one and all, slurring his words, yet he'd been on the wagon a year. Sober, he played a better sot than he had with half a case of beer polluting his bloodstream. "Vamoose, Mo. We're swapping war stories, me and Mac. You can't handle this."

"Lars thought you were a bit presumptuous, Mr. Fontana," Mo said sternly.

"Hell, I was downright contemptible."

"Vamoose, Mo," said Bounty. "We're talking shop here. You're liable to toss your cookies, you hear some of this stuff."

"Gimme a break." Mo Costigan hitched her green dress up beyond her knees and dragged over a chair from another table. Spinning it on one leg until it was backward, she straddled it, stacked her fists on the back, her chin on her fists. "Fire away, you bastards. Can't gross me out." She had had a few drinks. "I'm going to be a volunteer. I've always wanted to volunteer. Mac says I can't do it because I'm squeamish. So here's my chance to prove you can't gross me out."

Bounty looked at Fontana and winked. "I was just telling Mac about Elaine Spitzer over at the grade school. Sneezed in front of her class of third graders and blew her eyeball clean out of its socket. There's nothing but a couple of strings holding the little bugger in, you know that? Blew it out like a potato out an exhaust pipe. When we arrived, it was kind of dangling there on her cheek. Sent the class into hysterics."

Mo had already heard the story. "That's not so awful. To scare us, my grandfather used to pop his false teeth out."

"For months we had these plastic eyeballs laying around the station. People used to drop them in your coffee," said Bounty.

Mo Costigan sipped from the drink she'd brought with her, kept her eyes on the glass.

Fontana said, "I remember this guy got caught between two cars. They were playing bumper tag with him and smashed his legs. It was raining when we got there and started doing CPR. No pulse. No breathing. His brother was there. His wife. It was

---

ugly. My second year in. We're in this rain gutter pumping on this guy's chest and bag masking him. Worked like sons of bitches. About five minutes into it my partner says, 'Wait a minute,' and he pulls up this tarp the cops had draped across the guy's lower legs. Legs are gone. The arteries are open. We've been pumping all the blood out of his body into the ditch. Pumped the Dugan dry. So we look up and here's his wife and brother, waiting for us to save him. They're still hoping. They don't realize what we've done. So we throw the tarp back and keep working."

"He die?" Mo asked.

"Of course. It seemed like every time we went out in uniform we ran into somebody from his family, and they always made a big deal about how great we were and how hard we'd worked to save this guy."

"I'm not squeamish," said Mo, without removing her chin from her stacked fists. As she spoke, her jaw pushed her head up and down. She swung her saloon-direct eyes from Bounty to Fontana. "I'm not."

"First one I ever had that was really bad was a guy put his head in this little window to see if an elevator was coming. The glass was broken out, and he thought it'd be cute to put his head in and look for the elevator," said Bounty, absently tracing an index finger around the rim of his stein. Nobody said anything for ten beats.

"Was it?" Mo asked.

"What?"

"The elevator. Was it coming?"

"Well, no. Not at first. His problem was he got his head stuck in this window. Couldn't yank it out. When he heard the elevator machinery click on, he panicked. We got there he was just laying in the hallway. This big smear of red on the little window."

"You get sick?" Mo asked, wincing.

"No reason to. I didn't have to touch him."

"Last time I remember getting nauseated on an alarm," said

Fontana, "was Christmas Eve. We had this idiot kid about eighteen showing one of his friends this sawed-off shotgun he'd rigged up. I mean, we've got Uncle Phil and Grandma and the twins and everybody crammed into this tiny apartment and he pulls this shotgun out to show it off and blows most of his own hand off.

"We found two of his fingers and then somebody spotted the third one stuck to the wall and then one of my guys peers under the bed and there's this Christmas puppy with a little red ribbon around its neck. Tail wagging. A bloody thumb hanging out his mouth. So we're chasing him under the furniture in this bedroom, trying to get this guy's thumb, and somebody opens the door and the pup scats out between their legs and he's running around the apartment, tail wagging, red ribbon flapping in the breeze, carrying this guy's thumb like it's a rubber bone.

"The family didn't figure it out at first. All these firemen chasing their Christmas puppy. When they realized what we were doing, everybody pulled their feet up from the floor so the dog wouldn't spit the thumb down their socks."

"That's awful," said Mo. "But it's not gross." Fontana thought she was turning pale, but it was hard to tell in the semidark.

Warren Bounty said, "I saw a lady in Hong Kong with three thumbs. Used to keep a pen between two of them."

"Yeah? Knew a guy back East had three testicles."

"Dogs'll do the dangdest things," said Warren, sipping from his beer stein. "Guy had a heart attack. His Rottweiler wouldn't let us in the house. We're standing on the porch watching this guy turn blue. By the time the animal people got there he was long gone."

"We had a man in a pickup truck once," said Fontana, "went up an embankment at about sixty, rolled it over, and slid it down the street on its side. You know how on the old ones the gas tank is behind the seat, and the spout's right next to the driver's window? Gas went everywhere, and then sparks from the sliding metal set it off. Big fire. This fella had a Doberman pinscher inside with him. In the flames it panicked and grabbed this guy's leg and wouldn't let him out. That's how we found them after we tapped the fire. He's reaching for the window, frozen, and the dog is fastened on his leg. Burnt to a crisp, both of them." Fontana made himself into a reaching statue.

"People do funny things when they fall," said Bounty.

Mac swigged down some beer. "Worst I ever worked on was a suicide. An elderly lady jumped off a building. Maybe seventy stories. Landed on her back in a rose garden. Buried three feet in the soft soil. Just this cookie cutter hole with her at the bottom staring up at us. Like a sack of Jell-O when we took her out."

"Gawd," said Mo Costigan, draining the remainder of her drink. "Was she dead?"

"They buried her. I guess she was."

"My worst was a painter fell about a hundred and fifty feet off some scaffolding on the underside of a bridge in California," said Bounty.

"I don't think I want to hear this," said Mo.

"Landed in some woods. Must have been loam down there or maybe it had rained recently. Landed feetfirst, and the impact drove him into the ground like a nail in a board. There he was talking to us. Still alive. This head sitting there on the ground saying"—Bounty went into a falsetto— " 'Help me. Help me.' "

Mo Costigan's head rolled off her hands and thunked onto the table. She was limp.

"She faint?" Bounty asked.

"Think it was the head in the woods."

"I bet it was your dog story."

"That one happened."

"You saying mine are made up?"

"*The talking head on the ground?*" Fontana raised his eyebrows, and they both started laughing.

Fontana picked up a strand of her dark brown hair and lifted it away from her nostrils. They were grinning like imbeciles when Lars Ereckson and party arrived. Ereckson's wife was twenty-five years his junior and looked like a little girl playing grown-up. Ereckson gave Mo Costigan's limp form a glance and said, "Excuse us. We've come to collect the mayor. We have another engagement."

"It's too warm for this much dancing," said Ereckson's wife, fanning herself with a cow plop contest flyer she'd found at her table. She didn't take her eyes off Mo's leaden form.

Bounty and Fontana glanced at each other.

The two couples stared. Nobody seemed to know the proper procedure for extricating himself from this social swamp. Bounty and Fontana concentrated on keeping straight faces, avoiding each other's eyes. "She'll sober up in a couple hours," Bounty advised. "She don't usually go out on us this early."

"Want us to carry her out to your car?" Fontana made a move. "What kind of upholstery you got?"

"Good Lord." Mrs. Ereckson pivoted and headed out of the room, followed by the second woman.

Ereckson said, "Maybe you could . . ."

"Take care of her?" Bounty asked. "Sure thing, pal."

It was their laughter, particularly Warren's booming guffaws, that brought her out of the stupor. Fontana thought Warren might have been the loudest laugher he'd ever known. He didn't know why, but he liked listening to it.

"Wha—what is it?" Mo asked, bringing her head up and loudly siphoning up some of the surplus saliva in her mouth. "I'm not grossed out." She sat up. "Did I hear Lars?"

"Mo, darlin'," said Mac, "Mr. Ereckson and his friends came over, but we told him you were ripped out of your skull."

"Come on, what happened?" Mo asked. "I fell asleep. You guys think you're pretty funny. I gotta go find Lars. Supposed to be showing him the sights."

"He's seen it all now," Warren said.

28

SLAM DANCING
IN THE ALLEY

Fontana was headed outside through the rear exit. In an effort to get Mo off his tail, he'd stopped in the dark in the back room, where Velma kept the paintings to be auctioned off Saturday mornings. It hadn't worked. She'd followed him into the shadows. Through another door Fontana watched the mingling couples in the main ballroom.

The rotating silver spheres on the ceiling lasered splinters of light through the doorway. Johnny Mathis warbled "Misty."

"Was a time Warren never left anywhere without being sloshed," said Mo. "He's gone a hundred and eighty degrees. Last year we all thought sure he'd die."

"Someday you'll do something about *your* drinking problem."

"What are you talking about?" Fontana opened the back door. "Mac, where are you going?"

"Warren went out this way. I think I hear him." The moon

cast an eerie, warm whitish glow on the four struggling figures, their shadows stark and intertwined. They seemed to be moving in slow motion. Three burly figures in ski masks, slacks, and dress shoes were wrestling with Bounty. Warren wore a childish, scrunched-up look on his face. Warren Bounty was a large man, beefy, packing a gut. During his stint in the Army, he'd lifted weights, had continued for years. Ten years ago he would have been able to toss these guys around. Mo crowded behind Mac in the doorway, trying to hip him out of the way.

"Call the cops," Fontana said.

A gray Chevy van sat in the alley, facing east. The side doors were open. Motor running. Somebody had spackled mud across the license plate and doused the courtesy light.

"Dammit, Mo. Call the cops."

Bounty was putting up a feeble fight. The three had him immobilized. Almost in the van. One on each arm, the last gripping him in a headlock from behind so that he could have broken Warren's neck with an easy corkscrewing motion.

As he ran for the scuffle, Fontana ripped the lid off a garbage can. They were too intent on their struggle to notice him. Fontana slashed the lid sideways like a machete, clipping the headlock man across the side of the skull. It made a loud thwack. The man's knees buckled, and he slipped backward. Fontana whacked him two more times before one of the others swerved to square off.

Mac waved the lid to distract the second man and tried to kick him in the groin. An experienced street fighter, he blocked Mac's foot with crossed forearms. The move lowered his face toward Fontana. Cutting sideways, Fontana creased his head with the lid. The second man's body rolled to the side, and his legs buckled. Fontana punched him twice in the face.

The last man was still wrestling Warren. Fontana grabbed him by the back of his wool ski mask, bunching it up in his fist so the eye holes became misaligned. Blindfolded by his own costume, the third assailant grabbed the hood with both hands. He kicked out with his foot. Mac slashed the lid directly across his face where he judged the man's nose to be. Then across the throat.

Out the corner of his eye Fontana spotted the second man reaching under his shirt. He whipped the edge of the lid across the man's forearm, pinned him against the trunk of a Dodge, slicing, slashing, battering. A gun fell out of the man's waistband. When he saw it, Mac lost control. He struck the hooded figure repeatedly. Each blow snapped the man's head back and made it drum the car dully.

The bloodied man raised his arms only to have them struck with the twanging lid. Inside the mask he spit and coughed. Crimson splashed across Fontana's bare fists, speckled the rear deck of the Dodge.

Fontana didn't see it coming.

Just felt the horrible crushing pain in the side of his rib cage. Sensed himself tumbling.

Somebody had executed a flying kick into his side. He was on the ground, between cars. When he tried to move, he realized his knees were badly skinned. One knuckle raw. There were three assailants. And perhaps a driver he hadn't seen. One of them had recovered and kicked him.

Standing shakily, Fontana couldn't believe how much his ribs hurt.

One attacker was climbing into the driver's seat of the van. Another was running helter-skelter west down the alley. With incredible audacity, considering how large everyone in the scuffle was, Mo was trying to help. She had grabbed one of the assailants by the arm, trying to tug him away. He backhanded Mo across the face and looped Warren's left arm behind his back. Bounty was breathing like a racehorse. Mo dropped to one knee, touching her face in an attitude of prayer as if she couldn't believe what had happened.

When Fontana stepped forward, the last attacker bulled Bounty around so the ex-sherrif was between them. Bounty's eyes bulged from the pain. He was too old and too worn-out to put up a fight, and the knowledge of this showed on his face.

Pulling both men forward, Fontana pushed Bounty up against the van and jerked the other man around by the sleeve. The man took a backhanded swipe at Fontana. Fontana fed him two quick left jabs to the chin, buried a hard right in the man's sternum.

The man collapsed and backed away, brushing his buttocks up against the Chevy. Coughing. The driver gunned the engine. The van rocked but didn't take off.

The man backed up against the side of the Chevy said, "Not yet." Fontana could see the driver behind the wheel. Mask in place. The third man had faded around the corner at the end of the alley.

The assailant brought a hand up.

He pointed a .38 revolver, snub nose, at Fontana, and Fontana suddenly felt his guts churn. He was a tenth of a second from his last pulsebeat, and it made him angrier than hell. God help him if he turned the muzzle away for an instant. Without taking his eyes off Fontana, the man with the gun reached down and picked up his friend's fallen weapon. When Mo made a chirping sound and tried to rise, the gunman didn't move the muzzle from Fontana's midsection. Fontana debated whether to tackle the bastard, gun and all.

The gunman whispered, "Ain't so tough now, are we?"

Mo Costigan said, "Kill him, Mac. Kick the gun out of his hand and kill him. Dirty asshole." Her words left a dead space in the air. The wind ceased. The gunman looked at Mo. She didn't flinch.

After what seemed an eternity, he sat inside the door of the gray van, pulled his feet up, and said, "Now!" The Chevy burned rubber.

Mo reached Warren Bounty first. "You all right, pumpkin?"

She cradled his face between her hands. Though her own lower lip was bloody, her first thought was for Bounty.

———

"Okay, Warren?" Mac asked. Bounty was sitting on the ground wheezing.

"They didn't really do anything to me. You got here too fast."

"Get him inside," said Mac. "And call the cops. I'm going for Satan."

Station One was a block north and a block east. He sprinted, keeping alert. The town was quiet except for the muted music from the dance hall and the chatter from two squabbling couples coming out of the tavern attached to the Bedouin.

Satan was in the run behind the station, pacing.

"Come on, boy," said Fontana. "Bad guys. Come on. Bad guys." The dog leaped up against the cyclone fencing, whined, and curled in circles. Fontana stopped in the parking area behind the station and popped the driver's door of the GMC. Leaning inside, he removed the sheriff's badge from the ashtray, pinned it to his chest—his white shirt was dappled with blood—then unlocked the Remington. He pulled a handful of ammunition out of the glove box and jammed the cartridges into his pockets.

He jogged back to the Bedouin and, rather than mess up the track, went through the building via a narrow hallway. Mo Costigan and Warren Bounty were still in the alley. Fontana said, "I thought I told you—"

"Somebody came out," said Mo. "They're calling for us. Warren's got chest pain. And a broken finger."

"Just where the guy thumped me," said Bounty. "I know what a heart attack feels like. This ain't it."

"You sure?" Fontana asked.

"Swear on my mammy's grave."

"Mo, darlin'," said Fontana, "you were wonderful. Don't ever do anything like that again."

"What did you say?"

"I said, 'Don't ever do anything like that again.' "

"No, before that. The other thing."

"You were wonderful."

"Hey, what was that crack supposed to mean? About my drinking problem?"

Fontana picked up a shoe from the darkness. "Must have come off the guy ran this way." He held the brown tasseled loafer out toward the dog and said, "Satan. *Suche! Suche!*" Tail up, good ear pointed, Satan got a snootful and began tracking along the ground at their feet. It didn't take him long to head west up the alley.

Without hesitation the dog trotted around the corner and toward the main doors of the Bedouin. Inside, nobody paid them much attention. Except Velma, the owner.

"We got trouble, Mac?" Velma asked, taking in the gun and dog. She was a heavy woman with a pocked face and a passion for makeup and jangling jewelry.

"See anybody? He was wearing a ski mask outside. Would've been a little beat up."

"Your shirt's a mess. There was a man in here. Looked like a tomato hit by a truck. I'd never even recognize him if he washed his face." She glanced at the shotgun. "He was in and out. Made a call and disappeared out onto Main. Thought he'd been in a car wreck."

Satan was nosing around the base of the pay phone. Fontana spotted red stars on the floor. A galaxy of blood. The dog headed back to the main doors.

Muzzle to the blacktop, the dog headed across Main and east along the dark shopfronts. The track went north past the side of city hall, detoured through an alley, zigzagged through a backyard, and up Peach Street. They were moving quickly now, Fontana and the dog. Satan knew he was on to something. Knew it was important. When Fontana and the German shepherd came out on Staircase Way, the van was three blocks north.

He caught sight of a man climbing into the Chevy, which was pointed south, Fontana's direction. He ducked into Lyle Wentworth's front yard, knelt behind the bole of a weeping willow.

"Satan," he hissed. *"Bleib!"*

Tail lowered, the dog obediently came and sat beside him.

The van puttered up Staircase Way, then sped up and hooked a quick right at the intersection. They'd been alerted somehow. Fontana leaped the three-foot picket fence in the front yard, thumbed off the safety, and let a load fly at the van. It blew out most of the rear window.

29

THE SECOND GATE OF HELL

Mo's lower lip had swollen into an ugly slug, and her green dress was split down the length of one shoulder, exposing meaty arms. One of her high heels was broken, so she walked like a pendulum hitting a wall. The three of them were positioned behind the aid car in front of the Bedouin. Working the aid car were MacKelroy and a new guy named Smitts, who was employed in the service bay in Truck Town. He had been a volunteer in Pacific County before relocating in Staircase. MacKelroy was a male nurse at St. Joseph's in Tacoma.

"Who would want to kidnap you, Warren?" Mo asked.

"All I can think is somebody who had stock in a beer company. Now that I'm off the suds, profits have to be down." He smiled. Nobody joined him.

Bounty sat heavily on the rear deck of the aid car. His shirt was shredded down the front; his shock of hair, mussed. Perspiration beaded up on his face. Smitts was splinting the middle finger on Warren's left hand. Warren stared at the ground in front of Fontana's feet.

"They were trying to kidnap you," said Mo Costigan. "Your daughter got money?"

"Don't get ahead of ourselves here," said Fontana, trying to breathe deeply against the ache in his side. "Warren?"

"I stepped outside for some air. This van pulled up in the alley. Two guys come around the back of the vehicle and head towards me. At first I think it's a joke. You know? A couple of volunteers trying to give me a hard time. But they looked dead serious. I scoot for the Bedouin. I figured I could take 'em in a fair fight, but I didn't see how it's gonna be fair. You know the rest."

Two county patrol cars had responded from the substation below the mayor's chambers. Fontana gave a description of the van and related the evening's events. Before they screeched off into the night, they radioed for reinforcements. This would be a carnival night. County cops beating the backwoods for a van chockfull of kidnappers. It wouldn't be difficult to spot a late-model gray van with no rear window and double-aught holes in the sheet metal. On the other hand, it was a big county with thousands of dirt roads crisscrossing the moonlit hills.

Mo said, "But, Mac, you were going to decapitate that guy with the garbage can lid. You went Looney Tunes."

"Not really."

"You did, too."

"It wasn't that bad, Mo." He didn't like the way these people were looking at him. Mo. A battered and respectful Warren. Smitts and MacKelroy getting an earful of fresh gossip about their commander in chief.

"I only pray you never get mad at me."

"Darlin', don't be silly. I get mad at you every day."

"No. I mean, really mad."

"That's what I get, Mo. Really mad."

The fifth county car Fontana had seen since the incident came in off the old highway, tires whooshing. He spoke to the uniformed cop and watched him peel out. After the volunteers had buttoned up the aid kit, Fontana pulled Bounty aside. "Warren, you gotta have a hint."

The older man hung his head and examined the tops of his shoes. "Don't have the vaguest, Mac."

"What did they tell you they were doing?"

"Nobody let out a peep. 'Cept me. I hollered a couple of times." He'd sounded like a stuck pig.

"Anything like this ever happen to you before?"

Warren shook his head.

Pete Daugherty poisoned. Shots fired at Kingsley Pierpont. The ex-fire chief nearly kidnapped. Somebody was weaving a tapestry, but the design was beyond Fontana's comprehension.

At a few minutes past midnight Fontana and the dog were combing the parking lot. How had they known Bounty was coming out the back? It made Fontana wonder if the kidnapping had been random. And if so, why? Terrorists? A group of mad interns after organ donations? He had already taken Satan to Bounty's rented house on American Avenue under the maples. The dog worked but found no track.

As he scoured the lot behind the Bedouin, Fontana ruminated on the fracas, replaying it frame by frame. Even Mo had remarked on his ferocity. If Mo was noticing, things were bad. Mo had her own agenda and wouldn't notice a python in her purse.

Squatting between two automobiles, Mac swept his flashlight back and forth, searching for cigarette butts, pennies, hairpins, matchbooks, anything the three might have discarded. As he conducted the probe, Caitlin and company emerged from the back of the Bedouin into the hot wind, into the moonlight. The dance hall's music boomed momentarily and then phased out as the doors closed.

Without knowing why, Mac flicked the flashlight off and stayed low. He watched them stroll to a pair of cars forty feet away.

"*Platz!*" he whispered to Satan. Flicking one ear, the dog lay down beside him and gave him a curious look.

The visitors got directions from Jim Caitlin and drove off, and then Rainy and Jim were alone. Caitlin fired up the Jaguar and idled it in place. "Sure," Fontana whispered to the dog. "Pollute the state. Shut off your damn motor if you're not going anywhere." Without moving his head, the dog rolled his eyes up. The Jaguar slowly reversed out and began creeping away. Fontana rose in time to see the Jag screech to a sudden halt.

Inside the car Jim spoke animatedly. Rainy answered from time to time, her blunt-cut hair flopping around her face as she moved. He could tell from the manner in which their heads chirped back and forth that they were feuding.

The Jag pulled forward and stopped again.

This time the door on the passenger side opened three inches, but before anything else could happen, the Jag ripped out of the alley. As the car slid through the corner on Peach, the door clicked shut. Caitlin was angry and drunk. The Jag's tires squealed. With half a dozen sudden angulations, three right angles, no streetlights, and a history of fatal accidents, the Moon Valley Road was nowhere to screw around. Last autumn a car and driver had gone off into the woods and hadn't been discovered for two days.

"Come on, Satan, old boy," said Fontana. "Let's make sure the lady gets home."

By the time he fetched the GMC, locked the shotgun in the rack, emptied his trousers of shot shells, and cranked the engine over, he figured they'd be well on their way home. They weren't. On the North Fork Road he spotted a pair of taillights, the Jaguar's. He pulled over and pushed the knob to kill his headlamps. Two minutes later the Jag pulled away, spewing gravel, fishtailing across the double yellow lines.

30

CONFESSIONS OF A PEEPING TOM

The road wormed east directly toward the face of the mountain along a flat valley floor, drew close to the dark monolith, then jogged north, tracing the swell at the base of the mountain. The Mamas and the Papas were singing "California Dreamin'" on the truck radio. Caitlin's Jag was long gone. A small hunched animal darted out in the road and got vacuumed into the headlights. Fontana swung wide to avoid it.

He made one slow pass, spotted the Jag cooling in the driveway, turned around a quarter mile later at the dead end. The only light in the house shone from a side window, their bedroom. He motored slowly, glanced at the house, and saw a brilliant flash of light. Heard glass breaking. Caught a glimpse of a thrown lamp demolishing the bedroom window.

Somebody'd bulldozed a road through the lot next to the Caitlins'. Fontana turned and drove until he was parallel with Caitlin's house. When he switched off the ignition, Shelley Fabares was softly singing "Johnny Angel."

He was eighty yards from the Caitlins' bedroom window, now shattered. He could hear shouting but couldn't distinguish the words. He picked up his field glasses as an electric current stropped up and down his spine. He planted his elbows on the hood of the truck and peered through the glasses through a smattering of underbrush. More yelling.

Naked, Jim stood with his broad, fleshy back to the window. Rainy faced him across the bed. She wore a white terry-cloth robe, clamped high at the neck with her good hand. They had changed in a hurry. Fontana could see one of her shoulders and half her face, Jim's buttocks shadowy in the window. Somebody slammed a door somewhere. Possibly in another house.

Now they were moving. The whole thing took only seconds. Jim leaped onto the bed, cornering her against the closet door. She dodged left, right, not sure how to play this mad game. He hurled himself off the bed and pressed her up against the closet door, bodies close, Rainy's obscured. Fontana's fingers were slick with sweat. A pulse drummed in his throat.

They wrestled. She squirmed out of his grasp and got a length away before he reached out, grabbed her by the arm, and whirled her hard against the closet door. The door slid askew.

Jim Caitlin pushed her onto the bed, peeling the robe off in mid-flight. Fontana saw a flash of tanned woman freewheeling through the air. She was out of sight below the level of the window. Neither of them moving.

A calm Caitlin turned to the closet and took out something, not visible from Fontana's angle, adjusting with his hands in front of his chest, working it. It was hard to see. Backside toward the river, Caitlin moved to the window.

Suddenly his right hand went up like an orchestra conductor's and came down swiftly. A door-slamming sound. A woman's shriek. The arm went up and came down again. Five or six times.

Yet Caitlin stood perfectly straight. Damn! He was flogging her! With a straightened coat hanger? Fontana dropped the field glasses onto the hood of the truck, dashed around the open driver's door, grabbed the shotgun, and flopped across the hood with it. He put the bead front sight square on Caitlin's torso.

"Raise your arm one more time, bastard," he whispered. But Caitlin didn't raise his arm. He heeled around, stared at his reflection in the broken window the way some people stared into the mirror after they'd done something of import, just to see what they looked like doing it. He strode around the bed past the sprung closet door. Fontana followed him with the shotgun, finger tight on the trigger. The first round was a rifled slug which would rip a hole in a buffalo. Caitlin manhandled the door back onto its running tracks. Even from a distance, Fontana observed a look of smug satisfaction on Caitlin's handsome face. He left the room, shutting the light off on his way out.

The Alsatian, who seemed to have an instinct for when Fontana's life was going awry, hunkered beside him and let out a soft, high-pitched whinnying. In this hollow tucked under the mountain the wind was only an occasional hot puff. Sometime later a deer tripped through the woods and drank from a pool in the river.

He started the truck and drove home in a daze. It was too bizarre. Lord, he had to get her out of there. When he parked the Destroyer, a bat flitted through his yard. With Brendan gone for the night, the house seemed like the loneliest place on earth.

31

NORTHWEST SOUP COMPANY BLUES

"You put Wanda in your will?"

"Sure, I put her in. What? Ya think I'm stupid? I don't want my brothers gettin' everything, do I?"

They were in the beanery. Lieutenant Allan, grousing that Pettigrew weakened and eventually collapsed all the chairs in the station, had decreed his own pet chair off limits to Pettigrew. Taking advantage of Allan's suspension, Claude overwhelmed it this morning. On his lap lay a section of newspaper peppered with sunflower seed hulls. Periodically he spit out another mouthful of mouse-colored splinters, making tiny "stub, stub" noises with his tongue. Watched too closely, Claude could make a person ill.

"But Wanda?" Bounty waved his good arm in Pettigrew's face. "You put her in your will?"

"Whatsa matter with you, Warren? I thought you liked Wanda."

"I like her. But I wouldn't trust her with the change from a pack of cigarettes. How much you giving her, for christsakes?"

Fontana was at the sink, enjoying the patter. Brendan was home with Mary. He'd skinned an elbow at his friend's house. That morning Fontana had slept late before checking on the phone with a Seattle fireman he knew. Caitlin was at work today, Saturday. He'd been at work in Seattle on Tuesday night, too, the night somebody'd fired at Kingsley. But he'd gotten the evening off on merits, reported back to duty around midnight. He could easily have made the ten-thirty shooting. Fontana called Rainy, too, but no one answered.

"I ain't givin' her all of it, if that's what yer askin'," said Claude. "Just my savings and all my clothes and such. I bought her this here ring, too." He held up a diamond and cracked his mouth into a smirk.

"Your savings? You might as well put a bounty out on your head. When did you do this?"

"Yesterday."

"Not two or three days ago before the poisoning?" Fontana asked.

"No way, José."

"I hate to ruin your stomach when I know you just ate breakfast and you're sitting here waiting for lunch, Claude," said Bounty, "but Wanda's taking you for a ride, Clyde." Bounty's left hand was in a partial cast, the middle finger plastered so that it stuck out in an obscene gesture. "Take her to bed, for godsakes. Take her to the movies. Take her for a walk in the rain. But don't take her to the bank."

Claude Pettigrew gave Warren a hard look. The ex-chief let some air escape out his nostrils and shook his head. He tolerated Pettigrew, as did everyone around the station—there was no choice—but he didn't have to coddle him.

"What's Wanda going to do with your clothes and such?" Fontana asked. "I mean, she could take that shirt you're wearing, but she doesn't own a sailboat and she never goes camping, so what's she going to do with it?"

Warren Bounty's laughter erupted like an avalanche. "Yeah. What . . . she going to use your shoes for crossing quicksand? Your Jockey shorts for a parachute? You don't have any clothes worth leaving, Claude."

"I got a black suit," Claude said seriously. "You ain't seen it. I'm gonna be buried in it."

"I doubt she's going to want it after you get yourself buried in it," said Bounty.

Claude hadn't let up on the hard look he'd been giving Bounty. "I know what your trouble is. Your goddamned trouble is you're jealous. Both of you."

"Jealous?" said Warren. "I wanted Wanda I could have her. Right back there in that bunk in the cell just like I used to do with all my gals."

Claude Pettigrew launched out of his chair, kicking it over backward with the force of his rising. He went nose to nose with Bounty. Underneath his bland disposition, Pettigrew had a temper that got away from him every once in a while.

"Battle of the Titans," said Fontana, enunciating through a makeshift megaphone he'd formed with his hands. "Come one. Come all. Watch the stomachs bounce."

"Ah, crap," said Pettigrew, turning around woodenly and righting the chair. His knees were so bad he couldn't stoop, had to lean over from the waist. The newspaper and sunflower seeds had spilled across the floor. "I got trouble and I need you guys' help."

"What sort of trouble?" Fontana asked.

"Wanda. I had her at the dance, but she just kinda drifted off on me. I called her place. I been all over looking. I ain't been to sleep."

"Well, the Navy's not in town, so I don't know where she'd be," said Bounty.

Claude didn't rise to the bait. "She ain't never done this. We was supposed to spend the night together. Today we were going outa town. She shoulda been here."

"What do you want?" Fontana asked.

"Find her, for christsakes. It's gotta be tied in. Think about all this stuff been happenin'. Pete. And last night Warren gettin' into that ruckus. Something mighty fishy's going on, and I'm afraid Wanda got caught up in it by mistake."

Warren said, "If she's caught up in it, it's no mistake."

"Bullshit."

"Who is Harold Glass?"

"I dunno."

"Maybe you better find out. He's sleeping in Wanda's bed. He uses the big H. You ever wonder where all that money you've been shelling out goes?"

"I know where it goes! The Northwest Soup Company!"

"Calm down, Claude," said Mac.

"We planned to be going to British Columbia this morning in Mom's Buick."

Fontana had never seen Pettigrew this agitated.

"I'll drive into Seattle right now."

"Would ya, Mac?"

"Yeah, sure."

"And Mac, Warren was lying about some guy sleeping in Wanda's bed, wasn't he?"

"You asking or telling?"

"Asking."

Bounty turned around and walked out of the room. Fontana inhaled deeply. "I haven't been there at night, Claude, but from what I could see of the setup, it's like Warren says." Pettigrew bowed his head and ran both huge mitts through his greasy, thinning hair. "Still want me to find her?" Without looking up, Pettigrew nodded.

Outside, Bounty chucked Satan under the chin. The dog leaned into it, eyes half closed in pleasure. "I'm coming."

"Why not?"

"Stop by my place to get some armaments?"

"We're not heading into a pitched battle, Warren."

"Easy for you to say. You didn't have three men trying to throw you into the back of a van last night. Now I got this finger all bunged up, I don't mind telling you I'm nervous as a cat in a house full of rocking chairs."

Fontana sighed. "You pull a gun without my say-so and it'll be you and me."

"Understood."

All night Fontana had tossed and turned, casting theories. Jim Caitlin harbored a great deal of resentment toward Kingsley Pierpont. In the beginning Fontana had mistakenly thought it had something to do with their personal histories. Jim had been raised in the South, as had Kingsley until he was five. There just might be some tenuous connection between Kingsley and Caitlin. Fontana had phoned Kingsley that morning, awakened him after a night out, and if there was a connection, Kingsley couldn't fathom what it was.

"Thing is," said Kingsley on the phone, "I been thinking about Lieutenant Allan."

"Yeah?"

"Bobby Joe got drunk one night during his divorce, bitching to me about some broad he thought his wife was sleeping with. You know, she left him for a woman. Know what he wanted me to do?"

"I won't even guess."

"Kill her."

"For real?"

"Well, he kept sayin', 'Supposin' some good friend of this gal's husband found out how bad the husband wanted this dyke out of the way. Supposin' he did the job. The husband'd probably give him five hundred bucks jus' outa sheer gratitude.' See. He didn't come right out and ask me to ice the bitch, but that's what he meant."

"Danced around with it."

"Exactly. Thought all us black dudes were killers. A lotta white folk think that. After I considered it, it made me mad. But he was drunk. He never said anything about it again."

"What are you getting at?"

"You suspended him. Maybe he knew it was coming? I'm not accusing him of anything, but if he did put that poison in the meat, maybe it was some sort of revenge. Or maybe he wanted to get rid of you. You was supposed to eat with us."

"What you're saying is," said Fontana, "under times of stress Allan's got a history of resorting to murder. At least in his head."

"Well, I s'pose that is what I'm saying."

"Kingsley. Watch yourself."

"You know I'm watching this old black ass every second." They both laughed.

Bounty hustled out to the GMC lugging a thin suitcase, stashed it on the floor at his feet, and climbed in. "Take the old highway up by the winery. There's an old logging road up there. I need to test this out before I go carrying it anywhere."

"What'd you bring, a bazooka?"

32

SERPENTINE

"I'd give up my front seat in hell to find out who those guys were and what they were after," said Bounty.

"You got close to who killed Pete. That's gotta be it."

"I ain't spoke to hardly anybody you ain't spoke to. Nobody knows zip squat." He gazed out the window for a few moments. His mind wandered. "You know, Mac, I didn't have a whole lot of luck when I was a kid. Once when we were walking across a golf course one hot summer afternoon, some big kids chased us. They made me eat horse biscuits. 'Eat 'em and smile,' they said. I didn't smile; they punched me. And then there was my little sister dying in that fire. Mom harping on it all the time. I guess she thought if she could punish me adequately, Elsa might come back. Even though I can't remember doing it, Mom never let me forget." Mac sensed Warren's memory of his mother was one of those things he ratholed for late at night when he was alone, along with the accidents he'd caused and the friends who'd gone wrong on him. "Right up until she died three years ago, Mom was squawking about me starting that fire and killing my baby sister. Don't s'pose if she was still kickin' around, I ever would have sobered up."

"You've been doing a lot of thinking."

"Right over there. Just pull in. I gotta test-fire a few rounds."

Fontana drove two hundred yards up a gravel road. To the south was a small foothill. To the north were the freeway and the chirring sounds of traffic. Five or six years earlier the area had been clear-cut, had only a stubble of scrub brush now.

After Fontana had turned the truck around and shut off the motor, Bounty climbed out, reached back in for his suitcase, and began walking. Mac followed him. Satan followed Mac. They gathered at a small clearing off the dirt road.

Resting the case on a stump, Warren flipped open the two chrome snaps. Inlaid with purple velvet, the case contained a Mac-10 machine pistol, a hefty cylindrical suppressor, and three extra clips. The case was custom-made, each piece with its own jigsaw cutout. Bounty, who wore a paternal glow on his face, removed the dark machine pistol, fitted the suppressor, then heeled a clip in and shoved a round into the chamber.

"I can't believe you own one of those," said Mac. "You need a license in this state for automatic weapons. They sell this crap for jungle warfare."

Using the forearm on his bad arm, Warren braced the weapon and fired three rounds single shot. The hot brass whirred up and back, pinging on the rocks at their feet. "Three-eighty," said Warren. "Sounds like a book being slammed shut, don't it? You get the nine-millimeter version and the bullets actually break the sound barrier so you have two noises to put the damper on: the blast from the barrel and the sonic boom of the speeding bullet."

Warren emptied the clip on full automatic, toppling a pair of saplings twenty feet away. Belly out, Warren strutted over to inspect the damage. The air reeked of gunpowder. Mac sat on a stump.

Three-eighty-caliber courage, thought Mac. Bad enough to be an ex-sheriff. Ex-fire chief. Ex-MP. Ex-drunk. Worst of all to be an ex-tough guy.

"Nobody's going to be standing around like a tree waiting for you to cut 'em in half," Mac said. "More than likely, you pull that cannon, they'll pull a bigger one."

"Yeah, and if I don't have mine, I'm gonna feel mighty lonesome. Ain't I?" Warren was walking back across the clearing, through the knee-high saplings. He began jogging right, left, dodging like a broken-field runner. He was clumsy and skidded in the rocks so that Fontana thought he was going to take a tumble.

"Serpentine," announced Warren, laughing loudly, perhaps at his own ingenuity. "Saw it in a Peter Falk movie. Never move in a straight line. Always serpentine. That's what separates the dead from the living."

"Serpentine?" said Mac, smiling.

"Always serpentine."

Warren stopped and let the swirling wind under the hillside lick him dry. The short jog from the bullet-splintered sapling had drenched him. Finally he looked west at a small lake to their left, only partially visible through the trees. Few people knew it existed.

"Funny about being a firefighter," said Warren, his voice rumbly with phlegm. "You learn all kinds of things about an area most people never discover. Lotta bad shit happens in these hills. Serial killers dump dead girls. Hunters disappear. Strange lights get spotted by campers. Hadda tow a Mazda RX-7 out of that lake once. Dead guy in it without a mark on him. Just went into the shallows. Medical examiner's office never did figure out what killed him. Wrote it up for natural causes. Strange."

Seattle was hot and overcast when they got there, the sort of weather that bamboozled people into wearing sunglasses even though the sun cast no shadows. They parked in front of the Ritz.

Upstairs Wanda's door was ajar. Mac waited for Warren to catch his breath from the two flights, then rapped, pushing the door farther open with each rap. He stepped inside. Harold Glass lay sprawled on a sofa on his back, shirtless, barefoot, an empty bottle of wine on the floor beside his dangling fingers. Something beige and spotty had dribbled down one leg of his jeans and dried.

Beyond him, in the half open bedroom door stood a man in maroon Jockey shorts, black socks and a turquoise sleeveless tee shirt. The man hopped on one foot tugging one of his socks up. He held a .44 Magnum.

33

ROGUE HAIRSTYLIST

"**H**owdy, Gil," said Warren.

Gil Cutty wriggled into his Levis. The .44 Magnum with the eight-inch barrel remained in his left hand. "I ain't got nothin' to do with any of the goings-on around here. This was my first visit and I ain't plannin' no more."

Warren headed directly for the room. The window was wide open, but the room smelled of booze, cigarettes, and hair spray. Wanda lay on her back in bed. A hypodermic syringe and spoon bent double and blackened on the underside lay on a table.

A longtime volunteer in Staircase, Gil Cutty was forty years old, small and wiry. Through a combination of too much sun, twenty-five years of tobacco addiction, and spray painting cars without a mask in his garage, he looked nearer sixty. Gil reckoned masks were for sissies. Even Survivairs. Frequently he neglected to open the garage door when warming up his Roadrunner. He owned a small ugly dog and drove everywhere with the mongrel in his lap.

Born and raised in Staircase, Gil Cutty addressed women in a slow drawl, "Hey, sweetlips. What's shakin'?" He had traveled, spent a month in Reno every winter.

"What happened to your hand, Chief?" Everybody connected with the volunteers still called Bounty chief.

"Had to teach a couple of guys a lesson." Warren Bounty watched Gil button the fly on his jeans and scrunch into his cowboy boots. "Boy, you been busier'n a pickpocket in a school for the blind."

"Stayed the night, was all. Part of the night. *He* was here the whole time." Gil Cutty gestured at Harold Glass in the other room.

"And we can see what a fine upstanding chaperone he is," said Bounty.

Cutty grabbed his shirt and tried to leave the room. Fontana threw his arm across the doorway. "Just a friendly question or two, Gil."

"I s'pose." He looked uncertainly at Mac with his remarkable James Stewart-blue eyes. The reddish tan made them even bluer. He scratched his forehead with the fluorescent-orange sight of the .44.

"Claude thought sure Wanda got herself kidnapped."

"Kidnapped?"

"She was planning to spend the night with Claude. They were driving to Canada first thing this morning."

"Aw, shit. She never told me none of that."

"Why the gun?"

"You seen the people in this building? There's a five-year-old up the hall'd roll you for a rusty church key."

"See you, Gil." Mac dropped his arm against his side. His ribs still hurt.

At the front door Gil Cutty cranked his head around. "You ain't gonna tell Claude, are you?"

"We ain't gonna tell Claude."

"I ain't afraid of that blimp. Just, I don't see stirrin' up trouble for no good reason."

"Course not," said Warren. "Claude does get wind of this, remember. Serpentine." He threaded his good hand through the air. Fontana tried to keep from laughing.

A few seconds later Warren reached down, ripped the sheet off Wanda, and let it parachute across the room. "I'll be dogged." Wanda wore the same thigh-high black leather skirt and frilly white blouse she had last night. When she came to, she bustled into the bathroom. Twenty minutes later she came out in a new outfit. She'd labored on her hair, but it was apparently unmanageable. She carried a comb and a spray can. Legs splayed, she stood in front of the mirror in the living room and sprayed. Fontana stepped toward the hallway and took a deep breath away from the mist.

"Dammit," said Fontana. "You trying to make Claude nuts? You're supposed to be driving to Canada with him right now."

"Oh, shoot. Forgot about that. No wonder the phone's been ringing all night." She gave the spray can a couple of pumps and began slashing at her hair with a comb.

Warren stepped forward and immersed himself in the cloud. "We just found out this morning Claude put you in his will. Interesting turn of events, wouldn't you say, Wanda? I wonder when your first inkling of it was?"

The more nervous she got, the harder Wanda pumped the spray can. She and Warren were beginning to look like an out-of-focus picture. "I didn't know nothing about no will until just last night. Claude . . . I don't know about him. I got this creepy feeling. Jeez, Warren. What happened to you?"

"Bet a guy a dollar I could arm-wrestle a tractor. Tell me about your creepy feeling."

"Claude's really been turning the screws lately. Like we can't go together anymore if we're not married."

"Gonna be kinda hard with three of you in the same bed." Warren nodded at Harold Glass.

"Oh, don't you start in on me." She fanned her wet hair with a slab of newspaper.

Fontana said, "Wanda, remember Monday when I went to go up the mountain? You came out and practically begged me back in to eat with you."

"I didn't know anything was going to happen. You think I woulda stuck around that long if I'd known something was going to happen? I spent more time in the slammer than everyone in Staircase put together. First person they were going to finger was me."

"When was the last time you saw Caitlin?"

Wanda turned on a heel and faced Mac. "Look. If I tell you, I don't want it comin' back on me."

"It won't."

"What's this? Saturday? I guess Wednesday I saw him. Late he came by. We went out." Consigning her lungs to Clairol, Wanda pumped the hair spray again. "He came up and took me to some swanky place out in the sticks. We had dinner lookin' out at the river. He knew the guy owned it."

"The River Palace?"

"I think that was the name of it. Near Fall City. I know Claude's pissed. Will you take me back out to Staircase and explain to him?"

"I'll take you. I'm not explaining diddly."

They got as far as Mercer Island before Wanda said, "You gotta stop, Mac. Need to use the ladies' room bad." She was breathing through her nose in a whistling rasp. Fontana got off I-90 and pulled into a Denny's restaurant parking lot.

"Surfin' USA" was on KVI when she went in, but they had already hiccuped along with the Bobbettes to "Mr. Lee," and walked like men and sung like girls with the Four Seasons before they got suspicious. Fontana found Wanda in the lobby, looped, ricocheting off the wall, smiling drowsily at anyone who came into focus.

He picked her large handbag up off the floor and escorted her by one arm out to the truck. A red-headed waitress scrutinized the transaction as if she couldn't decide whether or not to call the gendarmes. Wanda's pupils were specks in a sea of gray. Fontana toted her purse out behind the restaurant, removed her wallet, change purse, keys, Tampons, and dumped the rest into the trash.

"It was all the money," said Wanda lethargically. "I'm not addicted or anything. I can handle it." She started to nod off, head lolling. Warren shored her up with his shoulder.

"You know who owns the River Palace?" Mac asked.

Warren said, "They built it since I went away. Down on the lower Snoqualmie? Near Fall City? I ain't even seen it."

"Lars Ereckson established his new regional headquarters there." Mac elbowed Wanda Sheridan until she stirred. "Wanda, darlin'. What'd you guys do at the River Palace?"

"Lobster," she murmured. "I ordered lobster and Jimmy had steak. Made 'em take it back 'cause it wasn't done right. Jimmy expects the best."

"You meet anybody there?"

She tried to titter, but it sounded more like a cat coughing up a fur ball. "Now you mention it, some older guy came to the table and wanted to talk. They went off together."

"How long?"

"I dunno. Twenty minutes. I hadda eat mostly by myself. Jimmy got back his steak was all cold. It was okay, though."

"Why?"

"Because Jimmy wasn't hungry anymore. We left then."

"What'd the guy look like? The older man who came to the table?"

"I dunno."

"His name Ereckson?"

"Doesn't sound like it."

"Lars?"

"Yeah. Lars something or other."

34

THE UGLIEST MAN
NORTH OF SAN FRANCISCO

S ituated at a bend of the river below Snoqualmie Falls, the
River Palace sported an unparalleled view of the lower Snoqualmie that allowed patrons to observe a quarter mile of rapids
in either direction. People said the area resembled the New En-
gland countryside. Jigsaw puzzle companies snapped pictures of
the spectacle. To enhance the charm of the place, somebody had
constructed a covered wooden bridge half a mile up the road.
Despite exorbitant prices, an aggressive television campaign fea-
turing local sports celebrities had bloated customer interest until
the restaurant had weekend bookings a year in advance.

Lunch traffic was still thick as Fontana pulled into the large
blacktop parking lot. A Honda Accord cruised out past them.
Then a white Ford van, plastic steer horns mounted over the cab.
As both vehicles came abreast, he found himself face-to-face with
Bobby Joe Allan.

Instead of the enmity he expected to see, Fontana detected only uneasiness. Caitlin had been here Wednesday. Bobby Joe Allan Saturday and none too thrilled to be discovered.

Parking in the shade, they left Wanda to slumber in the truck, Satan to guard over her. On the trek through the parking lot Fontana espied a second van. He veered through the parked cars and ran his fingers along four buckshot holes the size of .22's beneath the rear window. Double-aught.

"This it?" asked Warren. "The van from last night? Christ, I'll get my weapon."

"Forget it. We got no license number and no real description of the men. If we do prove this was the van, you can bet whoever owns it will have loaned it out last night to a guy whose name he can't remember."

"So we can't *prove*. We'll *know*." Fontana scribbled the license number on a notepad. Tucked under a clip on the sun visor, he found the registration slip. Kowalski, Thursday. On the floor of the back seat was a dried puddle of blood. Leaning in behind Fontana, Warren whispered, "Let's burn it."

"Get real."

"You see Bobby Joe Allan as we were coming in?"

"Yup."

"Suppose he had anything to do with this?"

"What are you getting at?"

"Maybe he hired somebody to get you because you suspended him. Got me by mistake."

"We don't look much alike, Warren."

"So three guys ask around for the fire chief and somebody points to me. It could have happened that way."

"Guy name of Thursday Kowalski owns it. Works for Lars Ereckson. I've seen him with Mo. Something's wrong here. Corporate lawyers don't go around breaking arms."

"We should torch it."

Slamming the door of the van, Fontana walked toward the

restaurant complex. A score of white flags fluttered in the hot breeze, each affixed to a different gable of the tall building. "We get out, we'll take Satan over it. He might be able to tag the guys if they're hanging around."

"I'm getting my piece," said Warren, heading for the GMC.

"Not with me, you don't."

"They're inside, Mac!"

"Yeah, and nothing's going to happen. Not here in broad daylight."

"I'm not going in without my piece."

"You can be arrested just for carrying that thing."

They glowered at each other before Fontana turned and walked alone past the white-uniformed parking attendants and through the front door.

A man had just come to the main desk to speak to the woman behind it, a clipboard in his hand. He was startled to see Fontana but did his best to conceal it. Medium height, dark hair. Gruesome stitches laced both lips. A deep laceration festooned his left eye. Fontana said, "Next time you box with a horse, get some gloves for the horse."

"We still have a few tables, sir," said the woman behind the desk. "For one?"

Fontana flashed his badge, realizing a tarnished cutout of chrome and him standing there in jeans, hiking boots, and a T-shirt with a logo of spilled breakfast weren't likely to impress. He addressed the man. "I'm more interested in how your face got to look like that. Last night. Where were you?"

"Would you like to speak to our manager? I'll be glad to get him." The dark-haired man reached under the desk and picked up a pink phone, punched buttons. Fontana could see by the way he wetted his lips with his swollen tongue that his mouth had gone dry.

"I can have the King County police here for backup in five minutes."

The man averted his eyes, feigned interest in a passing waitress. "I was in a car accident."

"I doubt it."

"I have witnesses. Several of them."

"Go on."

"Including Ereckson himself."

"Where is old Lars?"

Ereckson's office was two floors higher in what, had the establishment been an apartment building, would have been the penthouse. Floor-to-ceiling windows exhibited blue sky. Trees. The river which was only a trickle in the drought. A hawk, harassed by a flock of crows, winged over a distant field, tilting this way and that to exploit the thermals.

As Fontana entered with the man from the front desk, a pretty young woman in a carmine skirt exited. Lars looked up from the young woman's bottom and glanced at the man with Fontana. "That will be all, Neil." He left. "I understand you've been asking some questions of my personnel, Chief Fontana."

"Dugan just left looks like he got hit in the face with a garbage can lid."

"Neil had an accident."

"I met a guy like that last night. Funny thing was, the guy I met last night was trying to kidnap one of my friends."

"I can understand why you'd be upset, but you're mistaken." Lars wore a dress shirt, the sleeves bunched at the elbows. His eyes didn't look too deeply at a person. He was more concerned with the way others were perceiving him.

"Funny thing is, we found a vehicle outside matches the one involved in our skirmish. I found four double-aught holes in the back of your vehicle just about where I put them."

"*My* vehicle?"

"In your lot. Belongs to one of your people."

Ereckson's voice grew chilly. "Who would that be?"

"Kowalski."

Ereckson sat heavily in his padded swivel chair and punched a button on his executive phone set. "Thursday. Come in here a minute."

Ten seconds later Thursday Kowalski burst into the office, gave a start when he saw Fontana, then shot a quick look at his implacable employer. He wore a Hawaiian shirt and shorts. Medium height and stocky, he fitted the physical characteristics of the man Fontana had doubled over the car trunk, the one he might have killed if he hadn't been intercepted. His head looked as if it had been stuffed and sewn by a flunking student taxidermist. One eye was puffed shut, the skin around it blue, black, and a shade of cucumber green. A doctor had sewn the rip in his left cheek. His lower right jaw was bruised and lopsided.

"Thursday," said Lars Ereckson, "Chief Fontana thinks some of my people were involved in a set-to last night. Says they were trying to abduct one of his friends."

Speaking with lips only, Thursday said, "Why would anybody want to do that?" When his lips separated, the steel in Kowalski's mouth glittered. Kowalski's jaw was wired.

"Jeez, would ya look at you," said Fontana. "You gotta be the ugliest man north of San Francisco. Knew a guy once got his mouth wired like that. Went out on a boat and got seasick. Hell of a way to buy the farm. I was you, I'd keep a pair of wire cutters handy." Eyes cold, Kowalski fished a pair from his pocket.

"Thursday, Neil, and one other man were with me last night from ten-thirty on. We were involved in a slight traffic mishap. Whatever else you may be thinking, you're dead wrong."

"All three of us know I'm not."

"I think, uh, you may be persuaded to change your mind."

"Just out of curiosity, what's the third man's name?"

"That will be all, Thursday."

"You sure you want to be alone with this guy, Lars?" Thursday tapped an index finger to his temple.

"I can handle things."

Ereckson tilted back in his rolling chair, knitted the fingers of both hands together, and surveyed Fontana with cool gray eyes while Kowalski departed. "You're an interesting man, Chief Fontana. You have a lot of skills someone in my employ might find useful."

"*Have* a job."

"Pays twenty thousand a year. I know. I asked your mayor. My clothing bill is double that. How'd you like to earn eighty? With a signing bonus of a hundred thousand. I can get it to you tax-free. I've got lawyers."

"Ugly ones."

Ereckson smiled patronizingly, reached down, and punched his intercom. "Thursday?"

"Sir?"

"Open the safe. Prepare a signing bonus for your new co-worker."

The line fizzed. "How much?"

"One hundred."

"Forget it," said Fontana. "I don't get it, Lars. What do you want from Staircase? You took a hell of a big risk last night. Why gamble? Bounty doesn't know shit from Shinola. What could you want with him? There must be a million little towns like Staircase. Why not go ruin another one?"

Lars Ereckson laughed, but the activity was infrequent enough that it was brittle and grating. "I could use a fire suppressions expert. A hundred and fifty a year, choose your own hours. Two hundred to sign."

"You don't get it, do you?"

"Three hundred to sign."

The phone buzzed. Ereckson picked it up, listened, and spoke to Fontana. "An overseas call. You'll have to excuse me in a moment. I'm not trying to buy anybody. I see good men and I hire them. That's how I got where I am."

"You got where you are sending people around at night."

"Consider my offer."

"I'll be back."

"Good."

"You won't like it."

"My wife and others will vouch for the whereabouts of those three last night."

Fontana left the room. Damn. These guys had sterling alibis. Even if he roped them for the kidnap attempt, County would pay hell getting a conviction. He could probably jam a couple of them into a cell, but they'd be out in an hour, and he wouldn't know any more than he knew now.

Outside in the lot the van was missing. Wanda was still asleep, Warren beside her with the Mac-10 and suppressor draped across his crotch. Fontana said, "You see 'em move the van?"

"Two big Samoan goombahs. Both packing. I could tell that much. Looked like trouble."

"You let 'em take it?"

"I let 'em take it."

"What's the matter?"

"What dya think? You coulda come out and found me splattered across that Seville. Or worse."

"Not with that cannon in your lap. And Satan."

"You gonna call the cops and get 'em crawling all over this place or what?"

"Not now."

"Why not?"

"What's your connection to Ereckson?"

"Ereckson? I don't even know the man. None of these folks. I don't know any of 'em."

"Sure?"

"Let's get the hell out of here."

Fontana drove to the fire station in Staircase. Fontana lugged the shotgun inside. Satan followed. Warren stayed with the GMC, cooing to Wanda.

Inside, Fontana found Bobby Joe Allan in the beanery, meticulously filling a cardboard box with personal articles from his food locker. When he saw Fontana, he slammed the locker door. Allan wore razor-creased rayon pants and a golf shirt. His wife had lost a button on her sundress and hadn't combed her hair. She had been across the room at the TV, but she abandoned that and made a beeline for Fontana. Satan let out a low growl, stopping her short.

"*Fuss!*" commanded Fontana. Satan was quiet.

"What is your problem? You've got a hell of a nerve."

"Lady, I call 'em like I see 'em. I'm not going to apologize for that. You want the straight skinny, come to the hearing."

"There isn't going to be any hearing. We're taking you to court."

"That'll be interesting."

"Bobby Joe told me about you, but I didn't believe it."

"Honey," said Allan in a broken voice. "Just leave be." Sandals spanking angrily at her heels, she tromped to the front door and slammed it behind her so hard the blinds got snarled.

"Need to talk," said Fontana. "About Pete."

Allan picked up the carton and traveled toward the front door. "Ain't got time."

"What were you doing at the River Palace?"

"Never had the pleasure."

"Jeez, Bobby Joe. You saw me look right at you."

"We had lunch." He started through the watch office.

"I talked to Lars a few minutes ago."

Bobby Joe Allan halted, set the box on the desk in the watch office, and stared at the floor in a trancelike manner the way people did when they hadn't been getting much sleep. Fontana let the silence bloom. Satan lay down on his front paws. Outside, an automobile drove noisily past in the street. Allan finally said, "What did Ereckson say?"

"You tell me."

"Lars offered me a job."

"Me too. Must need a lot of firemen in the construction business, huh?"

"I'm in a hurry. We have to pick up Laura's sister."

"We'll be talking, me and you."

"Just tell me one thing," said Allan, after pulling the front door open and wedging it with his foot. "Was it the kitchen police sicced you on me?"

"We could have been on a deserted island, just you and me, Bobby Joe, and I still would have suspended you."

He mulled that over. "Gonna fire me?"

"Yes. I'm telling you so you can make plans."

"Kitchen police" referred to Kingsley Pierpont. KP. People had been calling him that since he signed on. He didn't like it much. Across the street in Allan's van, Allan and his wife enmeshed themselves in a rather long and heated discussion before driving off.

35

MY DOG READS DICKENS

F ontana felt like a loose wheel on the freeway.

On the refrigerator he found a note taped to the door. He recognized Claude's squarish printing from seeing it on so many crossword puzzles. "Got to take Mom to Snowqualmi Hospital for her lombaego. Tell Wanda to wait at the Bedonin. She knows there will be no retrabution. Claude." Claude ciphered over crossword puzzles religiously, did them in pen, and misspelled just about everything to make it fit. If he grabbed the morning paper before Bobby Joe, the lieutenant would be in a funk all day.

Midafternoon, Saturday. Blinds drawn against the afternoon sun, Mo was secluded on the second floor of the small municipal building. He climbed halfway up the stairs to her office before she said, "Come on in, Mac. Jeez, Satan again? Why do you take that dog everywhere you go? He's old enough to be put to sleep."

"He's not old. He's just worn-out."

"But you hate dogs."

"This dog reads Dickens. Otherwise, I'd shoot him myself."

It was the first week of August, and from behind her desk she reigned in an empty building in a half-empty town. In shorts and a sleeveless raspberry-colored sweat shirt she looked flushed despite the room's arctic air conditioning. He'd brought her a dew-beaded can of Pepsi from the machine in the fire station.

"Thanks." After tilting back in her swivel chair and popping the aluminum tab, she sipped at the eruption of foam. "You lost it last night, Mac. You might have captured all three of them if you hadn't gone berserk. You gave the others just enough space to gather their resources. You really do have this beastly temper. Maybe you should see a therapist? Mine is very intuitive. She's a gay activist, but I think you'd like her."

"Satan's my therapist."

"But you had that trouble back East and got pushed out of a job you'd had eighteen years."

"Mo, honey. Can't you get anything straight? I didn't have trouble and get pushed out. I had trouble. I rode it out. Then my wife died. I rode that out. Then I looked at my life and didn't like what I saw. Then I quit."

"Have it your way."

A dialogue with Mo was like a walk on the beach. It wasn't over until later when you got the sand out of your shoes, until you unraveled all the double meanings and ascertained which of her comments was uttered from ignorance and which from cunning.

"You showed courage last night, Mo."

"Pardon?"

"Those guys were intimidating, but you waded in like an old hand. I was proud of you."

Mo sipped Pepsi and eyed Fontana over the cylinder of the can. In front of her on the desk rested a pair of sunglasses with wobbly arms. "Thanks, Mac. You don't often say nice things to me."

"You don't often deserve them."

"That's more like you."

"A simple thanks would have avoided it, Mo."

"See what I mean? You're always twisting the knife."

"Quit backing into it, and I won't have occasion to twist it."

Despite her obvious intelligence and attainments in business and politics, Mo was smart and thick, wise and idiotic, intelligent and just a bit stupid. Recently she'd saved the township $165,000 when a contractor tried to bilk Staircase for a new set of storm drains in the downtown area. But for Mo's eagle-eyed inspection of his records, he would have plundered the city coffers. Still, Fontana frequently saw her driving to work with a coffee cup on the roof of her Porsche.

"I'm here about Lars Ereckson."

"I knew after you met him, you'd change your mind. Funny, I had a rather peculiar telephone conversation with him just this morning. He seemed to think I was ill last night. What did you tell him?"

"I couldn't say, Mo. The three guys who attacked Warren in the alley. I found two of them and the van."

"You did?"

"At the River Palace. They work for Lars."

"No!"

"They do, Mo."

Dripping configurations of slobber onto her office carpet, the dog sat. Sunlight beyond the drawn drapes bathed the room in a dim, suffused glow. She got stern, trying on schoolmarm to his lying truant. "That's *very* difficult to believe."

"Watch my lips, Mo. *They work for Lars.*"

"Okay, so maybe they do. Lars is extremely anticrime. Did you advise him of it? He's very scrupulous about keeping everything on the up-and-up."

"Lars said they were with him last night. All three of them."

"Well . . ."

"He was lying. He offered me a full-time job and three hundred grand as a signing bonus."

"What are you . . . Lars is . . . Sure you're not going off half cocked? If Lars says they were with him, Mac, then you've got the wrong three."

"The two I saw were beat up. They recognized me right off."

"Have you thought this through?"

"The van's owner is Thursday Kowalski."

"Now you have really gone and done it. You didn't accuse Thursday? He's a Yale lawyer, for godsakes. Graduated third in his class. He could work anywhere he wants. A guy like that's not going to be running around dark alleys in the middle of the night wearing a hood."

"Next time you see him, ask him who broke his jaw."

"Well, he might be . . . You can't prove he was one of the three men from last night."

"What would Lars want with Warren?"

"I know Lars wouldn't do anything illegal."

"Just answer the question. Is there anything on earth Lars or his Palace Corporation might want with Warren?"

Pressing the cold Pepsi can to her brow and rolling it from side to side, she thought a minute. The wetness pasted stray hairs to her brow. "Warren? Lars? They don't even know each other. Mac, how are we going to get this town into the twentieth century if you go off on Lars?"

He felt his face heating up. "You don't care that he might be up to his elbows in kidnappings and murder? You just want what's good for the town, right?"

Mo didn't breathe for a few seconds. She batted her lashes as if fending off tears. "You know I want what's good for the town."

"Mo, sweetheart, do me a favor. Don't go up in the hills with anybody who has more than ten fresh stitches in his face."

———

"Now you're scaring me, Mac."

Fontana looked down at the headstrong mayor, who looked Napoleonic at the moment. Satan stood. Mac reached down and scratched the German shepherd behind his bad ear. "And don't be telling people what I make."

"I never—"

"Lars knew it."

"Lars is guiltless in all this. You'll clear him yourself. See if you don't."

The engine was out drilling with the volunteers when Fontana returned to his office. He heard hurried whispers and a tinkling that sounded suspiciously like the tine of an open belt buckle. Warren Bounty shuffled into the open doorway of the single-bunk jail cell opposite Fontana's desk. Wanda lay on the bunk, bare feet toward Fontana, peering dispassionately at him over painted toenails, pale, knobby knees, naked thighs. Warren was hoisting his trousers up around his hips.

"Hey, Mac," Wanda said huskily.

Fontana picked up his shotgun and left. "Now don't be like that." Warren rushed down the corridor behind him, fiddled with his trousers, crab-walked around the beanery table. The lugubrious look on Warren's face was pathetic. He was shoeless, zipper open, all dignity out the window.

"She's stoned, for godsakes," said Fontana. "I mean, that's a lot like rape."

"What?"

"In *my* office. What's wrong with you, Warren? I thought you had some sense."

"Mac, I'm . . ."

"You hate Claude that much?"

"I don't hate Claude at all. I'm . . ."

Fontana walked out on the rationalization.

———

36

IN WHICH NAKED
LADIES RUN IN A FIELD

Five hours later a sheep-eyed Warren showed up after dinner. He brought a present for Brendan, who hurtled into his arms as soon as he rolled, huffing, out of his Pinto. "Uncle Warren!" squealed Brendan. "You haven't been here all week."

"Been busy catchin' me a killer," he said, setting Brendan down carefully so as not to bump his plastered hand. He dug an activity book out of the Pinto and presented it to the boy.

After thanking him, Brendan said, "How do you make an elephant float?"

"Couldn't guess, pardner. How?" Warren was squatting on his heels, eye level with the boy.

"Add two scoops of ice cream and some root beer." Warren made the booming noise he passed off for laughter and pushed himself up with one hand.

"Just came over to apologize, Mac. Had no business doing

what I did. I left Wanda over at the Bedouin. Called Pettigrew's, but nobody was in. Gave her some quarters for the phone and left her in the bar. She's okay."

Warren booted a loose rock in the drive and gazed out through the alders at the base of Gadd across the river, at the distant Douglas firs on the slopes.

"Apology accepted." Warren presented his good hand. They shook with the awkward silence of a couple of schoolboys after a scuffle. "I phoned Bobby Joe. He said he had somebody to meet, but to come in an hour. Tag along?"

"Wouldn't miss it."

When Mary Gilliam arrived, she said, "I hope you know I'm missing my belly dancing class." She'd spruced herself up, lipstick and a handbag, enough perfume for a car full of thirteen-year-olds headed for their first dance. Combed her wispy hair. She had a fondness for Warren that embarrassed him.

Allan lived five miles away, north of Snoqualmie, on a small, overgrown farm his uncle had bequeathed him, high on a plateau and within sniffing range of the wood mill that employed Claude Pettigrew and five hundred other locals. A warm, dry dusk was quickly settling over the valley. It would be dark by the time they saw Allan. Fontana took the back route, past Moon Valley and out along Dabney Road.

"I'm thinking Bobby Joe's afraid we're going to nail him with something on Daugherty's death," said Fontana.

"You know," said Warren. "Maybe we should have played scoop and run with Pete. But look at it this way. Who was in charge? On a medic alarm if there's a paramedic, he's in charge of the medical aspects of the run. And Caitlin was there. Not from the beginning, but almost. I tried to tell him it was arsenic, but he wouldn't listen. You know Caitlin. I haven't thought about this before, but he was acting sort of weird."

"What do you mean?"

"Wouldn't listen to nobody."

"Even medics get nervous when a firefighter goes down."

"I'm not sure that was it."

Miles from the nearest highway, it was a small, rural community on a loop country lane that snaked up into the foothills over Tokul Creek. A double-wide trailer here. A ramshackle house on twenty acres there. Allan's spread began at the twisty road and stretched north. Fontana couldn't remember if he had a hundred or two hundred acres. It was mostly wooded, new growth, with two large horse pastures he leased out to neighbors. Most of his property was a hundred feet below the plateau and the road.

Fontana halted in the gravel and dirt and stepped out of the truck to unlatch the gate. The GMC motor purred as he swung the heavy steel gate parallel to the road. The hinges screaked. A robin chirruped bravely in the trees. He could see twenty yards up a rutted lane that was umbrellaed by drooping maples. The earth was dry and cracked. A breeze made the trees talk. Fontana thought he heard something foreign amid the natural sounds. Back at the truck, Don and Juan were crooning "What's Your Name." He switched off the radio.

"Warren. You hear that?"

"Too many sirens in my time. What?"

Fontana turned off the ignition and cupped his ears. The sound came again. A keening noise. Like an animal crying. A woman screaming. A buzz saw.

Fontana clambered into the truck, started it and moved it twenty yards into the narrow lane, killed the motor, and stashed the key on top of the handkerchief in the unused ashtray. Nobody could drive out now, not unless he moved the Destroyer. And certainly not in a hurry. He unlocked the Remington from the rack and grabbed a fistful of extra shells from the glove box, poked them into his pockets.

"Satan! *Fuss!*"

The dog whimpered and leaped out of the truck, sniffing the air for danger.

"What the hell's going on, Mac?"

"Through here."

Breathing heavily, Warren grabbed his Mac-10 case and followed. They prowled through a short forested stretch and emerged on the brink of an incline obstructed by six ancient cedar stumps, each six to eight feet across. The hill ran down into a rolling pasture, green as Kentucky despite the drought. Sheltered from the wind, nothing in the pasture stirred. The ground oozed warmth in the dusk.

The keening noise came again, on the far side of the pasture, amid the trees and a row of stumps that nobody'd bothered to dynamite. And then a man's voice, in the same area seventy yards away. A barking voice. Fontana blinked and squinted.

Sprinting through the brush toward the road was a naked woman.

"Looks like Allan's wife."

"I don't see. Where?" Bounty should have been wearing glasses, had commented on it often enough.

"Opposite. Running around the rim of the field."

"Allan was gonna set me up with her sister. Is she naked? They only been married a few months. Newlyweds. I bet old Bobby Joe's busier'n a cat trying to bury shit on a tin roof."

"Shush." Fontana saw her again, a white flash between the birches. Then another flash behind her. Sheltered from the breezes in this tiny valley, Fontana could hear quite clearly now. Two women. Both shrieking. The second woman burst from the trees and skirted the rim of the far side of the pasture at one o'clock. Fontana and Warren were at six o'clock, halfway down the hogback, thirty yards higher than the uneven pasture. The second woman wore black sweat pants and nothing else.

"Damn," said Warren.

"Somebody's behind them."

"Bobby Joe out here playing sex games?"

"I don't think this is any game," said Fontana, pushing the crossbolt safety on the shotgun.

———

Behind the women a dark figure ran in the same direction, left to right. Chasing. As the figure crossed a clearing, Fontana got a better look. A man, taller and fleeter than either of the women. He wore a hood. One hand was held awkwardly, as if he were carrying something small and heavy. They were in the field now, both women cutting directly across the pasture toward a spot below Fontana. The skirling sounded as if somebody were letting air out of a very tight balloon.

"I'm going for *him*. See if you can corral those two. They'll be wired."

"That's a plan," said Warren, obviously at a loss.

"Satan. Stay here! *Bleib!*"

Fontana crouched and went around the stump. Zigzagging down the hogback, he stayed behind brush. He crouched behind the bole of a tree at the edge of the pasture. Neither woman had seen him or they would have veered off. Their pursuer had just come out of the woods, bounding across the rolling grass, picking up speed as he loped. Fontana shouldered the shotgun so that it was pointing up. The first round, a twelve-gauge rifled slug, was enough to bring down a moose. The remaining six shells in the Remington were double-aught.

By the time she reached Fontana's position Laura had stopped caterwauling. He recognized the other woman now, her sister. They were both squat and heavy of thigh. They had a look of determination you didn't often see in humans. The wild-eyed flight of a wounded gazelle. Both were barefoot, legs bleeding and tracked from thorns. The man in black behind them had gained on the open stretch. He carried a pistol.

As the two panicky women neared the first thickets leading onto the wooded slope, the man yelled, "You bitches, stop. I'll kill you."

Whirring past Fontana's position, Laura's sister came so close he could smell her perfume. Then came Laura, the ground thudding under her heavy galloping gait. With the women safely past,

Fontana stepped into the path of the hooded man, now twenty feet away.

The recoil rocked Fontana's shoulder. The man landed on his back, firing rounds into the grass at his side even after he was down. He snapped off all six shots in the revolver, and then the hammer clicked on empties. All noise ceased while the echo came back at them from across the pasture. He twitched, hands and legs. After that he was still except for some agonal breathing.

"Hey, Dugan," said Fontana softly, "stop or I'll shoot."

37

THE MAN WHO LIKED
BATHROOM HUMOR

"**H**ot damn!" said Warren Bounty, lumbering over to the
fallen man. "Look at that. A nickel-plated Colt. Musta
been firing it off in some sort of autonomic response. He'd been
jerking off, he probably would have come after you shot him."

Both women had ceased flight, Laura cringing behind a nearby
stump, her sister ten feet away, hands clasped over her pale breasts
as if propriety were all she had to worry about.

Fontana was facing opposite the dead man, trying to calm the
women, both of whom stood like deer momentarily hypnotized
in a cone of headlights. Laura's sister, who had seemed a shade
less terrified and more in control during their pell-mell getaway,
was still gasping for air, whimpering, her dark eyes moist with
flight.

"You all right?" Fontana said. "We'll get you a blanket from
the truck."

"Is he dead?"

In the thickening darkness Bounty flashed his teeth. He was busy absorbing the spectacle in front of him.

"Who are you?" Laura's sister asked.

"Fontana. Acting sheriff of Staircase. Where's Allan?"

"Bobby Joe?" She glanced around. "Back at the house. They were going to murder all of us."

"Satan!" The dog leaped over a high stump on the hogback, galloped through a blackberry bramble, and ran to his side. Obedient as a cyborg, he would have stayed up there until tomorrow morning.

Kneeling in the grass, Bounty used two fingers to pull the wool ski mask off the dead man. The slug had struck him under the nose. "We ain't ever going to identify this."

"Dugan I saw at the River Palace," said Fontana, kicking the dead man's foot. "Name is Neil."

Scanning the trees across the darkening pasture, he turned and faced the women. Huddled together now, they comforted each other.

"How many more?" Fontana asked.

Eyes glued to the corpse in the grass, Laura Allan left her sister and sidled forward. When she got close, she spit. The globule didn't launch properly, trickled down her chin, and dangled in a silver whip. Determined, she spit again.

"How many more?"

She faced Mac, but her dark blue eyes didn't focus. "I was afraid to stay in the woods, so I followed Lisa into the pasture." Her sister, Lisa, palmed her breasts in either hand.

"*Suche!*" said Fontana. The dog took off, sniffing the ground. He didn't know what he was searching for, but then, neither did Fontana.

The woman in the black sweat pants said, "One other guy. He's got a gun."

"In the house?"

"They tied Bobby Joe up and ordered us to take our clothes off. When the first guy turned his back, I tripped this one, and we ran out the kitchen. The storm door latched, and he went through the glass. That's the only thing that saved us."

"Take care of 'em," Fontana said, jogging along the left side of the pasture toward the house. Aware the second man could be drawing a bead on him even now, Fontana stayed close to shelter. The dog was almost out of sight.

"I'm comin'," said Bounty.

"Get those two blankets from the truck, radio for help, and stay here."

The house was log cabin style. Single-story. No lights on. To the south of the building he spotted a small red Toyota which he knew belonged to Laura. Another foreign car parked beside it must have been her sister's. Bobby Joe Allan's van with the steer horns on the roof had been ransacked, contents strewn in the yard.

In front of the house in the huge graveled drive sat another van, same as the one he'd seen last night and again this morning at the River Palace. The motor was idling. Satan was already next to the driver's door, paws scratching the paint.

A shot rang out.

Instinctively Fontana flopped onto his stomach and raised the Remington to his shoulder. Gravel spurted from the rear wheels of the van. The engine growled, and the vehicle slewed from side to side, racing down the hill to the rear exit on Highway 202. A paper bag was taped over the license. He sent two rounds of buckshot at the van, which disappeared down the hill, a fog of dust and airborne dirt hurrahing its escape. Satan chased after the van. Fontana whistled and brought him back.

Ramming three cartridges into the Remington from his jeans pocket, Fontana made a careful approach to the house. The front door was wide open.

Accompanied only by his heartbeat, Bobby Joe Allan lay on

his face, mouth gagged, ankles and wrists tied behind his back with scraps of clothesline.

Bobby Joe watched Fontana and the dog without moving. Blood oozed from a chest wound, frothy and pinkish. The room reverberated with the sound of the stereo, Anne Murray singing sluggishly.

"Suche!" commanded Fontana. "Bad guys!" Satan was off, bounding through the rooms.

Removing the Buck knife from Allan's belt, Fontana sliced the bonds restraining Allan's wrists and ankles. He pulled the two-inch band of adhesive tape off his face and removed a pair of women's panties from his mouth. Allan gasped and lay still while his heart pumped a washed-out vermilion onto the floor. Allan had cataloged a plethora of frightened looks since Fontana had known him, but now he had finally given up being anxious. After all, it was here. With a bullet in your chest, what else was there to worry about?

"They all gone?" Fontana asked.

Allan nodded feebly. Fontana cut his shirt away, then rose and foraged through the kitchen. A pistol wound. The pinkish blood meant that a lung had been punctured and that Allan was suffering from pneumothorax. It meant that each time he inhaled, air escaped from the lung into the pleural space, compressing the space and compacting the lung until it got smaller and smaller. The lung sac would soon be two inches in diameter. Nonfunctional. If both lungs had been punctured, he'd suffocate in minutes. He might anyway. Working quickly, Fontana located a plastic bag, held it over the bloody hole, and trimmed it with the knife. Lacking tape, he held it in place with his hand. Three sides tight. One loose.

"Bobby Joe, I got help right behind me. You know those guys?"

Almost imperceptibly Allan shook his head. Pink froth appeared on his lips. Fontana palpated his chest on the other side, searching for an exit wound. For blood. Nothing.

Hauling the body of the phone over by the cord, Fontana punched 911, gave them the address and problem. They said they had already received a call, were sending medical help, but he knew the cops would be dispatched as well. Bounty had got to them on the radio.

Allan burbled again. Fontana leaned low. "What are you trying to say, Bobby Joe?"

"Laura."

It surprised Fontana that he would think of her. Bobby Joe, the epitome of selfishness, was dying, and he wanted to know how his wife was. "Warren's got 'em. The women are okay."

Allan didn't want to believe him, tried to utter something more. It was apparent he and his abductor had heard the faraway shot.

"Yeah, I know, Bobby Joe. There was a guy after them. I fixed him."

Allan's face relaxed. On the couch across the room lay Allan's .357, cylinder pushed open, bullets on the floor. "What did they want?"

"Gettin' a big score," said Allan wetly, and with great effort.

At that moment Bounty came bumbling through the door in a low crouch, his bulky Mac-10 pointed at Fontana. He swung it around the room in jerky arcs. He tramped from room to room like a raiding storm trooper and sixty seconds later was kneeling behind Fontana, studying Bobby Joe's face.

"Place is clear, Mac," said Bounty, fighting to catch his breath.

"Satan went through it." Fontana could feel the lung on the wound side slowly collapsing under his hand. Cyanosis was setting in. "Come on, Bobby Joe. Try to talk to me."

For a moment Allan looked as if he wanted to tell Fontana something; then his eyes swerved to Warren Bounty. He grimaced and squeezed his lids shut. Shrouded in an old army blanket, Laura limped in and knelt beside Fontana. "Oh, Bobby Joe, darling."

"He's not going to do much talking," said Fontana. "One bullet to the lung. He's having a hard time."

"I love you, Bobby Joe. Please be all right. I love you, baby."

In the back of the room Laura's sister hastily snatched up her clothing, shuddering as she climbed into it.

"You see 'em?" Warren asked.

"A van went down the hill to the other gate. The license was covered with a paper sack. I let one go at his tires. He might have a flat."

"I should probably stay here in case he says something."

"I'm controlling the bleeding. I got ears, too."

Warren Bounty gave Mac a dubious look—Mac was giving a lot of orders tonight—then lumbered out through the doorway in his distinctive gait. Fontana had a feeling, machine pistol or no, Warren wasn't raring for this sport. "Satan," said Mac. "Guard Warren!" Ears pricked up, the dog was off, spinning a throw rug out from under his hind paws.

Eight minutes later, as the first of the volunteers arrived, Bounty returned, shaking his head, Satan trotting at his heels. He'd ditched the gun somewhere out in the dark. The house would soon be crawling with cops, and an illegal weapon would only complicate matters. Allan had lost consciousness.

Staircase's aid wagon showed up without Caitlin on board, so the volunteers grabbed Allan and headed for I-90, administering O_2, and assisting his breathing with a Laerdal bag mask after they'd taped Fontana's makeshift patch in place. The house grew thick with cops.

Fontana scrubbed his bloodied hands in the kitchen sink and spoke softly to Laura's sister, Lisa, who for some reason had begun following him around the cramped house like a puppy. After clumsily dressing herself in one of the bedrooms, Allan's wife, Laura, collapsed onto the sofa and went mute. The volunteers driving the aid car had refused her passage. Relatives got in the way. A cop would take her to the hospital with red lights and siren.

"You all right?" Fontana asked the sister.

"They've only been married three months. Is *he* all right?"

"Gonna be touch-and-go. The men? What'd they want?"

"Bobby Joe was expecting them. At first I didn't know why he'd answer the door with a gun. But they came right in with those crummy hoods on, two of them, and pushed him around and just took his Ruger. On TV you hold a revolver on someone and they got some respect. Bobby Joe aimed it at the tall one, but he just walked right over and took it out of his hand. Kept punching him in the face. Laura started to get hysterical. She thought Bobby Joe could save her from anything. They were supposed to be business acquaintances of Bobby Joe's. He told them he thought he knew where it was, and that's when they tied him up."

"Where *what* was?"

"Nobody ever said what. They just kept asking, and he kept hedging, and finally I guess he got nervous enough to tell them."

"What'd he say?"

"Something about somebody else had it all. He wouldn't say who."

"Then what?"

"They forced us to undress. I think they wanted us without our clothes so we wouldn't run. And so it would frighten Bobby Joe. He thought they were going to molest Laura. I could tell that was the last thing on their minds. They were going to kill us."

"What was the meeting about?"

"I thought maybe it was about him getting fired. But it wasn't. Bobby Joe kept talking about buying a cabin in Montana. And a plane to fly there. Talking about buying a Cessna cash."

"Think you would recognize the one who got away?"

"Maybe his voice."

Across the room Bounty looked shaken. "This is a hell of a deal, Mac. What did any of us do to deserve this?" Mopping his face with his hands, Bounty sank back onto the sofa. A volunteer was patiently bandaging Laura's feet. The entranceway was dappled with bloody footprints. The phone was black with blood from Fontana's handprints.

Out back Fontana looked at the hot tub. Allan had spoken of turning into a prune in the tub, sipping beer and potting pinecones off the stump in his backyard with his .357. His ideal afternoon. One round of adolescent pooh-pooh jokes after another, too. Allan liked bathroom humor. Inside the house the Carpenters dropped onto the turntable. Maybe that's what happened when you played that sort of music. Maybe somebody gunned you. I should talk, thought Fontana, whose favorite singer was Shelley Fabares.

When the first King County officer asked if he'd obtained the license number of the van, Fontana removed a scrap of paper from his wallet and read off a license number. Bounty gave a curious, scrunched-up look.

"You sure that's it?" the officer asked. "You said it was getting dark."

"Positive."

"Shouldn't be too hard to get an owner off this."

From the divan Bounty grinned crookedly, his face looking particularly shopworn. Warren somberly escorted a contingent of brown shirts out across the pasture to show them the body. The medical examiner was called, Dummelow paged. Fontana led the dog outside and had him perform a general search. Two hundred yards from the house he located the Mac-10 stashed in some tall dry grass near a seldom used outhouse. There seemed to be nothing else to find. A reporter and camerawoman arrived just before Dummelow did and were told to wait at the edge of the graveled drive. They began filming Allan's plundered van from different angles, a bank of bright lights on a hand-held post bestowing an eerie glow to the otherwise dark yard. A zigzagging bat flitted in and out of the light.

Caravanning behind a couple of marked county cars, Dummelow showed up with Claude Pettigrew in his back seat. Even from the front porch, where Fontana waited, it was clear that Pettigrew had his hands manacled behind his back and that he was drunk.

"What's the story here, Mac?" Dummelow asked, climbing wearily out of his vehicle. He wore a gun at the waistband of his rumpled slacks, a pink striped shirt and tie.

"One dead. One on his way. Looks to me like the same guys who attacked Bounty last night out behind the Bedouin. This time they meant business."

"Dammit, I thought once we got the cuffs on the poisoner you people out here could relax."

"Him?" Fontana eyed Pettigrew in the police cruiser.

"All but confessed. Although I'm beginning to think he's a congenital liar."

"No doubt about that." Claude used to get potted and show off nude photos of a girl friend nobody else had ever seen or believed in. He'd found a mail-order house that supplied made-to-order Polaroids. Once he invited everyone in the department to his mother's for a picnic, roast pig, the whole bit. The volunteers bought the pig with money he'd supplied them. The kegs, etc. Two hundred and eighty bucks. Claude never showed. Two hours into the bash, with no food on the barbecue and everyone wondering what had become of him, Gil Cutty showed up with Claude in the back seat of his Roadrunner. He'd been sleeping off a bender in the alley behind the Red Fern Tavern. Since then Claude mailed out lots of invitations, but nobody ever came.

38

$512,000 IN HARD-WON WELL-SCRUBBED CASH

"I was suspicious of him from the first," said Dummelow. "After all, he was the chef at that little party where your man swallowed d-CON. He kept telling me nobody but he could have put anything in it. I thought it was possible he had this plan to go out in a blaze of glory and take you all with him. Maybe Wanda was writing him off. You guys had been razzing him about her. Get you all in one fell swoop. Himself, too."

"He didn't actually confess?" Mac asked.

"Not exactly. His room at his mother's house is full of materials on poisoning. We went to the Staircase library here and dusted all the books on the subject. Found his prints on almost all of 'em. He's got two cardboard trays of rat poison."

"That's all circumstantial, Chuck. He could have skimmed those books after the event. That would have been natural."

"Thing is, the town librarian called us. We dusted all the books she said he'd been reading. Then she brought one out of the back room that had been on the repair shelf for three weeks. Had his prints all over it. Tells all about arsenic. Give me a chance to go over his story with him. Guy's a screwball. I never saw so many X-rated videotapes. You know he corresponds with three different porno actresses in California? Mails them earrings and things?"

"There's a dead guy down in the pasture."

"Oh?"

"He was chasing the women with a gun. The other Dugan stayed here, and then, when I showed up, he shot Bobby Joe Allan. All I could do was put a couple of loads into his van as he was leaving."

"Who killed the one in the pasture?"

Fontana shrugged. "He threatened to kill the women. The gun was in his hand."

Pursing his lips, Dummelow turned and faced Fontana squarely. "You tell him to drop it?"

"Gave him three verses of 'Dixie,' Mirandized him, and signed him on with the local Moose lodge. Wasn't a whole lot of time. He could have shot me as fast as I shot him."

"I'll take a statement and run it by later to have you sign. So who were these guys?"

"Business acquaintances, according to the wife's sister."

"How'd you get here?"

"We were coming out to interview Allan. This whole thing is mixed up with the Ereckson organization."

Dummelow rocked on his heels and jammed his hands into his trouser pockets. "You talking about Lars Ereckson?"

"The same."

"Whooee."

"Mind if I talk to Claude?"

"Be my guest."

"You tell him about the library books?"

"Yep."

Fontana turned away from Dummelow and walked to the cruiser. "Hey, Claude," he said, after he'd leaned up beside the half-opened window.

"Can you believe this bullshit?" Claude didn't look up.

"Which bullshit?"

"This. Me. Arrested for trying to kill people."

"Not for trying, Claude."

"Well, I ain't done nothing."

"It looks bad, Claude."

"It was that damn woman."

"Say again?"

"Wanda set me up. I don't know how she done it, but by God, that gal set me up. I swear she did."

"How?"

"Look, will you look after my two gals?"

"How did she set you up?"

"My mom needs somebody to look out for her. Promise?"

"Yeah, I promise," said Mac, recognizing that the only lonely soul in the Pettigrew family who needed looking after was Claude. His mother waited on him hand and foot. With Claude in jail, she was in for a vacation.

"And Wanda. See to her, would you, Mac? You're about the only guy around I trust. Everybody else wants to bang her. You give me your promise, I know she's safe. You're a man of your word."

"I thought you said she set you up?"

"She did, goddammit. But I still love her." Pettigrew stared ahead and seemed to drift off in a fog of alcohol.

"How did she set you up?" Claude, who could sleep in a Tijuana bus station, began snoring. "Claude?"

It was midnight before County cut them loose. They drove to Fontana's in the GMC. Allan's place had been teeming with reporters and camera crews. A news helicopter overhead filmed the body in the field. Dummelow's troops obtained an ID on the owner of the van: Thursday Kowalski. Bounty had been wavering between contentment and an unwholesome irritability. Dummelow informed them that Claude Pettigrew had $512,000 stashed in seven different savings accounts across the state. That nine years ago Pettigrew had been arrested for assaulting a prostitute he claimed he'd been "dating." He assaulted her with a meat cleaver. Though badly beaten and cut, she refused to press charges. The thinking had been that Pettigrew's mother paid her off.

Shortly before they finished at the farm, Dummelow got a phone call from the hospital. Bobby Joe Allan had died on the table. That made two Staircase firefighters dead at Overlake Hospital in a week.

At Fontana's place Mac killed the motor in the GMC and said, "Warren, I've been thinking about this. Pete, Kingsley, Allan, and you. Who are you four? The basic response unit out of Staircase. This could easily be connected to some alarm."

"How are you figuring Ereckson into that equation? Pettigrew did the poisoning. They already nailed him for that. Leave Pete out of it. It being Pete who died Monday was clearly happenstance. It could have been all eight of us. It could have been two or three." Warren ran a meaty paw across his scalp. "No way has it got anything to do with the basic response team out of Staircase."

"We could go through the records. What else have we got?"

"Ereckson's who we've got. You're grasping at straws, Mac. They caught Claude. He'll confess. He mighta taken the shots at Kingsley. He might have hired these guys tonight. Or maybe Bobby Joe screwed Wanda. That would have set Pettigrew off. Hell, with his kinda money Claude coulda hired henchmen. You imagine five hundred grand stashed in seven different bank accounts?"

Fontana watched the ex-chief lumber to his Pinto in the dry midnight breeze.

"Mac?"

"Eh?"

"It all seems like a dream, don't it?"

"Sometimes."

"No, I don't mean just this week. I mean, everything. We're living a dream. None of it's real."

In the morning Brendan bounced onto Mac's bed earlier than Mac would have liked, squirmed onto Mac's chest, and said, "Waffles or pancakes? You're cookin', Mac."

"Pancakes, little man," said Mac, rolling over and trying to steal another couple of winks.

After breakfast he and the boy tossed rocks into the river, watched the dog wet his paws, then drove to the station. Mac kept the Remington by his side. At the fire station he used the telephone in his office.

"Jane?"

"Chief Fontana? Thank you for the flowers and the card. It was thoughtful."

"Jane, I hate to bother you . . . "

"If it's about Pete, anything I can say. Claude did it, right?"

"Where'd you hear that?"

"Gil Cutty phoned me up last night. Guess Claude got himself thrown in jail."

"I guess he did."

"So what can I do to help?"

"You been thinking about the last couple years with Pete?"

"That's all I been doin'."

"He had some grandiose dreams about suddenly coming into wealth?"

"Thought he was going to own a race car and things. And he was uneasy, too. Real uneasy. But how could he have known somebody was going to poison him?"

"He couldn't. When did this start?"

"Couple months ago."

"You think it might have been as long ago as a year?"

"Maybe a year ago. Yeah. It was in the winter because when we got the bad weather, he was talkin' about jetting to the Caribbean. I thought he was jokin'. I asked him how we was goin' to the sunny Caribbean when we couldn't afford dinner out at the Homestead. He just smiled. You know that smile Pete had." She was sniffling.

"I'll never forget it, Jane."

Kingsley Pierpont answered on the twentieth ring. "This better be good," he grumbled. Fontana had awakened him.

"You all right? I called you last night late, but you must have been out."

"I heard it on the news this morning at the cocktail lounge. I got my piece right here."

"I'm sifting through all the alarm records for the last three years. Since Pete got in. A lot of the narratives aren't complete. I want you here to explain the ones you can remember."

"What's goin' on, boss?"

"Don't know yet.

"Be up there in an hour."

39

HIS BEST FRIEND'S MOTHER

Fifty minutes later Kingsley showed up with his girl friend. Sunday morning. May's spirits rose when Fontana introduced her to Brendan. From the start they got on famously, if not flirtatiously. Brendan took her on a tour of Staircase, to include the popcorn machine and model rockets at the Mountain Hardware.

Fire and aid reports were warehoused in the bottom of a locker in the officer's room, each year bundled separately with thick knotted twine. Before examining the narratives, Fontana coordinated the record of alarms in the old daybooks with the chief's journal. None was missing. Lieutenant Allan couldn't fight fire, but he could put a judo hold on pen and ink.

Fontana had skimmed the narratives, sorted them. State fire reports NFIRS 1 in one stack. County aid forms in a second. He singled out as low priority any where none of the four—Kingsley

Pierpont, Pete Daugherty, Warren Bounty, or Lieutenant Allan—had responded. He marked anything attended by Caitlin.

"What's with Caitlin?" Kingsley muttered, after he'd settled down in the chief's office with a cup of coffee and his second toffee bar. He picked flecks of candy off his tan slacks and silk maroon V-neck shirt.

"Call it a hunch." Kingsley arched his thin brows. "Before we begin. Jane Daugherty said Pete was talking about sudden wealth. Allan, too. Know anything about that?"

"These boys dogged me from jump street. They got into some shit, odds are they didn't want me knowing. And there's no way they gonna share dinero with yours truly."

"I guess it's possible somebody shot at you to complete a sequence."

"Oh," said Kingsley. "Don't be thinkin' I'm just part of a sequence. Somebody fires on this black ass, I take it Mighty Joe serious."

Fontana had experimented with the high refrigerator in the beanery and discovered the only individuals tall enough to have pushed the d-CON tray to the back of the reefer without spilling the contents and without drawing attention to themselves by using a chair were Caitlin, Bounty, and Pettigrew. County had come up with no usable prints. Even Bounty had had to stand on tiptoe to expose the d-CON that first day. Allan, Daugherty, and the two volunteers who'd been present were too short. Wanda Sheridan was too short. Kingsley was too short, except that he had unusually long arms. Yet with people bustling through the station unexpectedly, the d-CON had to have been administered and put back with a certain degree of haste.

They had just over four hundred runs a year to sort through. Three years since Daugherty had been in. They eliminated false alarms where nothing of consequence occurred: outdoor burning mistaken for brush fires, etc. They whittled the piles down quickly, discarding repeat aid customers: Barbara, who routinely smacked her hubby with a skillet and had once speared him with a lamp; two winos, the Hutchinson brothers, living together near the library, who fell down every couple of months; oldsters with CHF; the DOAs in the nursing home."

Two hours into their search Dummelow showed up with his family, looking as though they'd just come from church. Fontana hadn't yet disinterred anything in the reports. Dummelow abandoned his heavyset wife and two teenage daughters in the car and walked into the station. "Chuck," said Fontana.

"Thought I'd stop in, have you sign this. Taking the family for a drive up to the pass while I got some time."

Fontana perused the typed statement, made and initialed two minor corrections, and signed it. "What happened with Claude?"

"Asked for his lawyer and clammed up. This afternoon I'm gonna rake his girl over the coals. I hear she's a pip. Thursday Kowalski? Lives in Redmond. Got his house staked out. The whole state's looking for that van. Physical evidence in the house? Nothing yet. We got tire tracks, some good ones. But no fingerprints. The bullet they dug out of your friend was a three-fifty-seven Federal jacketed soft point. It's torn up, but they may be able to match it to a gun. Trouble is, we need a gun to match it to. Phone records? Allan called the switchboard at the River Palace eight times yesterday."

"What about the guy I shot?" Pierpont cocked his head back and elevated his eyebrows. Fontana hadn't told Kingsley about the man in the pasture.

"No ID yet. Listen, I gotta hustle, the women are getting crabby. You, uh, be in touch." Dummelow stopped on his way out and looked out the window. "You know, for years I never visited this town but I always had a picture of it. When I was a kid, I was a ski instructor up at Crystal and one of the other instructors had come from here. Told me he screwed his best friend's mother. That was weird. I always used to think of that whenever anybody mentioned Staircase."

———

223

"And now?" Fontana asked.

"Now I still think of it." All three of them laughed.

When they were alone, Kingsley got serious. "You didn't tell me you was running around icing people." Fontana explained. When he finished, Kingsley said, "Don't want to rain on your parade, but I don't think this search is getting us anywhere."

"Mind if we keep looking?"

"I have an idea. Let's keep looking."

Kingsley looked as if he'd been dragged through a knothole. He yawned intermittently and was having a hard time staying awake. At two o'clock May and Brendan came back, wilted by the heat. Fontana and Kingsley were grasping at straws now, scrutinizing the reports two and three times. Nobody had made threats against firefighters. They found few alarms that had cost anyone a great deal of money, except for two houses that had burned to the ground. One belonged to an elderly woman descended from the O'Hallarans, who'd been among the first settlers in the area in 1858. The other had been a family of four who'd ceaselessly praised the department's valiant but misdirected efforts to save their house and puppy. Before Staricase FD could get to it, a $150,000 Ferrari had burned to cinders on the highway, but the driver had been insured.

They broke for lunch and a short walk to the South Fork, where they removed their shoes and dangled their feet in the river. Satan remained onshore and watched as if they were deranged. By the time Kingsley and May were ready to leave the sun was sliding low. They agreed to a barbecue at Fontana's: grilled hot dogs, stale jokes, and a begging dog that ate only from Mac's hand.

The brainstorm came just before dark.

Pierpont and May were still there, the four of them reclining in lawn chairs as a dwindling gaggle of teenagers splashed and frolicked a quarter mile upriver in what the locals called the Blue Hole. Another swimming spot was situated at their feet. The dike road didn't stretch this far, and Mac had posted the land for Mary.

The posting and the knowledge that Satan resided nearby kept trespassers at bay.

"Look," said Mac. "We've been trying to get a hook on these alarms all day, and we've come up with zilch. I think I know somebody who can help."

Relaxing with a Harvey Wallbanger, Kingsley shrugged. "We got time. Day is shot."

"It's so beautiful out here," said May, watching the setting sun color the mountain.

"Up for a drive, Brendan?" The boy scrambled out of his chair, rubber thongs beating his heels. They drove out the Moon Valley Road. The red Cherokee was in the driveway. The Jaguar wasn't.

When he pushed the doorbell, she called from out back. The entire front yard was shaded by the house and the tall trees. It took a while for her to come around the house. When she saw who it was, she slowed.

"Mac, what are you doing? Hello, Brendan."

"I'm in a bind, Rainy. Lieutenant Allan was killed last night."

"It's been all over the news. They think there may be a vendetta against firefighters in this town. The mayor was on the radio talking about calling in federal help."

"Mo can build a clock, but she can't tell time. Your husband around?"

"I don't know when to expect him."

"I'd like your help, Rainy."

"What on earth for?"

"You told me once you keep meticulous diaries."

She seemed hesitant, brushed an errant strand of hair out of her face. "And?"

"You said you kept every thought in there. Your moods. Who you talked to. How tall Benny was getting. Whether you had a quarrel with your husband."

"I didn't say that last."

"I extrapolated. Do I have the general idea?"

She nodded.

"I don't want to intrude on your private thoughts, but I'd like to know whatever they tell about Jim. Four people from the department have been attacked this week. Two are dead. I'm trying to track down the alarms they went on together. I've got it down to about sixty alarms I'd like to collate with your diaries. If I could give you the dates and you could look in your diary and tell me whether Jim was feeling or acting unusual, it might be a big help."

"You think somebody's going to try to kill Jim?"

"I don't know, Rainy." He had a sudden picture of last night's horrors visiting this house. Around the corner Brendan was chasing a hummingbird. "Brendan, get back here."

"You want me to spy on my husband?"

"It might save a life."

"You think Jim is involved? He was at work last night when Allan got hurt."

"In a general way, he's involved."

"Why don't you ask him?"

"He wouldn't tell me. You know that. Besides, your diaries are bound to be more accurate than his memory."

"What about the other people? Kingsley?"

"Kingsley's at my place."

She mulled it over. "I'll come, but only if Jim doesn't find out."

"My house?"

"Let me get something else on."

40

CHINOOK

F ontana's life was a series of aftershocks. It rocked him when
he faced Rainy in her yard and glimpsed her calm demeanor.
It rocked him beyond any of the recent tremors: Pete's death; the
bloodbath last night; the killings. In fact, shooting the man last
night had dissolved into a watercolor memory, something that
had merely needed to be done.

Sooner or later he realized the enormity of that event would
erode his tranquillity. He hated to believe that he, or anybody for
that matter, could kill so casually. Surely when things settled
down, the mental recriminations would ignite. For the deaths.
For what had happened to Rainy Friday night. For his inability
to ameliorate her pain.

At Fontana's a quaint coal-oil lantern threw a bleaching light
on their faces. Plugged into headphones and listening to a Sibelius
symphony, May lay on the divan in the living room. They hud-

dled around the kitchen table: Rainy, Kingsley, Mac, and a heap of paper work from the fire station. Mac would read the date off an alarm, Rainy would riffle through one of half a dozen palm-size journals, trace her index finger along the jottings, and pronounce everything normal that day and the next.

Tuckered out from an afternoon of showboating for May, Brendan slumbered between cool, tight sheets. Satan lay across the doorway on the porch, letting the chinook curry him. The drapes in the living room rustled.

Rainy had changed into shorts and a long-sleeved blouse, which partially concealed her prosthesis. She looked frazzled. Half an hour into their odyssey, she said, "Sorry to be obtuse, Mac. What are we looking for again?" Kingsley made his face go long and his eyes go big.

"Behavior of any type that is out of the ordinary. Any kind of mood swing. Either way."

"Jim does a lot of that."

"If he did it on or around any of these dates and you recorded it . . ."

"It would probably just be coincidental."

"Maybe."

Fifteen minutes later they struck pay dirt. January 12, two years ago. "Jim," said Rainy, "was in a reckless way for a couple of days on the thirteenth and fourteenth. I remember because we still had a lot of snow in Moon Valley and that usually depresses him. He refused to drive his Jaguar in it, so he ended up taking my Jeep to work."

"How about the twelfth?"

"Twelfth, thirteenth, and fourteenth. I don't know why I wrote it. 'Jim's been singing show tunes all day.' " She glanced at Kingsley, who was fingering his gold necklace. "Jim's pretty phlegmatic around the house."

"What else?"

"Just little things. Personal things." She seemed embarrassed.

She swung her head, threw her bronze-brown hair out of her eyes, and gazed directly into his face in a way that made him wish they were alone.

It was an aid report. Fontana skimmed the skimpy narrative. "DOA found in Mazda RX-7 WA. lic. #387-BCR. Rigor set in. Wallet on body gave ID as Campbell Sundt. 48 yr. old wt. ♂." The location said only, "I-90 EB at winery turnoff." In attendance: Lieutenant Bobby Joe Allan, Staircase FD; P. Daugherty; K. Pierpont; and paramedic J. Caitlin.

"Remember this one?" Mac asked, handing the nearly illegible gold carbon copy to Kingsley.

Kingsley slipped on his reading glasses, held the page at arm's length, and wheezed while he read. "We had maybe six inches of snow. I was driving. Up by the winery. Some kids cross-country skiing out by that lake up there called it in. Lake Renalt, I think it's called. Little bitty thing. They met us at the end of the road. I didn't want to take a chance on getting the Seagrave ditched up there on a logging road, so I stayed with the rig and the others hiked in.

"Not too many showed up, being snowy and all." Kingsley was alluding to the fact that volunteers were required to make a specific number of alarms a year or lose their status; thus all volunteer and off-duty responders were listed on the form, even if they had to make a tally on the back. There was a roster in the officer's journal as well. Regulars got overtime for each call attended while off duty. Allan made a lot of money on night calls, as had Daugherty, who had often slept over for the twenty bucks sleepers were allotted.

"What happened?" Mac asked.

Kingsley shrugged. "Like I said, I was with the rig, but I guess it was a DOA sitting behind the wheel of his car halfway into the lake. They walked up to it. Somebody snagged a rope on the Mazda and hauled it out. Took forever."

"What'd they say when they got back?"

"Not much. I figured they had that long walk to yak theirselves out."

"Anybody on that alarm besides Jim Caitlin, Daugherty, and Lieutenant Allan?"

"If that's what the form says."

"What'd this guy die of?"

"Guy didn't die of nothin', was just dead."

"Why would a guy be up there in the snow in the middle of nowhere?"

"Maybe he was getting his ashes hauled and croaked."

"Anybody see evidence of another person around the car?"

"Not that I recall." The trio squandered another half hour poring over the rest of the reports. They found nothing else that correlated with anything in Rainy's journals.

By the time May and Pierpont left it was almost dark. May was anxious to get back to Seattle, said she had papers to go over before work tomorrow. Fontana bade farewell in the driveway. When he turned around, Rainy was watching him from the porch with one of those looks women gave. He didn't know if it was motherly, womanly, or mere casual appraisal. In the west the sky was a deep royal blue, the first two or three stars winking overhead. Warm as it had been at noon, the wind tousled her hair.

"Show me your river," she said.

As they walked toward the Middle Fork, he absentmindedly raised a guiding hand to the small of her back but dropped it before it made contact. Satan tagged along. The lights of the house were barely visible through the poplars. He'd latched the front door to keep raccoons out. Brendan was asleep.

They reached the bank where they'd had the barbecue, four lawn chairs half sunk in the sand, the metal grill long since cooled on the rocks. The river was silvery. Shortly the moon would peep over the south-slanting wooded ridge of the mountain.

The river swooped into a bend as it reached Fontana's property, formed a sandy hole forty feet across, then churned out again, rippled over the rocks, and rounded the bend toward Mary's property. In better times kayakers cavorted in these rapids. Now the white ripples near the far bank were shallow enough for an adult to wade. The last burnt apricot cloud to the west had turned slate.

"God, it's hot," Rainy said, with an uncharacteristic lack of piety. "Feel that air coming down the pass as it picks up speed? It's like a blow dryer." She raised both arms, fluffed her hair, and stretched. From behind he watched the arch of her back, the graceful swing of her hair.

"You okay, Rainy?"

She pivoted in the sand and gave him a curious look. "Why wouldn't I be?"

"You've been hiding out."

"Don't be silly. We were dancing at the Bedouin just two nights ago."

"Jim seemed put out Friday." She turned toward the river. He could smell perfume intermixed with the heat from the hills. "Why don't you leave him, Rainy?"

"What did you say?"

"Why don't you leave Jim?"

"Stay out of it."

"I know I'm risking our friendship. It's because of that friendship that I'm saying this. I wonder about Benny."

"Benny's all right!" she stammered. She glanced at him and then back to the river, surprised at her own sudden emotion. Satan was at the water, testing it with a paw. "You swim here or what?"

"Couple times a week when it's this warm. Leave him."

"This is not a topic for discussion. Certainly not us two alone here."

"He's hurt you, Rainy."

She wheeled and made an effort to walk back the way they'd come. Fontana grabbed her good arm and held it firmly. "Please take me home," she said.

"You need money? I can loan you five thousand."

"You don't know what you're talking about." She was close to tears.

"Damn you, Rainy. You're suffering."

"You don't know anything about it."

"I know what happened Friday after the Bedouin."

Alarm fluttering in her blue eyes, she stepped back, lost her balance in the soft sand, and almost toppled. "What do you know? There's nothing to know."

"You've got to leave. He beats you."

"You're guessing. I don't need to hear any more of this." She tried to wrench herself away. He grasped her shoulders. When his fingers touched her back, an involuntary gasp escaped her lips. He released her. "Mac, you don't want to get involved."

"I am involved."

"Jim is different from anyone you've ever known. I can guarantee that. You don't know what you might be letting yourself in for."

"I can't imagine an intelligent, independent woman like yourself sticking with that cretin."

"He isn't. It's just . . . so very private."

"Your back must be a mess."

The pitch of her voice rose in disbelief. "What?"

"He was driving erratically. I was afraid you were both going to end up in a ditch, so I followed. I saw what happened in your window. I didn't want to, but I was there."

She didn't raise her hands from her sides. Tears tripped off her cheeks, striping her shirt, dropping into the sand. He wished he could undo everything that had happened. He groped for words. She began fumbling with the buttons of her shirt, working from the bottom.

"What are you doing? Forget it, Rainy."

Working the buttons, she refused to look up.

"Forget it."

When she finished, she pulled the shirt open, shook it out

where it'd been tucked into her shorts and dropped the sleeves off both arms simultaneously. The material wafted to the earth. Avoiding his eyes, she turned and showed her back. At first he couldn't discern anything but her silhouette. Then he saw the long red welts. Half a dozen of them. Uglier than he'd imagined, they stretched in parallel rows from her shoulders down along her right flank.

Without turning, she heeled her shoes off, dropped her prosthesis, and took five careful steps into the pool below. When she was far enough out, she knelt and launched herself into the depths, head held above the surface. Satan saw it and plunged in. Swimming out in a long, graceful arc, she submersed herself, then dipped her face forward, raised her head, and wiped the excess water off her cheeks and eyes. Now he couldn't tell what was tears and what was snowmelt.

"I thought you liked to swim," she said so softly he almost did not hear.

He stripped off his shirt, doffed his shoes and walked into the pool in his shorts, dived under, and surfaced, blowing water across the smooth, flat plane between them. His blowing stippled the glassy pool with droplets of spray. It wasn't nearly cold enough to erase the heat of the day. Rowing her arms below the surface at her sides, she watched him as he swam toward her.

"You know I'm not going to sleep with you," she said.

He kicked back and floated face up. "Then we'd better not make love. I always fall asleep after making love."

41

THE STRANGENESS

Paddling in a quick, bobbing rhythm that was surprisingly graceful, Satan circled the duo. He swam east until he'd hooked into the gentle rush of the stream. He let the current spin him around in a large arc that propelled him back across the water hole. Steaming past Fontana, he beelined across the pool, climbed out, and shook himself raggedly on the bank.

Great, thought Mac, you old booger—you're going to stink all night. After gnawing at a flea on his flank, the dog wandered back up the path toward the house as if he owned the property. The breeders and trainers called it self-right. He knew he belonged. It was a quality no dog or human could fake. Not an ounce of uncertainty in that canine. He could walk into any room and look powerful, confident, afraid of nothing. Should the boy awaken and call for Mac, Satan would howl. Should a car approach the house, the headlights would be visible through the trees.

———

Bright enough to read a newspaper by, the moon rose slowly. Submerged so that only her head showed, Rainy swept languorously around the pool, watching him. The stars began to emerge in the sky, pinpoints growing more pronounced as the deep blue-black turned darker. But for the moon, the stars would have kidnapped the night. Together Rainy and Mac fell into a torpor.

Rainy swam close. A nighthawk darted over the pool, scooping insects out of the air. The moving part of the stream to the east gurgled. Treading water, he moved in close to her and bumped his nose against hers. She kissed him, a mere peck. The moonlight made the hair wetted back on her head appear blond.

With a small, sly smile of knowing she stroked out into the pool.

"You want to know about Jim? Why I stay?"

"I guess I do."

"I'll need that money you offered."

"Anything I have is yours."

"Some cash is all. You were right, you know."

"About what?"

"He abuses me." Dipping her head back in the water, she floated, then propelled herself partway back to him. Her hand made a kerchunk sound as it slapped the surface. The wet hair gave her face a different shape. It looked longer. "We've been married five years. I had Benny with Gordon. That didn't even last twelve months. So when Jim gave me his whirlwind rush, I fell for it without seeing the man behind the barrage of flowers and smooth talk and fancy restaurants. Oh, he was a charmer. After our wedding he was wonderful for about six months.

"I'd had the one bad marriage, and I was determined to make this one work, even if living with Jim was going to require patience. He'd had these moods before, but he'd leave the house when he got one. Once for three days. Never explained it. I thought it was something he had to work out on his own. Then over a period of weeks he grew worse. He mouthed off with things

I couldn't believe anybody would think, much less say. He claimed my girl friend wanted all three of us in bed together. Never any witnesses when he said these things. Always just him and me. But he kept threatening to say them to Rose if I didn't stop being friends with her. He puts on one face for the world, but beneath it all he's very different.

"Having endured several of his tantrums, I decided to visit a counselor. After one session on my own Jim agreed to come. It was the shock of my life. I figured I'd explain Jim's problems and then Jim would deny some of them and admit others and gradually the counselor would see.

"But he warped everything I said until I was the one who looked unhinged. While he wrapped that counselor around his little finger, I started to recognize phrases and attitudes he'd used courting me. He mentally seduced the counselor. Whatever I said came out sounding like I was in the wrong. Suddenly Jim wasn't having moods. It was me who was difficult. He even convinced her I was delusional, that I'd taken drugs before our marriage and was having flashbacks. He convinced her I'd been wild and that he had settled me down. Flat-out lies. Jim's always been a conniver, but that afternoon I realized he could talk his way out of a steel trap.

"As soon as we were away from the psychologist's offices in Bellevue, he pulled the car to the side of the road and without any warning put both hands around my neck. He hadn't said a word since we left. Neither had I. The look in his eyes. I just knew I was about to be murdered. He squeezed until I almost passed out. And this on the freeway. People driving by. People watching him. I saw them looking. Nobody stopped. Later I realized he'd done that on purpose, wanted me to see people witnessing it and to know nobody would help. He wanted me to feel helpless."

"Go on."

"When I started to pass out, he let go. I don't know why. Just like that he let go. Dragging him off to the counselor, he said, would never happen again. Or to the police or to anybody. Our problems would remain *our* problems. The look on his face. I knew he would murder me without batting an eye. It scared me so bad I didn't even want to think about running. I couldn't imagine what he'd do to me or Benny if he caught us. I settled down and tried to do the things Jim wanted.

"He'd come home from work and search the house for signs of a man. You can't believe how insecure he is. He'd put on white gloves and inspect for dust. Under the beds. If he found any, I had to do the house again, vacuuming, sweeping, mopping. The strange thing was, after he'd grabbed me by the neck, he went almost a year without another flare-up. I was grateful but still frightened. Yet over time I convinced myself that it wasn't going to happen again.

"For a while I was stupid enough to believe he'd scared himself by how close he'd come. About a year after we'd seen the counselor I decided I'd had enough, that I was tired of kowtowing to this tyrant. I told him I wanted a divorce. God only knows where I got the courage. I must have been crazy. I'd talked to the pastor, and he'd promised to intercede if I had any problems.

"Jim said fine. A divorce was fine. But I'd have to wait two days before I left. He gave me some mumbo jumbo about having dependents in the house until a certain date for work. I was nuts not to get out of there that minute, with just Benny and the clothes on my back. Afterwards the pastor got concerned, and Jim had a long talk with him. From then on, whenever I tried to complain to Pastor Taber, he'd get real still. You know how people stare off into space when they don't want to hear what you're saying? Jim had seduced him, too."

"It's got to do with your hand, doesn't it?" said Fontana.

"You want me to tell it, or are you going to guess?"

42

KISSING DRY ICE

Rainy said, "I have this recurring nightmare that I finally gather up the nerve to tell someone and they don't believe a word of it."

"I believe you."

"Why?"

"I trust you."

"It was a Saturday afternoon, and he asked if I'd help with some yard work before I left. He was very polite. It did seem a little curious, but Benny was napping and I was done packing and I couldn't see the harm. I was weeding the flower beds, and he was running the lawn mower.

"I felt so stupid. I should have left on the sly, but my original arrangements caved in, and he was being so urbane about it all it put me off my guard. It was a rotary mower with a blade underneath that whirled around like an airplane propeller. God, it made that horrible metallic coughing sound lawn mowers make when they pick up something that doesn't belong in there. I can still hear it."

"Oh, God."

"When I looked up, Jim was grinning a little Cupid smirk as if he'd just pulled the cat's tail. He'd stepped on my arm, pinned it down, and just pulled the mower across it. Such a weird little smile for such a ghastly thing. Then the pain shot through me, and I started hyperventilating. I almost bled to death. He wrapped it in a dressing he had with him, walked me to the car, and went inside to wake Benny from his nap. Driving to Overlake Hospital in Bellevue, he went ninety the whole way. As if he cared."

"Rainy."

"Has Jim already convinced you I'm lying? He sets traps for me with everyone. No, don't say it. He told you that I lost my hand in a train wreck and that I'm a pathological liar. That I'm very touchy about the subject."

"Car accident. He didn't say anything about you lying. He said you were touchy. I knew that wasn't true. Half the time you go around without the prosthesis."

"He tells everyone something different. That's how he is. He's so confident he can gull you he doesn't even bother to keep track of his stories. And you know what? He's right. He can gull anybody. If you'd caught him in the lie, he would have come up with some glib explanation. 'Rainy told me to say it was a car accident. She doesn't like the visual image the other creates.' "

"But this is such a small town."

"You mean, he might get caught lying? He does. People just go right on falling into his net. He's like that. You know him. What did you think before you got to know me?"

"You're right. I didn't see it."

Fontana breaststroked close and cupped her teary face in his hands. He kissed each salty cheek. "You've held this in for what, three years?"

"We both knew the accident wasn't an accident, but we never spoke of it. Isn't that bizarre? Not a word. He said it was too bad I'd had my problem—meaning my hand—but if I tried to leave him again, he'd grab Benny. That I'd never see him again. He wasn't bluffing."

"What happened in the hospital?"

"Jim was affectionate in front of the doctors, blaming himself. They never even talked to me about how it happened. Oh, he was solicitous. A roomful of flowers. Chocolates. I hate chocolates. Cards. Balloons. The nurses thought he was a saint. The story went around that if he hadn't been with me, I would have died. That first afternoon, as he took Benny out of my sight, I'd never been so frightened. My hand all wrapped up. I was drugged to the gills. Jim carrying little Benny."

"So you lay in a hospital bed trying to figure out your future?"

"Don't kid yourself. I thought about burying a knife in his gizzard. I thought about it, but I knew whatever I tried I'd just pull back at the last second and he'd catch me. That's when I found the Lord. Jim knows I know he's a psychopath. He couldn't care less. He knows I can't leave. He'd find me. Benny would disappear. I believe that with all my heart. It's as if when I married him, I kissed dry ice. I can't get loose of it."

"How often does he hit you, Rainy?"

She looked around at the trees and hills, as if someone were going to answer for her. "Almost never. You shouldn't have been there."

"Couldn't help it."

"You know, early in the morning he came back and apologized? Wanted to make love. I told him if he touched me, I'd kill myself. I'd kill Benny. That I'd post letters to all of his friends and the authorities explaining why. I've got the letters written. I showed him one."

"Benny's in Tacoma with Jim's mother?"

"Until the end of the week. Florence has no idea what a creature she raised, though she's been exposed to enough clues."

While the fervor of her story subsided, they moved close, treading water, only their heads above the surface. The moon radiating off the river upstream was so bright it resembled the light from a car's headlights. They floated side by side on their backs. Stargazing.

It came without warning.

The projectile entered the water at the lip of the pool.

It made a zip sound like a small fish breaking water. Except this was too swift for a fish. One ear had been half submerged, so he heard it zinging above and beneath the surface. Quick and shallow like a sharp stick scratching the sidewall of a tent.

A bullet.

It sent a surge of adrenaline through Fontana. He wasn't sure of the trajectory, but he had a feeling it had come from upriver. He hadn't heard the pop, but he would listen carefully for the next one. If there was a next one.

"Rainy!" he whispered, grabbing her forearm and towing her quickly toward a large smooth rock overlooking the south end of the pool. Here the water was only waist-deep. The rock was half the size of a Volkswagen bug. If he was correct about the trajectory, they'd be safe until the shooter changed positions.

"What is it, Mac?" He'd never seen her so frightened. Shivering. Owl eyes. "Somebody's here? God. If it's Jim, he'll kill us. You don't know that man."

"Stay where you are." Fontana laid his palms on the smooth surface of the rock, still warm from the day's sun, and propelled himself around the west face of it.

The woods ran almost to the dry riverbed's edge. In some places saplings had sprouted in the riverbed. Seventy yards away the dike began, topped by a single-lane gravel road built up on a mass of trucked-in mountain rock. Designed by Army engineers and Washington State flood specialists, the graveled dike extended a mile before it branched off to the main road.

He heard the shot as a second bullet zinged past, zippered the quiet pool behind. The slug ricocheted smoothly off the surface of the water and bounced toward the house. He thought he saw the muzzle flash from behind a fallen tree at the end of the dike road. It sounded like a small-caliber rifle. Maybe a long-barreled pistol. In the moonlight he caught a glimpse of what looked like a white V-neck T-shirt. Then it was gone. Another muzzle flash. A bullet chunked against the sandy shore.

He cataloged his options. He was wet and shoeless. He had Rainy to protect. The closest weapon, the city's shotgun, was up at the house.

Another round whirred close to his ear and made a fizzing sound in the water behind. He turned and saw the ripples. Naked back propped against the slick rock, Rainy had half risen, arms at her sides, her body shielded by tons of river-smooth boulder. She was shivering violently. Mac slid in front of her and embraced her, his lips brushing hers as he spoke. "You're not going to die, Rainy."

"It's Jim. I know it's Jim. Somebody's shooting at us, aren't they? Jim's got a roomful of rifles. We're going to die."

Mac gave her another hug. "Don't count on it, darlin'." He turned his head, stuck two wet fingers in his mouth, and whistled shrilly.

When he peeked around the huge rock, he heard stomping in the woods, twigs cracking. The shooter was retreating. He knew what was going to happen. He knew Fontana. Knew the dog. Ears alert, Satan came bounding down the trail from the house, watching Fontana for cues. "Satan! Bad Guys. Out there! *Fass! Fass!*"

Satan perked up, took a few steps, and scanned the woods on this side of the river. "*Suche! Fass!*" shouted Mac.

The dog began running. Another bullet hit the rocks and chirred into the distance. He was shooting at Satan now. Fool. The dog would zero in on him in no time. Like all police dogs,

Satan had been trained to ignore gunfire. In the dark he'd be hard to hit.

"Stay here." Fontana waded to the sandy bank, snatched his moccasins in one swift movement, and ran barefoot down the well-packed path toward the house. He heard Satan barking in the distance. Damn. He hated sending the dog to what might be his death, but he had no choice. When he got to the house, he reached inside the front door and grabbed the Remington, jacked a round into the chamber, then slipped into his moccasins. He checked Brendan's room, stuffed a flashlight into his wet hip pocket, and jogged outside. He could hear the barking as it receded into the woods.

When he got back to the pool, Satan was deep in the woods. He heard the muffled woofing. He couldn't be sure, but it sounded to him as if the dog had gone in the wrong direction. Wouldn't the shooter head south and then west toward the road? Satan was due west of the shooter's original position. It had to be wrong.

"Rainy? You okay?"

Moonlight refracted off her wet skin. Rainy said, "What are you going to do?"

"Follow Satan. You go to the house and lock the door. Douse the lights. Don't open for anyone."

"I'll call the police."

"No phone. I won't be long."

He used the riverbank for cover for the first seventy yards. The barking had ceased now. It had been deep in the woods, so he wasn't worried about getting ambushed. Satan had chased the sniper into the thickets. When Fontana reached the end of the dike road, he spotted an abandoned pair of beat-up binoculars with a broken cord.

Behind he could see Rainy's half-naked form on the beach as she knelt to pick up her shirt. The dog remained silent. Maybe he had the Dugan in his teeth. A shepherd couldn't bark and hold an arm, too. Fontana found a trail through the woods. He knew it led directly to the macadam county road. A whiplike branch hit him in the face. Once he penetrated the trees they thinned. The underbrush became sporadic. He cut his bare legs on a sticker vine, could smell the sweet, sublime odor of rotting blackberries. He'd gone 150 yards, shotgun poised, when the dog came trotting back. Alone.

He knelt and patted the animal to see if he was hurt. He wasn't. "What's the matter with you, Satan? Where is he?" The dog looked perplexed, twisted his head, dropped his tail, whined. "Go get him! Get the bad guy! *Suche!*"

Satan spun around and began sniffing the trail with renewed enthusiasm, as if he hadn't a hint what he was looking for. Damn dog. It was obvious he'd contacted something a few minutes ago. But not the sniper. There were bobcats in these hills. Possibly a coon. Fontana had been cautioned about police dogs getting side-tracked. Perhaps he'd mixed up the shooter's track with one of the hundreds of other tracks that had been laid down in the past few days. All week these woods and the riverbank had been crawling with swimmers. Maybe the shooter had intimidated him with that potshot. It wasn't supposed to be possible, but Satan was full of surprises.

Stopping every twenty yards to listen, Fontana made his way through the trees. As he approached the road, he heard a car engine turn over. He sprinted through a copse and fought his way onto the pavement. Hundreds of feet away by now, the car was driving without lights. The silhouette was low-slung. Possibly a sports car. But it was too far to tell. The animal looked up at him, curled in a circle, and whined. Then Satan sat and gazed up at him expectantly.

"Damn your hide, Satan! What the hell did all that training do for you?" The dog hung his head and laid his ears back. His tail drooped. "I told you to search, damn you! Booger!"

Fontana leaned down and scratched his muzzle, but the dog turned away. It wasn't his fault he was getting old. You had to keep an animal like this in the business, or he lost it. Same with humans. In fact, he was just as rusty as the mutt.

With a low growl, Satan tracked some crushed grass near the edge of the road. Fontana went over to the dog, who seemed, to judge by his body language—the active tail, quick looks in Fontana's direction—to be telling him something. Fontana marched the flashlight beam along the roadside.

Two oil spots on the edge of the road. If the sniper had moved over another three inches, the oil would have dripped into the brown weeds and Fontana never would have seen it. Two speckles, one slightly larger than the other. The same thing he'd found in Seattle after someone had fired on Pierpont. He would come back and take samples.

43

I'VE KILLED FOR LESS

After scooping up Brendan, Fontana lugged his drowsy, blanket-shrouded form next door. Mary rarely retired before four in the morning. When he knocked, she was bickering with her mother over what to watch on the tube. As was her habit, Mary's mother sat three feet in front of the TV and commandeered a Gene Autry movie. A few months shy of a hundred, Mary's mother never dressed in anything but a nightgown and store-bought teeth. "Who's there?" the old dame asked, squinting. She was half blind. Almost deaf.

Mary yelled, "Oh, Mother, it's just Mac and his boy."

Rainy, who'd never met Mary before, smiled nervously. Brendan had conked out and from his stupor mumbled, "Mommy." It chilled the room to silence. Mary busied herself fluffing pillows on a couch for the boy. Rainy gave Mac a sympathetic look but broke it off when she saw his eyes.

When they climbed into the truck, Rainy said, "What if he's waiting at my house?"

"Don't jump the gun. It could have been anybody. At that range and at night I doubt the gunman knew for sure who we were. He knew my house was there. And he knew Satan. My guess is he was reconnoitering, wanted to get at me, saw us down there, and decided to do it then. You just happened to be there."

"But what if it was Jim?"

"We'll drive to your mother-in-law's in Tacoma. Pick up Benny."

"He'd call Florence and spook her. He could talk her into anything. Benny wouldn't be there. We need a plan."

Weaving shadowy strands of fact with needles of conjecture, Fontana began to wonder what information Rainy was withholding. The more he thought about her attitude, the more he thought she was holding something back. Was it possible she could prove Caitlin the poisoner? Was that why Caitlin had dragged his feet taking care of Daugherty? Or did it have something to do with Pettigrew and Wanda?

As he drove out the Moon Valley Road, Fontana picked up the binoculars he'd found on the dike road and dangled them by the broken strap. "Don't touch 'em. Recognize these?"

"Should I?"

"Thought Jim might have an old beater pair he used hunting."

"He does, but I wouldn't recognize them."

The warm winds had already dried Rainy's hair, frizzing it in the open window. She sat apart from him against the passenger-side door as if she were an awkward teenager after a bum date. In her lap she carried her prosthesis. He glanced at her profile. It wasn't hard to imagine eliminating Jim for her.

When they reached her house, the Jaguar was still gone. Rainy let out a sigh, her entire body relaxing until it went limp. "I think I'm getting paranoid, Mac."

"I'd say that's a reasonable reaction to getting shot at in the middle of the night."

"No, I mean about Jim. That wasn't Jim out there. You said it yourself."

"I didn't exactly say that. I said it could have been anyone."

"But it wasn't. How would he have known where we were? How would he have known I was with you? And even so, Jim wouldn't have handled it so crudely. Jim is a connoisseur of pain. He would have waited until he had me alone. If he was going to shoot at you, he would have done it after worming the facts out of me. And I don't think he would have missed. Whoever shot at us tonight was scared to get closer."

"Whoever it was knew about Satan. They didn't know where he was, so they kept their distance."

"It wasn't Jim."

"I'd feel better if you'd get a few things and stay somewhere else tonight. Leave him a note if you want."

"I'll stay here. I'm not ready for the final move." She was preoccupied with a letter somebody had tucked into the half-loop door handle. Folded around the letter was a piece of typing paper with a penciled message. Rainy read it. "From the Muhlhausers. Jim's been waiting for this. Now I know he wasn't here. He wouldn't have left this. It's got something to do with their business deal. Muhlhauser says here he came by at six. Just a few minutes after you picked me up."

"That makes me feel a little better."

After she'd unlocked the front door, Fontana said, "You know where he keeps his hunting gear?"

"The binoculars?"

"I'd appreciate it if you took a look."

She went into the garage and rummaged around out of sight. When she emerged, she said, "I can't find them."

When they heard the Jaguar, Fontana was in the driveway, preparing to leave, Rainy a bloodless shadow in the doorway. Caitlin pulled the red Jag up behind Rainy's Jeep, turned off the lights, let the car idle down, then got out. Caitlin had a large Doberman with him. When the dog leaped out, growling and straining at the leash, Satan's ears pricked up. He took a tentative step forward, barked throatily. Fontana had seen this before. Next was blood.

"Heel! *Fuss!*" Satan didn't heel, but he didn't attack either, heeding some sort of dog ethos barring assaults on a tethered animal. Husky as Caitlin was, he had a difficult time controlling the Dobe.

"Simba! Simba! Down!" He jerked on the leash and slapped the dog across the side of the skull with a thermos. The thermos imploded. Glass rattled inside.

Knotting up a handful of Satan's fur at the base of his neck, Fontana opened the GMC door and walked him in. The German shepherd vaulted the front seat, snarled, and bared his teeth in the back window. Fontana slammed the door.

Caitlin dragged the dancing Doberman around Fontana in a large arc before knotting his leash to a sapling at the corner of the garage. When her husband's back was turned, Fontana motioned to Rainy. He wanted her to leave with him. She gave a slow, grave shake of her head. She knew Caitlin better than he. It had to be her decision.

"My brother-in-law's Doby would have turned him to mincemeat," said Caitlin.

"Not bloody likely."

Caitlin glared at Fontana across the driveway, a practiced look designed to unnerve. For the first time Fontana saw what Rainy had been talking about. He'd never seen the stare before, not from smiling, joshing Caitlin. The look was a weapon.

Jim Caitlin strutted to the wall of the garage and took a chunk of wood from the woodpile, hurled it at the barking Doberman to shut him up, missed. His torso in shadow, he laid his arm on the woodpile, fist out of sight behind the lip of the garage. Fontana hadn't realized how bright the moonlight was until Caitlin stepped out of it. "What are you doing here?" Caitlin asked.

"Came to warn you. Somebody took a shot at me less than an hour ago."

"Your place?"

"By the river."

Caitlin absorbed the news, turned, and pitched the thermos at the savagely barking Doberman. It connected hard against his snout. The dog knelt and looked away. Satan had stopped barking.

"You're just making him mean," Fontana said.

"You train your animals. I'll train mine." Caitlin wore shorts, penny loafers without socks, and a T-shirt as if he'd doffed a dressier shirt. "Whatcha doing with the bird gun?"

"I get ticked when people shoot at me."

"Well, hell's bells. I didn't do it. Put the piece away." Caitlin's expression was lost in the shadows. "What the hell's going on out here, Fontana?"

Mac kept the gun and glanced at Rainy, who shied back from the doorway. "What do you mean?"

"I mean, all these people getting killed. Pete I could believe. Somebody screwed up and dropped rat poison into the chow. But Bobby Joe? I heard somebody shot at Kingsley, too. What the hell's going on?"

"You know as much as I do."

"Why would I know what the devil's got in his pocket? You're the sheriff."

"Allan was at the River Palace the afternoon he was killed. He called there several times after he got home. I understand you were there this week, too." Rainy stirred in the doorway. It was the first she'd heard of it. She glanced toward her husband's voice, but Caitlin was out of her line of sight in the shadows.

"You came out here and bothered my wife for this? Why didn't you call?"

"No phone. You know that, Jim. 'Sides, I wanted to warn you myself. Scout the area. This guy sneaked up on my house from the back, up through the woods."

"Sounds like a local."

"I thought the same thing."

"Like a hunter. You're lucky he didn't plug you."

"What do you know about the River Palace?"

"Had lunch there, Tuesday, Wednesday. I forget."

"You met Lars Ereckson?"

"Wouldn't know the man if I stepped on him."

"I've got witnesses who place you with him."

"They better not." The menacing stare again. " 'Cause I don't know the man." Still hidden behind the short wall, Caitlin's right hand moved slightly. It seemed a good place to keep a hideout gun. Or maybe he was just hefting another stick of wood to fling at the Doberman. "I don't like liars. Bring your grubby little witnesses and let me see them."

"We'll have to do that before this is through."

"Looking forward to it. So what happened tonight?"

"Like I said. Somebody shot at me."

"What else?"

"Nothing."

"Got any witnesses? You weren't alone?"

Fontana shifted the shotgun. "Yeah, I was."

"Get a look at him?"

"I chased him. I didn't get a real close look, no."

Caitlin smirked, shifted his stance. Fontana felt so very calm that it scared him. It reminded him of the deceptive calm of a small southern town before a lynching. Mentally he enumerated all the horrors Caitlin had wreaked upon Rainy.

"Yeah," said Caitlin. "Well, you told me. I'm warned."

"Been out working on a car with your dad?"

"I had things to do."

"Just asking."

"Well, I just had things to do."

Fontana felt an urge to level the Remington and let fly. It wouldn't have surprised him in the least to find himself standing over Jim Caitlin with an empty shotgun, no memory of how the gun had been emptied.

Glancing quickly at Rainy, Fontana tried to read her look without giving anything away, tried to pass his eyes over her as if he were casually sweeping his gaze around the yard. Clearly she wanted him to depart. He walked to the truck, got in, turned the engine over. When he looked back up at the house from the road, he couldn't see either of them. He felt as queasy as if he were falling through a mile of night sky.

Down the road kids were sleeping outside in a tent in the front yard of one of the houses on the main road. Behind him on this slab of the mountain, goats lived in caves, were frequently seen grazing on the high, impossible cliffs. "Teen Angel" came on KVI. Satan should have been baying. "Hey, old boy," said Mac, turning to the dog. Satan looked away, peered out the window as if there were something of special interest out there. "Hey, boy. Oooooooouuuuooa."

Satan didn't even flick an ear, refused to look from the window. You didn't call this dog booger without getting snubbed for it.

44

FIVE
BRAIN-DEAD FIREFIGHTERS

Heavy, thumping footsteps approached the front door. Fontana shielded his eyes against the naked porch light with a salute. "Mac?"

He wore only a half-zipped pair of trousers, his soft, hirsute belly bulging out the doorway. Warren Bounty's hair was sweaty and tousled. Earlier in the week he'd kept every door and window in the house open. It was a factor of his fear that the bungalow was sealed. The neighbors' houses were closed, too. Caulked with fright. Rabid paranoia in a town that didn't know what crime was.

"Sorry if I woke you, big guy," said Fontana. "Little less than an hour ago some Dugan took shots at me down by the river."

"God, Mac." Bounty wiped his perspiring face with a large, coarsened palm. "That's nuts. Did you get 'em?" Fontana shook his head. He recognized a pair of sunglasses with a broken hinge on Warren's coffee table.

———

"They screwed up when they ran off. Left some binoculars that are bound to have prints. Plus a couple of the slugs went into that pool under our beach. I'll snorkel around in there tomorrow with Brendan and we'll match them if we have to fire a bullet from every weapon in the county."

"Brendan's okay?"

"Yeah."

"I'm glad. Anything ever happened to that boy of yours, I think I'd want to die."

"I appreciate that, Warren."

"You know you two are like family. I talked to the county police this evening. They told me they haven't located the van from Allan's place yet."

"They will."

"Mac, when they do, I want first crack at the bastards," said Warren, scratching his stomach. "We gotta kill them."

"What happens happens, Warren. I'm not going to stand here and plan to kill somebody."

"Listen, Mac. Nobody's going to pat your back and flour your nuts because you turn this guy over to the police. Everybody wants to see dimes in his eyes."

"I warned Caitlin already. I'm gonna call Kingsley as soon as I leave here."

"I'll call him. Jim Caitlin? Been out there tonight?"

"If I get killed in the next couple of days, do me a favor, Warren."

"What's that?"

"Don't rule Caitlin out."

" 'Cause a you and his wife?"

"Because of a lot of things."

"They're trying to murder every firefighter in town, you know that, Mac? Reminds me of the time down south the whole dog-gone fire department ran out on the highway to see what this barrel was rolled off a truck. Turned out to be one of the most potent pesticides known to man. In concentrated form. Leaking all over the place. This was maybe twenty, twenty-five years ago. Every man jack touched that barrel ended up brain-dead. Five of 'em. The substance went right through their skin to their nervous system and ate their brains. The whole department from the chief on down ended up in the vegetable ward. Scary as hell. Trouble is, this shooting tonight blows your theory, don't it?"

"What theory is that?"

"You said this all had something to do with things happened before you got here. Now they're shootin' at you."

"I hadn't thought about that."

"You better. And you better start thinking psychopath while you're at it."

"What are you getting at?"

"You've been trying to unscramble this as if it makes some sort of sense."

"And you're saying maybe a psychopath is behind it?"

"Think about it."

"Warren? Warren?" It was a sleepy, throaty voice, the kind of female who sounded like a man on the phone. Bounty leaned back in the doorway and peered behind into the semilit living room. The move made his fatty breasts pucker like an old woman's. Fontana looked away, disturbed at how sickly and run-down Bounty looked. Mo Costigan shuffled into the room and blinked at the unaccustomed light. She wore one of Bounty's flannel shirts. Nothing else.

"Go back to bed, babe," said Bounty. He grinned when he turned back to Fontana. "Tell you the truth, I think me and Mo are gettin' serious. I do. How's you feel about putting on a monkey suit and bein' best man?"

"My pleasure, Warren," said Mac, though he felt Warren might be overestimating his own charms while vastly underestimating Mo's promiscuity.

"Don't sound too enthusiastic."

"I'll be happy for you both. Look, Warren, I talked to Caitlin tonight. He admitted going to the River Palace but says he never talked to Lars Ereckson."

"Wanda said he talked to some older guy matches Ereckson's description. Wanda doesn't have reason to lie. Not 'less she's part of it."

"We're getting close, Warren. Or they wouldn't be taking potshots at me."

"We don't all get killed first, we'll probably catch these bastards by September, huh, Mac?" Bounty laughed heartily, his belly bobbling. After enough of it, the laughter turned into coughing. Fontana glimpsed Mo Costigan behind the bedroom door eavesdropping. When he headed for his truck with the dog, Bounty said, "Let's not let this town end up like that one down south with all the fire hats in the vegetable ward. I'd like to have just a couple of us make it through the month."

"Scared, Warren?"

"Damn right. Ain't you?"

"I guess I am." Admitting fear was not something Fontana was good at. Lying about it was even harder. What he felt wasn't fear. He wished it were. It was rage.

45

TIME FOR ME TO DIE

Limbs sweating, torso puddled with it, Fontana lay awake on top of the sheets, contemplating his sins. He'd known the night hadn't finished keelhauling him. Satan snoozed beside his bed, snorted, and stood to stretch slowly when he heard the noise. Fontana leaped six inches—as if he hadn't been expecting another grisly scene in the middle of a hot night. His bloodstream carried so much excess adrenaline he felt like a sluggish nag doped for a win at Longacres.

"Time out zero-four-fifty-five. Medic response. Staircase Aid One. Bellevue Medic Two. Moon Valley Road. Medic response. Staircase Aid One . . ." Two rounds of information from the beeper. Then they added, "Man down. GSW." He could already feel the pulses hammering in his temples. He flopped back onto the bed, rolled over onto his face, and slowly pushed himself up. The anger had subsided somewhat, replaced by a quiver in his breathing, a catch in his conscience.

He tugged on pale tan shorts and a red fire department T-shirt. He gulped a drink of water to settle his stomach. Jeez, he'd blown it. Now he had to drive out there and pretend he didn't already know. Pretend to be shocked. Pretend he had nothing to do with the mess. Brendan had been left to sleep on Mary's davenport. At least he wouldn't have to wake him up twice in one night.

Satan rode in front. Control Ten confirmed the address, but he didn't need to hear it: 7755 Moon Valley Road.

When he got to Moon Valley, three cars cluttered the drive. The Jeep. The Jaguar. And Will Long's Cutlass. Will Long came cantering out the door of the house and met him in the driveway. A short, skinny, highly excitable volunteer whose hobby was computers, Will worked days in the Snoqualmie wood mill. He'd held on to his crew cut after high school. His clipped mustache made him look like a woodchuck.

"GSW right through the brainpan, Chief. Still warm. I don't know what the guideline is. Should we be doing CPR or what? I just got here, see. So we've only lost maybe thirty seconds. What is it? Six minutes and the brain goes?"

Fontana started to gesture and realized suddenly he had the Remington shotgun in his hands. He headed for the house, each step coming slower than the last. "Strangest goldanged night," said Will Long. "Never seen anything like it."

Fontana stepped inside over the corpse.

It appeared as if he'd opened the door, staggered backward a yard or so, perhaps in disbelief, or recognition, before taking the slug. The body lay on its back. The puncture was in the exact center of his forehead. No blood. No pooling. Just the hole. The entrance wound was tiny and not as precise as it might have been. Rainy was in a filmy floor-length aqua gown.

Clad in a pair of Jockey shorts and nothing else, his chest hairy and fleshy, Jim Caitlin clutched a revolver in his left fist.

"Course, he coulda been down half an hour," muttered Will Long. "I ain't got zip squat from her." Rainy stood in the doorway with the kitchen light behind her. Long didn't know whether to stare at her dead husband or at her lithe silhouette under her gown. "CPR, Chief? What? He's still warm. We should try, shouldn't we?"

Fontana gazed down at Caitlin. The slug hadn't exited. Both eyes were black from the trauma. Who could guess how many times the bullet had raced around inside his skull before coming to a halt? Will Long knelt beside the body now, readying the Laerdal facepiece most volunteers carried to avoid mouth-to-mouth.

"How long ago?" Fontana asked. Rainy didn't reply. Her hip was propped up against the doorframe. "How long, Rainy?"

She crossed her arms in front of herself, brushed a strand of hair out of her face. "I called as soon as I could," she said.

"Get your act together, darlin'. The police'll be here. You'll have to answer their questions. Forget it, Will. Even if we brought him back, and we wouldn't, there isn't anything left inside."

Knees cracking, Will stood. His mustache twitched. Outside, the flashing red lights of the approaching aid car bombarded the trees and sky. The siren had been muted half a mile up the road. "Chief?"

"Do me a favor, Will? Wait outside." Long left reluctantly. Fontana keyed his portable radio. "Chief Eighteen-ninety. Code green all units. Give us the police and medical examiner."

"All units responding to Moon Valley, code green. Code green all units responding to Moon Valley," said the female dispatcher. "Be advised Chief Eighteen-ninety. County is responding."

"Eighteen-ninety okay." Turning to Rainy, Fontana said, "You all right?"

Her nod was barely perceptible. "What are we going to do?"

"This isn't the time." Eyes listless, Rainy Caitlin stepped forward and examined Fontana's face, his brow, nose, lips as if memorizing it prior to a long voyage. "You'll be all right, darlin'."

"I can't think of a thing to tell the police."

"Tell them what you saw. You don't have to speculate. Nobody's asking you to speculate."

"Can't you handle it?"

"They'd badger you after I was gone. Best to get it over. They know what you've been through."

"Well," she said, "they know part of it."

"Just your own words. Keep it simple."

"Should I tell them we got shot at in the river?"

"I'm going to tell them. I don't have to mention you if you don't want. Are you thinking Jim fired on us?"

"I don't know what I'm thinking."

"Did he say anything after I left?"

"We went to bed."

"Tell the cops the truth."

"The river?"

"Yeah."

"And the rest of it? There's not much. The doorbell rang. Jim took the magnum from under his pillow and answered it. When he didn't come back, I got up and found him like that."

"Hear the shot?"

"I don't know what I heard. I heard something."

"Tell it just like that, Rainy. Don't elaborate. Most of all, don't speculate."

"Mac?"

"What, Rainy?"

She was at the doorway to her bedroom now, angled toward him in an attitude of supplication. "You came back. You killed Jim."

"What makes you say that?"

"I don't know."

"Rainy, you have to realize from my position, given what I know about you two, it has to look like you set this up."

"Me?"

"It might even look like you killed him."

"Why are you doing this to me? I wasn't accusing you, Mac. I'm glad he's dead."

"Just tell them what you saw and heard. And for godsakes don't tell anyone you're glad."

The uniformed cops showed first. Then three more volunteers, who were waylaid by Will Long at the mouth of the driveway. The sun was coming up, and even here under the shadow of the mountain it had whitewashed the sky. In back of the house the Doberman howled. Fontana had a feeling high clouds would scud in today. When Warren Bounty showed up, he said, "Christ. Somebody busted him good. Who?"

"You get the first guess," said Fontana, gazing up at the rocky mountain.

"Neighbors see anything?"

"Haven't asked."

"You all right, Mac?"

"Sure."

When Rainy emerged from her bedroom she wore her hand, slacks, a blouse, and a look of resignation. Fontana had found a sheet in the hall closet and draped it across Caitlin's body.

Charles Dummelow arrived soon after Rainy came out. He must have done a hundred on the empty freeways. Sockless, carrying his pistol and holster, Dummelow bustled over to where Bounty and Fontana stood over the body, Bounty pale in the dawn. The deaths were hitting Bounty harder and harder, perhaps because now he realized how lucky he had been the night of the kidnapping. He scowled when Dummelow squatted to peer under the sheet. Warren said, "You can't sink a ship with BBs, Mac. That's what we're trying to do. We ain't got nothing but guesswork. We need something to break. I'm telling you it's a psychopath. Or a gang of psychopaths. In a fortnight there won't be any of us left."

A news crew from KOMO-TV pulled up behind Dummelow's car. Will Long began chatting with the woman driving the van while a man in running shoes hustled around to the back and unloaded equipment.

Charles Dummelow glanced into the interior of the house, where a uniformed King County officer was interviewing Rainy and taking notes. "The wife?"

Fontana nodded.

"How do you figure this?" Bounty snapped out of his stupor.

"Chuck, I'm all worn out on figuring. I'll let you handle this."

Dummelow stepped close. "Something else happen tonight?"

"Somebody fired shots at me."

"See him?"

"No, but I've got physical evidence. I'll bring the package in tomorrow afternoon."

"Don't pop your cork. We're going places on this case. I got in touch with somebody from Cincinnati, where Lars Ereckson is from. They seemed to think that along with his legal enterprises, he imports drugs. My guess is Thursday Kowalski runs his enforcer network."

"You want the truth," said Bounty, "I think he did this. Same guy who capped Bobby Joe Allan."

"Trouble is we arrested Thursday Kowalski and a buddy about ten o'clock last night."

"What?" said Bounty.

"I think we're going to have to let his buddy go, but they're both in a cell right now."

"The guy owned the van?" Warren Bounty asked.

"Thursday Kowalski."

"He coulda had friends. Who knows how many are in on this?"

"I got a little piece of information might help," said Dummelow. "Then again, it might not. Mac? Guy you called me about earlier tonight. Campbell Sundt? Died two Januarys ago up here somewhere? His real name was Robert Gordon Kowalski."

"Wait a minute," said Bounty. His shirttail was out, and Fontana could see a gun butt in his belt. "Who is this guy you wanted him to check out?"

"Two years ago Staircase Fire found a body in a Mazda up by the winery. I asked Charles to check for aliases."

Dummelow said, "It was in the reports at the time. There was no need for you ever to have heard about it, but we came up with Robert

Kowalski. Not Campbell Sundt. Thursday Kowalski's brother, carrying fake ID. Natural causes. For whatever that's worth."

"Did he work for Lars Ereckson?" Fontana asked.

"Right-hand whipping boy."

"How the hell did you come up with that, Mac?" Warren Bounty was dumbfounded. "I'm not kidding. How did you ever come up with Campbell Sundt? Stop the world. Let's get us an answer here."

"A little intuition. A little guesswork. A little luck."

"A lotta luck, I'd say."

"Luck is the residue of design," said Dummelow, giving Bounty a squint-eyed look. He turned to the corpse, glimpsed Rainy in the kitchen still talking to the uniformed cop, and rubbed his thumb dryly across the fingers of his right hand, another of his nervous mannerisms. "Guy musta . . . let's see . . . the poor guy musta heard a knock at the front door, got his gun because it was the middle of the night, opened the door carefully, and still they got the drop on him. 'It's time for me to die,' he musta thought. What a creepy feeling that must be. Looks to me like he stepped back before he caught the slug. Despite the TV baloney, usually a guy gets shot, he falls forward."

Bounty had his hands jammed into the tight pockets in his jeans, was rocking on the heels of his cowboy boots. "You hit a guy high enough you can throw him into next Tuesday."

"Poor bastard," said Dummelow.

"Yeah," said Fontana, who had already turned to walk down the driveway. "Poor bastard."

46

SLAPSTICK COMIC
FROM HELL

The predawn portended the hottest day of the year.

Long before they headed home, the sun laddered the eastern sky and cast a haunting blue-green haze of shadow across the foothills. The haze would soon burn off.

County evidence specialists had dusted and taped for fingerprints, had picked through the petunia beds on hands and knees, looking for expended shells. Rainy explained that after Jim got out of bed, she'd heard a loud sound but hadn't bothered to get up. Jim was lugging his .357, and always, where Jim was involved, she assumed the adversity would be visited upon somebody other than her husband.

She'd been half asleep, the heavy bedroom door closed. He'd left the light on, so she had pulled the pillow over her head to shield her from the brightness, muffling sound as well.

Before they split up, Bounty said, "You got an alibi, Mac?"

"What are you talking about?"

"I mean, you're dancin' close with his woman, and a couple of nights later hubby gets his skull ventilated. They gotta be askin' you questions. Just a matter of time. I ain't saying anything, just hoping you have an alibi. You better find one."

In the morning, exhaustion robbed his thoughts of clarity. He'd been stressed all week. Had been endlessly computing and analyzing each convolution in this calamity. The visual images bouncing around his mind were of dead people. Pete Daugherty. Bobby Joe Allan. Jim Caitlin. Fontana's younger brother, who had died years ago in a truck crash. Linda. Phantoms obsessed him. He had a vision of Warren Bounty sprawled in a ditch with rigor mortis. He thought about last night. While Kowalski and cohort had been manacled in police handcuffs, somebody had been down at the river shooting at him.

Caitlin? There was still that possibility.

First Pete. The next evening came Kingsley Pierpont's attack. Someone had fired rounds through his kitchen window. An old girlfriend? No dearth of suspects there.

Fontana began cataloging every word and look he'd exchanged with Kingsley during the past week, the past month. Tuesday night he'd appeared genuinely worried. But then, how well did Mac know Kingsley? What if Kingsley had absorbed enough punishment during his eight years in the Staircase department that he'd opted for revenge? Some in town entertained that scenario. But then, the town was rattled. There wasn't a cockamamie theory under the sky it hadn't auditioned twice.

He was too tired. It might be Kingsley. Wanda. Maybe Pettigrew and unknown accomplices. Certainly Lars Ereckson's crew had murdered Allan. And they'd assaulted Warren Friday night. And perhaps one of them had assaulted him at the river. Possibly they had been after Kingsley. Hell. Maybe they'd done Pete. Although he still couldn't shake the conviction that Pete's killing was of a different sort. No. Pettigrew had probably done that. The slyness that makes someone a poisoner does not propel him to break into houses, hire bullies to kidnap two women and shoot a man. Nor did that slyness prompt a body to skulk through the woods and lob bullets at a swimming couple.

Wanda Sheridan. Could it be that some lethal boyfriend lurked in the background? Harold Glass? Maybe she'd been sent to Staircase by Ereckson? Then, too, now that she was in Claude's will, she had much to gain.

It was eleven o'clock. They were at the pool at the river: four of them—Mac, Brendan, Satan, and a King County cop named Bob. Brendan wore a multicolored swimsuit, a face mask, and huge swim fins. Every time the flippers flapped across the surface Mac chuckled. When he stood up out of the water, the boy's scrawny little body was speckled with droplets.

They'd already recovered one slug and dropped it into Bob's plastic evidence bag, were scouring the bottom for another. In his summer uniform shirt Bob was sweating. The mercury had already topped ninety. Satan had taken a quick dip and lay sopping wet in the shade of a birch, panting contentedly as he watched Mac and the boy. It was Monday, and only a few recreational swimmers had come down to the river.

Last night Satan had found lots of track at Caitlin's. He'd traced the Doby to the backyard, where the two had barked at each other. He'd tracked Warren's path around and out to his Pinto. He'd tracked something off into the underbrush in the woods alongside the house. He'd even followed a scent Bounty swore belonged to the killer. It led directly from Caitlin's front door across the lawn at a diagonal and stopped forty yards down the road, where the killer, Bounty opined, had parked.

"Know what I think?" Bounty said, hooking his thumb into his belt and drumming his fat fingers on his hips. "I think somebody saw all this commotion and decided if they wanted to settle an old grudge, nobody would know the difference. I think Caitlin didn't have a thing to do with all this. Somebody just tagged it on."

"That's a thought," Fontana said. Warren was hemorrhaging theories, a new one every ten minutes.

When he had picked up Brendan that morning, Mary had been preparing to take her decrepit mother out shopping for a nursing home. Said Mary drolly: "She's outlived her husband by fifty years, her income by thirty, and my patience by ten."

"What?" shouted her half-deaf mother from in front of the television, where she was engrossed in a black-and-white Bob Hope movie. She wore a drab nightgown, a yellow rose pinned over one ear.

"Forget it, Mother!" shouted Mary. "I love Mother, but dear God, she's been here a hundred years. Give somebody else a chance."

The past week seemed like a skit from hell.

He watched Brendan submerse himself, kicking his fins in the air so that first his little butt, then his legs and fins were the only things above the surface, then nothing. Brendan couldn't reach the bottom consistently enough to help sift the sand for slugs, but Mac was getting a charge out of his high jinks. Mac used a trowel and a flour sifter on the bottom.

When he surfaced, gasped, and shook the water out of his short-cropped hair, Mary Gilliam was standing behind the King County policeman. She was staring unabashedly at Fontana's half-naked form. "Mary?"

"Why don't you get yourself in shape, Mac?" she kidded. "Just got a call from Warren Bounty. Said it was urgent."

"Where?"

"His place."

"Thanks."

"Someday you're going to break down and buy a phone," said Bob. Fontana smiled. "Come on, squirt."

"You know where the key is," said Mary. "I'm taking Mother for a long drive in the country. If I'm lucky, the heat'll kill her."

"Ah, Mac," said Brendan, "can't we stay?"

"Uncle Warren wants to talk to me. We'll come back."

"If you're worried, can't Satan stay with me?"

Mac plunged into the pool, where Brendan was dog-paddling. He bobbed his face in and out and sluiced water through his teeth at his son. "Brendan, who told you I was worried?"

Brendan shrugged as if he'd been caught snitching cookies. Those wide-spaced gray eyes of his mother's worked on Mac like battery acid. He looked more like Linda every day.

"I *am* worried. I want you with me."

They had a problem with continuity of evidence already, so Fontana decided to leave Bob at the pool. Had somebody been watching from the minute the shots had been fired last night until the minute the slugs had been recovered, things might have been cleaner. As it was, even a simpleminded defense attorney would challenge whether or not the slugs they brought up had been fired the night before, two weeks before, or had been planted. It didn't matter that much to Mac. He wanted the sniper. Once he found out who it was, he'd frame the SOB if he had to. Besides, the more he thought about it, the more he thought it had to have been Caitlin.

"Warren?"

"Mac, old man. I got it figured. I know, goddammit. It all came together for me after I got home this morning. I was feeling lower than whale shit, and then all the facts started jumping through hoops. I don't know why we didn't see this before."

"Just tell me, Warren."

"Take hours. Besides, there's evidence at Allan's. We gotta get out there and pick it up before somebody else does."

"Cut the clowning, Warren. Who?"

"You won't believe this."

"Try me."

"Wanda."

Fontana didn't know what to say.

"I had my eye on her from the beginning, Mac, and I was

right. 'Member when we found Gil Cutty at her place? It was beautiful. It's all woven together, Mac. You gotta come out there and see what I'm going to dig up. I need a witness, dammit. I got a feeling they might have already got it. I'll explain the whole thing when you get there."

"Don't know if I can find a sitter." Fontana reached out and ruffled the boy's wet hair. They'd dripped puddles on Mary's floor. "Warren?"

"Bring my little buddy along. Won't take but a few minutes. I just need a witness."

After they'd mopped the floor and changed into dry duds, Fontana loaded the ancient GMC with the boy, the dog, his shotgun, and a couple of dozen twelve-gauge magnum shells. His jeans pockets were stuffed so that he had a hard time sitting. The next Dugan who ambushed him was going to think he'd hit the Alamo.

47

SERPENTINE II: THE SEQUEL

T he yellow crime scene ribbon festooning the front gate had been cut down and lay snaking through the wild roses. Fontana assumed Warren was already on the property. The Destroyer jounced over the rutted grass and gravel drive. The Coasters sang "Searchin'." At the window Brendan winged his hand in the slipstream.

Oddities were the linchpins of a case, and he'd been ignoring the first of this fiasco: Wanda Sheridan wheedling for him to stay for the clutch. During the past six weeks Wanda and Mac had been like arrogant cats in neighboring windows, neither paying a pinch of attention to the other.

"Light speed, Mac? Can we do light speed?"

"What?"

"Light speed?"

In second gear Mac jerked the ashtray as if it were a control knob while he goosed the accelerator, let the truck slow, did it again. Riding its soft suspension, the truck responded for a moment as if it had been slung from a slingshot.

"You gotta back off right away, huh, Mac? We'd go zooming. Right?"

"Clean into Snohomish County."

Bobby Joe Allan's house was locked and shuttered. His van, replete with plastic steer horns, sat in the drive. Bobby Joe's wife had flown to Idaho to mourn with relatives. She would return for the funeral.

Driving through the grassy tracks beyond the house toward the rear of the property, Fontana spotted Warren bounty's disreputable green jalopy parked twenty yards from a weathered latrine. When he killed the engine, Satan bounded out and began working. The dog's tongue hung pathetically in the heat, drool whipping off in nasty parabolas as he tracked from the Pinto to the outhouse, barked, turned, and looked at Fontana.

"Out in a minute," growled Bounty from inside the shack. Brendan grinned at Mac. Warren's first stop at their house was usually the john. Brendan and Mac always thought it comical.

After clambering down from the truck, the boy pursued a grasshopper through the tall brown grass. To the southwest only a sliver of the main log house was visible. The privy sat at the north edge of a rolling field. Years ago, when Allan's uncle owned it, the field had been cultivated in corn. Thirty yards to the north the woods and lower foothills began: fir, pine, and spruce saplings. Weyerhaeuser owned most of it.

The weed-choked field gave off a warm, moist heat that seeped into Fontana and slowly nudged him into a torpor. Yellow and black bumblebees serviced clover. The faded purple of thistles was exploding into white thistledown that caught and floated in the wind. Standing shoulder-deep in wild daisies, Satan circled the outhouse as if he had real business before glancing around at the empty landscape. Satan returned to Fontana's side for an affectionate pat.

From the toilet Bounty's muffled voice said, "Got a present for my little buddy."

Brendan had galumphed out of earshot, almost over the brow of a hillock. "He'll like that," Fontana said. Satan was back at the Pinto, sniffing. Fontana recognized the behavior with a start. The animal looked up at him, curled in a circle as if asking a question, and whined. "Oh, shit," said Fontana.

The Pinto was parked on a slight slope. Fontana popped the driver's door, sat on the sunbaked driver's seat, stepped on the clutch pedal, and released the emergency brake. The Ford slowly rolled backward. Fontana reset the brake, eased out, knelt, and contemplated the grass. Nose to the ground, Satan trailed him, whined, licked the side of Fontana's trim beard.

"Been just as confused as me, haven't you, old boy?" Fontana slapped the dog's flank. Dust mushroomed off.

"How's it hanging?" Bounty was ten feet from the outhouse. In his hands he carried the bulky Mac-10. The latrine door swung in a desert-hot breeze, hinges creaking.

Fontana didn't speak.

"Dog ain't as stupid as you thought, huh?"

"I'm the stupid one," said Fontana.

"Guess you, uh, figured it, huh?"

"Yeah, I guess I did, Warren."

"What can I say, Mac?"

"You were a friend, Warren."

"Everybody's got his fatal flaw. Now you uncovered mine."

"Satan chased you at the river, but you told him to go get somebody else. Time I got there, he was thoroughly confused."

Warren Bounty inhaled deeply and conjured up a weak grin, his belly thrusting against his shirt. "Surprises the hell out of you, don't it?"

"Only because I trust friends."

"Me standing here with this big old weapon. You standing there with your hands in your pockets. Ain't you scared, peckerwood?"

"You're the two-bit red-neck peckerwood. Lie to me. Trick me. But don't steal my lines."

The grin cracked wider. "I ain't so sure you ain't crazy yourself, Mac."

"I'm trying to understand why anybody would take shots at Kingsley. Why anybody'd fire on me and Rainy." Slowly Fontana rose from the grass, keeping his eyes on Warren while trying to locate Brendan in his peripheral vision.

"Is that who that was? Rainy Caitlin? You and Jim's wife playin' water sports. As an investigator, Mac, I was never fit to carry your jockstrap, was I?"

"Wouldn't know."

"I'm so lame, how come I managed to keep one step ahead of you?"

Bounty brandished the Mac-10 in both hands like a conquistador with a sword. "I heard back East you were some sort of legend. 'Cept you got into hot water with your superiors. Lost your temper and killed some babe. I heard about your temper. You skated in court. But you were good. They farmed you out to other cities when they got cases nobody could figure. The original pro from Dover. Gawd, I would have given anything for a talent like that." Fontana knew it wasn't talent, had never been talent. Monomania was what it was—a pathological obsession for each case. And rage, the same rage that was about to end Bounty's life. Or his own.

"Pete was *your* friend," Fontana said softly.

"You let me tag along because you felt sorry for me. Me? You wouldn't believe how many people knew little chips of the puzzle. It was important I was around, so I could keep them away from you. What turned me into a suspect?"

"If I'd suspected you, Warren, I wouldn't have brought Brendan. You know that."

Bounty fidgeted with the weapon. Any second he would be whirling, crouching, yelling. The air would be dense with the smell of gunpowder. Fontana felt an almost overpowering urge to rush him, take his hits, and wrap his fingers around that slack neck. Except he'd never make it.

"This ain't easy for me, takin' you on. Didn't have this baby, I never would have tried." He jostled the gun. "When I heard that car brake ease off, I knew it was all she wrote. Woulda got that oil drip fixed, but I ain't had time. Until just a minute ago I was almost going to forget you. But then, you would have got me sooner or later, wouldn't you, Mac?"

"Sooner or later."

"See the lousy position you put me in? You know I set fire to my baby sister when I was little. I don't remember it, but I guess I done it. I been reminded of it enough times. Some people are born with bad genes. I'm one of 'em. I don't want to hurt people, but I get put in these positions so's I don't have no choice. Only thing I ever did right was quit drinking."

"Don't stand there telling me you don't have any control over what you've done. You're no different from the rest of us. Any man is the culmination of his thoughts and decisions. Now you're trying to talk yourself out of culpability. Bullshit. Put the gun down. We were friends. Brendan's here. He worships you. For godsakes, don't do anything else you'll regret."

Without breaking either hand loose of the weapon, Bounty wiped an eye on the back of his wrist. A tear dribbled down his opposite cheek. Fontana would have made a dash for the shotgun except he still hadn't pinpointed Brendan. Also, he didn't want to make it easier for Bounty to ripsaw into him. "Just me against you, Mac. Nobody'll ever know. You two'll just disappear."

"Satan! Bad guy! Warren's a bad guy! Get over there!"

The dog obeyed quickly, slinking thirty feet to the right, casting wayward looks back at Mac. Now he would wait for the signal. With his son in the backdrop he and the dog didn't dare bungle this. They weren't going to get two chances. The instant Bounty turned his weapon toward the dog, Mac would scat. Or conversely, the instant Bounty turned the weapon on Mac, the dog would attack. Satan knew what a gun was, and he knew Bounty had one. He'd been shot before. Though he'd been trained to attack in the face of gunfire, Fontana wondered if his training hadn't been compromised by earlier shootings.

"You knew I was bringing the boy."

"Told you I feel bad about this."

"Warren, you're just another greedy bastard can't wait for that box seat in hell."

"Once I played that first card, I hadda finish."

A fully automatic weapon could wreak havoc even in the hands of a shaky fat man. All Bounty had to do was squeeze and point. It was going to be a miracle if Fontana could reach the shotgun before the Mac-10 tattooed the afternoon. For the Alsatian, it was a death mission. Even if Bounty missed at first, the .380 rounds coming like salt out of a shaker would cut the dog in half. No matter, Mac was determined Bounty wouldn't survive. He played the thought through his mind, programming himself. Automatic pilot. The adrenaline in his system had to keep him moving no matter what.

"I ain't had many friends like you, Mac."

Fontana smiled grimly. "Me neither."

"Couldn't be helped. I got myself in this jam a long time ago, before I met you or the kid. I got no options."

"And Brendan?"

"Don't be starting something messy, Mac. Been practicing with this thingamajig. I'm a damn sight better than I was the other day. It'll be quick. Don't worry about that." Mac realized that by mutual agreement they were gabbing until they could gab no longer, both of them delaying the moment of truth. An absurd collusion between assassin and victim. "Still don't have it figured, do you, Mac?"

"Money or drugs. Robert Kowalski's car must have been loaded. You were up there on that aid run. They didn't bother to put your name on the report because you were on salary. You didn't get paid extra for alarms. You told me you found a car in the lake. I didn't connect the aid run and you with the lake until just now. Kingsley said they put a rope over the car and dragged it out. Nobody's going to do that by hand. You must have used the Destroyer."

"You got that part of it, by golly." Bounty's bravado was accelerating. He needed Fontana to know exactly why this was happening. "That old Mazda was loaded down with cocaine. You never seen such a sweet deal."

Fontana's fists were slimy with sweat. His son tramped through the grass behind, too far to comprehend their words. He could see Bounty's face tightening, relaxing, tightening. Bounty wasn't sure he could go through with the killing. Good. It would give Fontana another bullet in the cylinder. The dog. The doubt.

Stomping after a grasshopper, the boy moved closer. First the clickety whirring sound of the insect, then the boy's voice softly calling, "Come on. Come on now," then more rustling footsteps in the hot, dry grass.

"The dog ain't going to help," said Bounty. "Stay! Satan! *Bleib!*" The dog glanced from Fontana to his former owner.

"*Eis!*" said Fontana, letting the tone of voice indicate the gravity of the situation. Brendan heard his tone, too, stopped. "Brendan! Hit the dirt!"

"Mac?"

The dog was already moving.

"Hit the dirt!"

"Are we playing a game, Mac?"

"*Eis! Eis!*"

Each step taking an eternity, Fontana found himself scrambling for the far side of the GMC. A slow-motion dance of bullets chased him. The sound of the suppressor was like somebody thumping a phone book in rhythm with a pair of steel hammers. The driver's door was open, and once he got there, he'd have the Remington.

He'd been running forever, and he still wasn't behind the truck. A spray of bullets blipped into the dirt and grass at his feet. Sounding like whips. He slid, kept his legs under him, felt shards of plastic bite into his face as a piece of the taillight on the GMC exploded, then caught sight of his son lying on his stomach twenty-five yards away. In a slight hollow, he would be okay until Warren moved. The firing stopped.

"Mac?" Brendan called.

"Stay down!"

The dog yelped. Windows on the truck cracked with quick, hard pockmarks. Fontana crouched behind five thousand pounds of insufficient cover. Bullets rained on the truck. The dog was either dead or had chickened out. Squatting beside the driver's door, he grasped the Remington, thumbed the safety off as another spray of bullets poured from the silenced Mac-10. Lead stitched the dirt at his feet. Warren was aiming for his ankles. He duck-walked to the front wheel, crouched. He didn't know if he'd been hit. As long as he could move. Off in the grass the dog whimpered. So did the boy. It grew quiet.

Exposing nothing but his hands, Fontana raised the shotgun, leveled it horizontally across the hood, and fired. The noise splintered the afternoon. The awkward angle of the recoil wrenched his wrists. He pumped the Remington and fired another round over the hood. The Mac-10 remained mute. "Stay where you are, Brendan. Don't move."

"Daddy?"

"Are you okay, Brendan?"

"What's wrong with Uncle Warren?"

"I'll explain later."

The spray of lead began in an arc in front of the truck, then swerved up into the side of the vehicle, plinking across the heavy-gauge metal of the hood, making it ring like a sorry cymbal, blowing out both front tires.

Acting on instinct, Fontana stood and fired at Bounty. He knew the move would be unexpected. It would also give him a line-of-sight target. Fontana's slug tore a hole in the corner of the outhouse as Bounty ducked behind it.

Small bits of light appeared in the wall of the outhouse as if a huge sewing machine needle were tracking across the wall. He could see sky behind. Tiny spouts of dust kicked up to the east of the truck making poof-poof noises. Bounty was guessing at his position, firing blindly through the outhouse wall.

"Mac? Mac? We gotta talk. Stop shooting for a second."

Fontana punched a load of double-aught buckshot through the center of the outhouse. He was through with the rifled slugs now, down to pellets. He sent another blast through the lower right side. Mid-level left. He thumbed six fresh cartridges into the gun.

A black object arced through the air and clanked on the dry earth thirty feet from the weathered shack. The Mac-10. Bounty woofed from inside the structure. "I'm hit, doggone it, Mac."

"Sorry to hear that, Warren," A load went through the top of the outhouse. Another slightly lower.

"Goddamn you! I threw down my weapon. I want a truce. You can't do this to me. You can't kill in cold blood. Not in front of your kid."

"I thought that's what you wanted, Warren. You wanted to blow this bastard away when we found him." Boom. A load hit the shack dead center. He listened for the sound of a falling body that didn't come. Fontana strode around the rear of the truck, jamming three more red twelve-gauge shotgun cartridges into the magazine.

"I'm hurting, Mac. Don't kill me. God, don't kill me."

"What are you doing, Daddy?"

The outhouse was beginning to look like Swiss cheese. Fontana fired another load into it. The front door coughed outward a few inches from the concussion, then flapped closed. Fontana was now directly east. He triggered two more loads into the structure, each lower than the last, then dug the remaining cartridges out of his pockets.

"Let me go, Mac. I'm arrested. I'm in your custody. I'm trusting your honor."

"Now we're talking honor?"

Shooting from the hip, Fontana jacked the action of the shotgun viciously after each round. Boom. Boom. From this distance each load tore a fist-size hole out of the building. He was gradually removing hiding places in the latrine. From inside Bounty yawped, "Damn you! There's no place. I'm on the floor. You'll kill me. Damn you."

Boom.

"I'm bleeding. I'll tell you the whole story if you quit."

"Talk." He thumbed the last two rounds into the Remington. He could see Bounty inside, in the lower left corner tucked into a ball.

"I ain't got nowhere to go, Mac. I ain't got nowhere."

"Serpentine, Warren," Fontana said. "Serpentine." He put another round into the box. The blast bit a hole large enough for a rabbit to jump through.

"Mac?" called Brendan from the tall grass. "What are you doing?"

From inside the john Fontana heard a new sound, a metallic rasping. Fontana walked up to the structure, then shoved the wall with his foot. When it toppled onto its side the shack broke into pieces. Dust bloomed up from the brown grass. The metal toilet receptacle had one ragged hole in the rim. Bounty had stuffed his bulk down the chute like Santa Claus. It didn't look big enough.

Fontana stepped close, almost put his head over the crapper to peer inside before he heard a click. He pulled back. Two rounds of pistol fire flew out of the commode. One went vertical. The other slanted and caught the lip of the commode, sent slivers of wood drifting into the air. A tiny fragment of bullet caught Fontana in the lip. He touched his face. Crimson dappled his fingertips.

"Mac? You out there? I didn't nick ya, did I? Mac? Brendan? Your old man still standing?"

"Old man's still standing, Warren."

"God, Mac, let me out. It smells like a rendering plant."

"You blew your chance to get out."

A grasshopper whirred in the distance. More hollow pops came from the pit. Bounty was shooting wildly. Six more rounds. He was in a panic, firing in all directions. Then the semiautomatic pistol bobbed out of the hole and plopped into the dirt on the opposite side of the base, its action jammed open, clip empty.

Fontana walked to the base and in one clean movement booted the metal receptacle off. It clanked down the slight slope and came to a tinny stop in the dirt. Remington butted tightly against his shoulder, he jacked the action. He had two rounds left.

"No!" shouted Brendan.

"God, don't do this. For the love of God, Mac, let me die in the hoosegow. I ain't got long anyway. For the love of God."

"Serpentine." He aimed into the muck next to Warren and pulled the trigger. "Serpentine."

Brendan was up tight against Mac's right leg now, clinging. "No, no. Don't kill Uncle Warren. Please don't kill him. Please, Mac. I love him."

Hysterical, Brendan wrapped his arms completely around Fontana's right leg and sobbed. The boy threw Fontana off-balance. In the pit Warren was weeping, though he hadn't taken his eyes off the hole in the end of Fontana's shotgun. His head was eighteen inches below the level of the outhouse floor, face canted up in the tight quarters. He had hunkered to get that low, sitting cross-legged, a crushed beer can, used condom wrappers, and other debris between his legs.

"Please," shrieked the boy. "Please, Mac. Not Uncle Warren. I love him."

Flecks of muck spattered Warren's pale face.

Fontana pumped the last round into the beer can next to Warren's crotch, turned, picked up his son in one arm, and carried him over to the dog. Panting heavily, Satan lay on his side. Blood matted the fur across his ribs. Mac petted the dog's neck, unsure whether the wound would prove fatal. The dog lay still, knowing his fate was now in his master's hands. "Settle down, Satan. You saved my ass. Good boy." He kissed Brendan's hot brow, then wiped the blood from his lip off the boy. Brendan clamped frail arms tightly around his father's neck.

48

THE THIRD GATE OF HELL

I n the dark sky the first explosion resounded so close the ka-
rumph shook them. Ten-thirty Saturday night. The final event
of Cascade Days. The annual fireworks extravaganza. People re-
clined in lawn chairs or flopped on blankets in the outfields of
the baseball diamonds. From behind the grade school David Werner fired off mortars. Eager spectators crowded close enough to
smell the powder and drifting smoke. Each time a payload exploded, hundreds of upturned faces could be glimpsed in the
strobe light.

Each year Werner hobbled through the mortar pits with his
cane in one hand, a road flare in the other, refusing to allow
anyone else to touch off the pyrotechnics. Gil Cutty crept around
behind him in the dark with a two-and-a-half gallon pressurized
extinguisher waiting for his trousers to light up the way they had
four years ago. Volunteers manned charged hose lines nearby.

Fontana hogged a grassy plot near the railroad tracks. In shorts and T-shirts Brendan and Benny sat cross-legged several yards in front, large child heads tracking the sky.

Propping herself with her false hand, Rainy lay on the blanket with Fontana. Mac watched the yellows and blues in the sky reflect off the planes of her face. After a particularly effective detonation they interrupted their lulling conversation to whoop with the crowd.

Though the chinooks had petered out, it was still warm. At night the temperature dropped to the fifties. A toenail of moon peeped over one of the mountains in the notch of Snoqualmie Pass.

"I'm not sure I understand all that happened," Rainy said.

"Haven't had much chance to talk, have we?"

"What with the funerals and all the loose ends. So who was Chief Bounty trying to poison?"

"Two Januarys ago on an alarm Daugherty, Lieutenant Allan, Warren Bounty, and your husband went up to Lake Renalt. Kingsley was driving but he never left the rig."

"We found the report together?"

"Uh-huh. Bounty wasn't listed on it. What they found was a man in a car that was half in the lake. Dead for twenty hours. He carried fake ID, but his real name was Robert Kowalski, brother to Thursday Kowalski, one of the ones who tried to kidnap Bounty. They both worked for Lars. The car was stuffed with dope. The four of them decided they had a couple of million bucks on their hands and it would be foolish to award it to the authorities. So they reported the car empty except for a dead man. Ereckson's people must have figured Kowalski got robbed and murdered. No reason to expect the cocaine was still in the car when the emergency personnel showed. They did send Thursday Kowalski up here to ask around afterward, after Bounty had been committed. That's why Bounty didn't know him. The others realized Kowalski and Ereckson were interested in the cocaine. One by one they tried to make deals with Ereckson.

"When I arrested Warren last week, I had no physical evidence until a county dog sniffed out the dope inside a wall in one of Bounty's rentals. Bounty's been trying to dump the dope on some local dealer for over a year. Then last week at the state lab the bullet they found in your husband matched slugs fired from Bounty's gun. The slugs I found at the river matched a rifle in his rental. The fingerprints on those binoculars were Bounty's. Trouble is, unless forensic pulls off a miracle, we may never prove he did the poisoning. So far we've got him for possession, assault, attempted murder, and first degree on your husband."

"When the people from Ereckson's organization tried to kidnap Bounty . . . they wanted the cocaine?"

"Nothing else."

"How is your dog?"

"He took two slugs. They wanted to put him to sleep but I wouldn't let them. Even a human who gets shot three times in his life doesn't come back a hundred percent. He may have a limp, but I think he'll be with us a little longer."

"So many people might have died from that poison."

"Jim, Daugherty, and Bobby Joe Allan were all on Bounty's list. Kingsley never knew what was going on. They'd apparently all agreed to sell the dope and split the proceeds without telling him anything about it. With Warren's law enforcement and criminal connections he would be the likely choice to handle the transaction. Before he could hawk it, though, alcoholism derailed him. Jim, Pete, and Bobby Joe must have been frantic when they couldn't find the cocaine after Bounty got put away."

"When Bounty got hauled off to the hospital last year, none of the others knew where the cocaine was hidden?"

"Else they would have peddled it. Pete might have destroyed it. I know people looked because Warren's house was torn apart.

If any of the four talked, the other three were sunk. Then, when Pete was poisoned, I think Allan suspected and Jim knew it was about the cocaine."

"But all the other people who might have died? Claude invited *me* to stay."

"Warren figured the more people got sick, the more it would look accidental. Once he'd murdered, the threat of somebody going to the authorities snowballed. Nobody did, though, because nobody wanted to queer the deal. Warren bet Wanda twenty bucks she couldn't get me to come back in for that lunch. He thought because I'd been an investigator, it was just as well if I swallowed my share of d-CON. Later he pointed out the container on the refrigerator. I thought he was helping, but he knew it was only a matter of time before we'd find it. He wanted to ingratiate himself so he could keep an eye on the investigation. I should have known he couldn't see over the reefer without standing on his tiptoes. And that note sounding as if it had come from a disgruntled lover? He tossed that in as an afterthought to muddle the situation. Tuesday in Seattle, when he took a potshot at Kingsley, there was no reason other than the jitters. Or maybe trying to give us a red herring."

"But those people tried to kidnap Bounty."

"By that time your husband had been out to the River Palace, trying to cut a deal with Lars."

"You're sure about Lars Ereckson? The police haven't arrested him."

"They booked his right-hand man. Another of his men was killed out at Bobby Joe's. In fact, that Friday night after the ruckus in the alley one of the kidnappers phoned the River Palace switchboard from the lobby of the Bedouin. Ereckson's insulated himself through layers of command, but sooner or later he'll get his. Never have liked developers."

"You're crazy." Rainy caressed his cheek with the backs of her fingers. He touched her lips, and she bit his finger playfully.

———

"When Ereckson learned Bounty had the cocaine, he tried to kidnap him. After I suspended Bobby Joe Allan, he got in touch with Ereckson, too. Bobby Joe must have made it sound as if he knew where the dope was. Bobby Joe always did like to pretend he knew things he didn't. This time it got him killed. Afterward Bounty was as befuddled as I was. He didn't know the cocaine belonged to Ereckson."

A red and silver flash detonated, then shimmered downward through the night sky. Half a second later came the thunder and the collective "Oooooo" from the crowd. Everyone went "Oooooo." Mac and Rainy laughed.

The boys were out of earshot. Rainy leaned close and kissed him. "I'm having some interesting thoughts, Mac. I might even act on them."

"Don't be shy."

After the fireworks they hiked, a caterpillar of four flashlights jouncing along the trail in the woods, to Fontana's place. Brendan announced the first to spot a bear on the trail got a prize.

"What prize?" asked Benny.

"A head start," said Brendan, breaking into laughter. He'd made the joke up himself and told it whenever they were in the woods. Rainy took Fontana's hand and said nothing. A shooting star stroked across the night sky. They slept together for the first and last time that night.

At the end of the summer Rainy announced she was selling the house in Moon Valley and moving to Redmond, which was half an hour away by car. She would seek work in Seattle or Bellevue.

Claude Pettigrew splurged on a romantic cruise in the Caribbean, just Claude, Wanda, and Harold Glass, who, Wanda said, "really needed the time off bad." Hornswoggling Claude again and again wasn't hard for Wanda.

A rumor circulated that Mo Costigan was sleeping with Lars. Some worried about her getting corrupted, but Fontana assured them Mo's bread always landed butter side up. Most Friday nights Mo danced close with Fontana at the Bedouin.

Mac. All he wanted was a quiet place to caulk the seams and rents of his history. A world where the wood stove hadn't been invented. Where strange dogs didn't shit in your yard. Where developers had consciences. A world where the department had a grass fire every other Friday afternoon and nothing else but an aid run with Mary Ann Pink punching out her boyfriend and locking him in the bathroom with their goat.

After the trial Brendan insisted they visit Warren at the Monroe Reformatory, and he wept when Mac balked. When they got there, Warren laughed his booming laugh and told funny stories. He had a chess set he'd carved for his "little buddy."

"Now don't you grow up to be a jailbird like your old uncle Warren," he cautioned, smiling as warmly as ever.

"No, sir," said Brendan.

"And you," he said, staring at Fontana. "I'd rather climb into a phone booth and ram a pat of butter up a wildcat's ass than tangle with you again."

"You know, Mac, I'd explain things if I could. You ain't gonna forgive me no matter what. I got into a bind. I saw my chance to make a million, and I grabbed at it. A guy like me doesn't get two pops at the brass ring. Then I got sent away sick. When I got back, Caitlin told me to shit or get off the pot. Said he'd go to the authorities and bring us all down if I didn't turn over the drugs to him. I believed him. I couldn't have that. Everything I did, I was forced to do. You can understand that, can't you?"

"What I believe is that you don't have any kind of conscience at all." Neither spoke for a while. "They taking care of you, Warren?"

"Of course." He laughed. "The state takes care of a guy just fine."

"Too bad."

Kowalski got twenty years for the murder of Bobby Joe Allan, which meant he was eligible for parole in thirteen. The man who'd been arrested with him was released—insufficient evidence even though he had sixty-three stitches in his face. Satan healed up enough so that Mo Costigan caught him oiling the hubcabs on her Porsche and didn't feel a bit of remorse when she spattered his hide with a dirt clod.

Rainy phoned one foggy morning and told him she'd obtained a position in an insurance company. Mac wrote an anonymous letter to the *Valley Times* asking for an ordinance to require beeping watches to be checked in at the counter of the local movie theater. He interviewed to fill the two vacant firefighter positions. In the front window of the station Pierpont taped up a reproduction of an 1860 poster recruiting pony express riders. It said: "Help Wanted: Orphans Preferred."

Mac bellowed at the council meeting when they approved Ereckson's development. Moses, the cat, continued to sleep on top of Satan. When "Teen Angel" came on the radio, Satan howled, and if no one was looking, so did Mac. Kingsley caught him at it one afternoon and said he should be on David Letterman.

Brendan, who had almost forgotten what his mother looked like, dragged out the photo album and studied it for hours. He continued to set three places at the table. When school opened, second grade inhaled him.

In the fall it rained torrents, and the heat of summer faded from people's memories. Mac and Brendan eventually finished their mammoth checker tournament. Mac lost.